WORSE THINGS
WAITING

Other books by Brian McNaughton

Fiction

The Throne of Bones
Downward to Darkness
Nasty Stories
Even More Nasty Stories

WORSE THINGS WAITING

Brian McNaughton

WILDSIDE PRESS
Berkeley Heights, New Jersey

Worse Things Waiting
A publication of
Wildside Press
P.O. Box 45
Gillette, NJ 07933-0045

www.wildsidepress.com

FIRST EDITION

At the door of life, by the gate of breath,
There are worse things waiting for men than death.
— A.C. Swinburne, The Triumph of Time

Chapter One

*A*my Miniter didn't want to live in her old home when she returned to Mt. Tabor, Connecticut, after an absence of four years, so she took an apartment in Brooksprite Gardens, a brand-new complex of two-story buildings, and furnished it with things from the house.

She sold the rest of the furniture for a tidy sum, donated all of the clothing, hers and her late mother's, to the Salvation Army, and cleaned the house from top to bottom in preparation for selling it. But the house had lain unoccupied in her absence, and it was in sorry shape. After pricing the services of carpenters and handymen, she went to work herself glazing broken windows, nailing down loose floorboards, and repairing leaks in the plumbing.

She had only just started on the wiring, planning to add a few outlets and replace the old fuse box with circuit-breakers, when she realized that it was time to return for her junior year at college; so she applied for a leave of absence and pushed ahead happily with her renovations. After painting the house inside and out, she sold it for $165,000. That was $30,000 more than a real estate broker, a colleague of her mother's, had assured her she could get for it in its original state, and she estimated her own investment, including her time, which she valued in accordance with the federal minimum wage law, at $5,000. Without even trying, she had found a career.

If she had stopped to think about it, it was a career she would have rejected. It had been her mother's, and she believed her mother had merely used it as an excuse to exercise her inclinations as a busybody and poke around in other people's houses. Amy had always thought of herself as artistically inclined, because her mother had always said she was, and had said it more often than not reproachfully. At college she had majored in dramatic arts, but it was soon obvious that she had no talent for acting. On stage, she felt nothing but an urgent desire to blend into the scenery; and any audience would have agreed that she succeeded in this brilliantly.

Other girls with her coloring were routinely described as blue-eyed blondes with fair complexions, but the only adjective that ever came to anyone's mind on first seeing her was *pale.* "You look pale this morning, dear," her mother had said to her almost every morning of her life (or so it seemed to Amy) and when teachers and friends concurred in that opinion, she accepted it as a condition of her existence. She began to dress, think, and act palely. Just as some inner pallor leeched the gold from her hair, the blue from her eyes, the bloom from her cheeks, so it sucked the color out of everything she wore. She could have bought the gaudiest dress in a bargain store run by color-blind West Indians and walked out looking like a librarian on her way to work.

To avoid going on stage at college, she had busied herself with jobs that nobody else wanted or could do. She became a pretty good carpenter and electrician, and she also unwittingly earned a reputation as a benign Phantom of the Opera, never directly seen, always flitting palely at the periphery of everyone's vision as she performed minor miracles to keep the show going on. She was sorely missed when she didn't return, although no one in the drama department could put a finger on exactly *who* or *what* was missing that year.

She had returned to Mt. Tabor with the idea of clearing up her mother's affairs, something she imagined could be done by spending a dull hour in a lawyer's office and signing a few papers. But she found that her mother's lawyer, George Spencer, had given up his practice and gone abroad — no one knew exactly where — leaving those affairs in a frightful mess. So Amy had hired another lawyer and taken the apartment, which lay within commuting distance of college, in order to be on top of things. It took her two months to learn that her mother had been holding four other houses and a large tract of undeveloped property as investments; and that a fifth house, because of George Spencer's inadequate instructions and a subsequent mix-up at the bank, had been sold at a staggering loss to satisfy the local tax collector. She began to realize that necessity, as much as inclination, was leading her into the real estate business, and that she could clear things up only by taking firm charge of them herself. As soon as her old home was sold, she began to make a detailed survey of the other houses with an eye to renovating them even more elaborately.

What surprised her most about her auspicious start in business was her previously hidden talent for selling. "You are psychologically incapable of saying *no,*" her mother would say in the course of some dressing-down; or, "Why can't you develop a smidgin of self-confidence?" With the memory of such criticism still rankling, selling was the last career she would have chosen. But she found it came as naturally to her as had the other skills. In making her pitch, she was talking about a house she knew thoroughly and about work she had done with her own hands. She had the facts in her grasp, and the words followed easily. Her prospects, disarmed by her youth and her initial diffidence, found themselves cornered by a passionate adding machine.

But the diffidence remained; and what really appealed to her about the work was the long hours she could spend alone in empty houses. Nothing was more congenial to her dreamy nature than mechanical, repetitive tasks like sanding a floor, or stripping wallpaper, or painting. While going through the hypnotic motions, she would people the house with friends and family she didn't have, even with the husband and children that, in cooler moments of reflection, she could never truly visualize for herself. She was glad that she had a talent for selling, but it wasn't a part of the job she looked forward to; it was more like a price she had to pay for the delicious pleasure of what her mother used to call, with high disdain for the mutability of slang, *mooning.*

Her dream husband was an older man, not entirely unlike Peter Jennings, big and confident and charming and handsome, whose business kept him out of her life most of the time. Most typically, he would be seated at the breakfast table, shaking his head in fond amazement at her latest triumph in real estate investment before going on to praise her eggs Benedict.

He never made an appearance in the bedroom. If she directed her full attention to the thought of touching and being touched by a naked man, it would make her sick. She would shake all over and break out in a cold sweat. "Boys are the nastiest, grubbiest creatures you could possibly imagine, Amy. It would make you ill to know what thought is constantly uppermost in their filthy little minds," her mother would say; or, when she she was a little older and her mother had thoroughly demoralized her with the vision of hell on earth that she called the Facts of Life: "Men simply don't *think*, Amy, all their actions are determined by the bestial appendage between their legs and the simple, brutal urge to stick it into something." Sometimes she would imagine her dream-husband as having been conveniently wounded in some war.

Amy's mother died when she was a sophomore in high school. Until then, she had never had a date, not a real one, and she managed to finish high school without ever going out with a boy. She'd had dates in college, mostly because her psychiatrist had seemed to expect it of her. She had wanted to prove to him, as well as to herself, that she could conform to a normal, acceptable standard of behavior. But the dates had been disasters. Everything her mother told her had been proved true. If you held a boy's hand he expected you to let him kiss you, and if you let him kiss you. . . .

The agent who had steered her to Brooksprite Gardens had put forward as one of its virtues the high proportion of young, single, fun-loving people who lived there, and she had reflexively balked. But then she reminded herself that she was young — at twenty, probably younger than most of the people in Brooksprite Gardens — that she was single, and that even though her idea of fun (taking a long walk alone in the rain or staying up until three with an absorbing book) wasn't the same as most people's, she loved it. Because of her continuing desire to prove that she was just like everybody else, she had taken the apartment.

At first, living alone there scared her half to death. It wasn't like college, where you either knew everyone or could get to know them simply by saying hello. She was on her own among menacing strangers. The young man next door with the motorcycle had be be a Hell's Angel. The man across the way with the shaved head and mirror sunglasses was a black revolutionary, making bombs in his apartment. A slamming car door or a loud stereo meant that yet another sex-and-drug orgy was about to get under way. The walls were thin, and the first night she spent there, she shivered in the closet for an hour clutching a hammer with which she planned to defend her life or virtue. She at last convinced herself that the voices she heard in her living room were in fact coming from a television set in the next apartment.

She calmed down after a week or so and began to take a less biased survey of her neighbors. The windows of her bedroom overlooked the parking lot and, across it, one of the twenty cookie-cutter replicas of her building that comprised Brooksprite Gardens. She had hung heavy brocade drapes from her mother's house at the windows and, positioning a wing chair beside them, could peek at the comings and goings of her neighbors while she was at home.

At length she came to the conclusion that they were perfectly ordinary people. The black militant was a security guard at a shopping mall; the Hell's Angel was a history teacher at the regional high school. Nobody but girls ever came to the orgies in Apartment 220, and they sat around a table for hours playing — she needed her binoculars for this — hearts.

Brooksprite Gardens boasted tennis courts and a swimming pool. Again trying to be one of the gang, Amy bought herself a swimsuit and a tennis outfit, but she never managed to get beyond the stage of putting them on and wearing them while she watched television or read a book with the drapes drawn and all her brand new locks secured.

The apartment complex hadn't been here when she was growing up. It had been built during her absence on the site of the former Mt. Tabor landfill, the town dump. An ominous desert of smoking piles and bad smells, the dump had suggested the surface of a hostile planet or a World War I battlefield to her active and somewhat morbid childhood fancies. It had provided a landscape for some of her more unforgettable nightmares. Through it had oozed a greasy, sluggish vein of liquid sludge that had undoubtedly given the apartments their name, and she shuddered to contemplate the sort of sprite that might disport itself in such a brook.

But the dump had been bulldozed and planted and sanitized. The horrid brook had been squeezed underground. The malodorous mountains of debris had been reduced to knolls swathed with lawns like putting greens. Silver beeches swayed among blacktop lanes meandering coyly among identical cedar-shingled barracks. She didn't even recognize the place for what it once had been until she'd signed her lease, and then it had been too late to change her mind. Child molesters, ax-murderers, and cannibals were only pranksters (her mother had impressed upon her) compared to the sort of people who broke leases.

But the apartment itself was neat and bright and logically laid out. Sliding glass doors in the living room led to a balcony where, one of these days, she might sunbathe in her new swimsuit. By peeking through the purple curtains she hung over this door, she often saw singularly hectic and refulgent sunsets above the wood that bordered the complex. It seemed that the scruffy little wood must hide the entrance to another and more glorious world, and sometimes the feeling that it really did became so strong that she would walk there after dinner on the chance of finding it; but beyond the wood lay only the unreclaimed section of the landfill.

She tried to make her apartment homey by selecting only those items from her mother's house that dragged no unpleasant associations along with them. Books and bookcases, her childhood escape routes, were acceptable, and so were the anonymous kitchen appliances. She'd also brought her bed, a familiar refuge, from home. Most of the chairs and sofas from her old living room brought back memories of her mother, enthroned for some stern lecture, so she'd sold them. She'd furnished the living room mostly with things from the attic that were rather old fashioned and mouldy, but with the drapes drawn, no one would notice. Taking the dining room table where her mother had nightly reconvened the Bloody Assizes would have been the equivalent of an escaped pris-oner's taking his rack with him, so she'd bought a new one.

The only real memento of her mother that she'd brought to Brooksprite Gardens was the statue of Bozo. It wasn't really Bozo (one of their many dogs, a combination boxer and golden retriever) but they'd always called it that because its lion's head resembled him. It was made of highly polished black stone, about two feet high, and it represented a heroic but sexually ambiguous figure standing on an egg with a crack in it. An endless serpent without head or tail was twined about its legs and lower torso, and from its shoulder blades sprouted angelic wings that reached to its ankles. In each hand it brandished menacingly a tightly rolled scroll.

Amy's mother, who had thought it was in bad taste but kept it on display for its comic value, said it was a gift from a former boyfriend, but she knew nothing of its meaning or history. The theriomorphic aspect suggested Egypt to Amy, but the style was definitely Greek, at least in inspiration: the wings were just like those of the Winged Victory, which she'd always admired in the Boston Museum of Fine Arts.

She had often imagined being borne through the air in the strong arms of Bozo, whose lion's mouth hadn't been designed for kissing, to some better place. Her mother might try to stop them, but those strong jaws would — but that was a thought she didn't dare think, not anymore. Her mother had been a fine woman, an inspiration, she had loved her, and she grieved deeply for her; that was what her mother would have wanted her to think now, and that was what she thought.

She enshrined Bozo in the living room of her apartment, on top of a case containing her very favorite books, with thick, drippy candles rising from ornate holders on either side of him. Only when she had put him there, the perfect place for him, did she realize that the pier glass behind him revealed his strong and unquestionably masculine buttocks to all the world. Should she remove the mirror? But she wanted the mirror there. Should she move Bozo? But that was the only place for him. Should she put something behind him? But she had wanted to reflect his wings and his strong back, to give him depth and presence with the mirror.

She fretted about these and similar questions for a week. Her heart stopped whenever the doorbell rang. It would be someone — some man — who would come in, take one look at Bozo's behind, and read her naughtiest thoughts. But the bell never rang for anyone but the mailman, salesmen, and Jehovah's Witnesses; people she could deal with through the security of her newly installed chain lock. At last she came to terms with it. This was her apartment, her very own home, and she could display whatever she damned well pleased in it. Her mother wasn't around to confiscate it, as she had sometimes confiscated unsuitable books and pictures (*The Catcher in the Rye,* a poster of John Lennon and Yoko Ono — "He was a dope fiend, she's a Jap, and they're both naked," she had fumed) from her bedroom.

Besides, her sophisticated friends — the writers and artists and musicians she would surely meet one of these days — would laugh at her obsession with bourgeois decorum. Having made up her mind to keep Bozo where he was, she began to feel worldly and bohemian. She toyed with the idea of drinking apricot brandy and smoking cigarettes.

For the first few months, while she was exhausting herself each day on renovating the house, she slept soundly in her new home. She would often be roused by slamming car doors and late goodnights in the parking area beneath her window, but she could always roll over and go back to sleep after a few dark thoughts about drug-and-sex orgies and the decline of common consideration for people who went to bed at the reasonable hour of ten o'clock.

But in June, when the house had been sold and she was only at the point of planning her next project — which would mean evicting current tenants, a task she had no stomach for, so she was in no hurry — she began to be troubled by strange dreams. The dreams were timeless, they had no specific locale, they had no real people in them: only voices, but less than voices, they were like overheard thoughts. She seemed to be eavesdropping telepathically on an endless and incredibly boring dialogue between two creatures who had little in common with the human race.

Amy thought about them a lot when she was awake. The voices had a reality, an individual flavor, a tone that seemed to remain consistent from night to night. One of the characters was hopelessly uninformed about the simplest aspects of everyday life; the other one, trying to educate him, didn't know very much, either, and her — almost definitely *her* — information was outdated and confused. She couldn't have cited examples, because it was only the tone of the conversations that she remembered, never the exact content.

In themselves, the dreams weren't frightening, not at first. They were merely irritating, extremely so. It was as if she were being forced every night to attend a lecture in some subject she didn't understand. What was frightening, to a person who had spent so much time under psychiatric care and whose confidence in her own sanity was none too secure, was that she should have a recurrent dream at all, regardless of its content.

Going to bed became a dreaded chore. She pushed back the time of her retirement to eleven, and then to midnight, but all she succeeded in doing was falling asleep on the couch, where she would have the same dream and wake up with assorted aches from her cramped position. She tried hot baths and warm milk. She tried re-reading Tolkien and C.S. Lewis in the hope of provoking comfortably familiar nightmares as counterirritants. Nothing worked.

Then the dreams got scary. One night she heard the droning voices and woke up. The voices droned on. She tried to open her eyes, but she couldn't. She was fully conscious, but she was paralyzed. She knew that she was lying in her bed and wearing her blue cotton nightgown, the one with the little red roses. Her left foot was tucked somewhat uncomfortably under her right leg. She tried to move it. She couldn't. And still the voices droned on.

> *Think of it . . . pictures. . . .*
> *Pictures?*
> *When I spread them all out on the table like this, you can see all the pictures at the same time. Amy on a pony. Amy on her fourth birthday. Amy's mother and father with their mechanical conveyance. The table is now covered with pictures; you can see them all at once. Now I put them in a pack and show them one by one. Try to think of each picture as a separate event.*
> *How can one event be separate from all other events?*

The horror intensified as she heard a car engine start outside and the darkness of her eyelids lightened. She knew that headlights were sweeping the ceiling, but she couldn't open her eyes to see them. The engine stopped and the car door slammed.

"Hey, Todd?" That was Toni, the woman in the apartment beneath her, calling to her husband, but Amy suspected that they weren't really married. "Did you remember the coffee?"

"Shit."

"You want to get it? Leiber's is still open."

"No, I don't want to get it, I just got here."

"I'll go."

"Fuck it, I'll go."

The car door slammed. The engine started. The car drove away. Amy had tried as hard as she could, but she hadn't been able to squeeze out a scream for help.

> *See? I deal from the pack: Amy on her pony. Amy at the beach. Amy on the swing. If you saw events this way, one at a time, one following the other, you would believe that Amy was on the swing because she had been on the beach, that she was on the beach because she had been riding her pony.*
> *I would not believe this.*
> *If you lived in time. . . .*
> *I am in time. Amy is on the beach. Amy is on her pony. Amy is lying on her bed in the next room.*

At these words — for the second voice, the male voice, was filled with a cruelty and arrogance that might not have been heard on earth since Attila the Hun last spoke — she struggled with maniacal intensity to scream, to get out of bed, to open her eyes, but she lay still.

> *This looks like a spider.*
> *It is a hand.*

The voices — not really voices, but thoughts — each had a distinctive, unmistakable character, and they were doing their thinking beside her bed. Her right hand shot up sharply into the air. The fingers clenched and unclenched. Hand and arm dropped to the bed, lifeless once more.

> *Uncover Amy.*

Independent of her will, her hands pushed down the sheet and blanket. She sat bolt upright. Her eyes opened. She saw the windows outlined dimly behind the drapes, she saw a murky gleam in the mirror above her dresser, but she could move her eyes neither to the right nor to the left. Her treacherous hands pulled her nightdress over her head and cast it aside. She lay back naked and stared at the ceiling, listening.

Amy is different from the creature in the pictures.
They grow larger and change as they grow older. This organ develops for the nourishment of their offspring.

Amy's hand clutched her breast.

Hair grows, here and here. This is a female, you see.
Amy's legs jerked abruptly apart.

Where are the offspring?

Todd Farmer's headlights swept across the ceiling. This time she could see them. They were extinguished. His engine stopped, his car door slammed. The front door of his apartment slammed, and she heard laughter.

She has no offspring. She has never known a male.

Amy's fingers probed her vagina painfully.

Bring a man to her, and show me what you mean.
I will show you at another time. It is time to go.
Time is not.

The droning voices argued this abstruse point as they receded. Released from paralysis, Amy screamed and screamed again. Remembering her neighbors, she pulled the pillow over her face and jammed it into her mouth before she screamed a third time, long and loud.

She pulled the covers over her head and lay curled in a tight ball, sobbing and shuddering uncontrollably for a long time. She wanted to call the police, but what on earth could she tell them? That she had been hearing voices, and that she had been sexually assaulted by her own hand? No matter how carefully or cleverly she worded her appeal, they would think she was crazy, and they might very possibly be right.

After a long time, she convinced herself that she had only been dreaming. She crept out of bed and tiptoed to the window, less terrified now by the creatures of her imagination than by the thought that the neighbors might have heard her screams. The dim lights in the entryways shone on a herd of glittering. empty cars. Everyone was home. Only a couple of lights burned in the building across the way, and no one was peering out anxiously or reproachfully for the author of the screams. Maybe she had screamed only as part of her nightmare.

She slipped into her nightgown and turned on the light. Sleep was out

of the question. She would make a cup of cocoa and read until morning
Dream or not, it took all her courage to walk out into the kitchen, and
she turned on as many lights as she could on the way.

Carrying a tray of cocoa and pecan shortbread cookies, she entered the
living room, snapped on the light, and screamed again. Her hands jerked
convulsively; the tray flew against the bookcase. The cup shattered against
the mirror and broke it. The statue of Bozo teetered. She lunged to save
it, but it fell and shattered on the floor. Her left wrist stung where a shard
of the cup or mirror had grazed her. Bright drops of blood dripped to
the snarling mouth of the statue's severed head.

In the living room, a chest of her most treasured possessions had been
forced open, its contents strewn about the Anatolian carpet. Her mother's
photo album had been taken from the chest and all of its pictures pulled
with destructive clumsiness from their plasticene sleeves. They lay beside
the coffee table in a ragged pack.

She paused only to make certain that all the locks were locked, the bar
drawn, the chain in place befdore dashing back to bed and hiding under
the covers, leaving all the lights burning. But she knew it didn't make a
bit of difference.

Chapter Two

*M*artin Paige expected Mt. Tabor to look like every other small town in New England. Bad roads would take him through a desolation of abandoned farms until he went down a hill and crossed a stream by means of a dubious bridge, passed a derelict mill and entered a deserted main street dominated by a picture postcard church. The centers of communal life would be a Dairy Queen frequented by kids and a garage run by halfwits.

He wasn't entirely disappointed. The farms were abandoned, the roads were bad; the hill and the stream and the iron bridge, circa 1910, held their appointed places. But the mill was a steakhouse — Rocco's Ranch, steak and all the salad you can eat, $10.95 — and the stores on the main street were open for business, some as trendy boutiques, others like the Super Duper Mart (PARKING FOR SUPER DUPER CUSTOMERS ONLY!) or Ken's Komputer Kingdom. The kids were all hanging out at the Dairy Queen, glumly plotting escape, but the man who sourly put three dollars' worth of gas in Martin's 1969 Mustang looked more alert and intelligent than Martin believed he himself did. He had at least shaved within the past couple of day, reminding Martin that he hadn't.

He even knew where the police station was, and although the question provoked a gleam of interest, he didn't ask why Martin wanted to go there. Martin didn't volunteer the information, as he often would to impress people with the glamorous and interesting life he led, because he was in a hurry. He wanted to wrap up the Mt. Tabor Massacre in one day. He would get $300 for it, and he owed nearly that much to people who could squeeze it out of him. When he got home, he would have to write a couple of fast stories for *Pussy* or *Spread* in order to pay the overdue rent and eat. So much for this week's quota of pages on the Big Novel, *Swords of Winbourne.*

He thought of his compulsion as he drove to the police station. It surely was a compulsion to tell people that he was a writer, because he dropped it into every casual conversation he held with a bartender or checkout girl. Apart from seeing the initial flicker of interest in their eyes — and that only sometimes — all he ever got out of it was a swift and sudden onset of black despair. They thought a writer was somebody rich and interesting like John Grisham. He knew it was nobody but Martin Paige, a bum living by his wits, one step ahead of lawyers, loansharks and tax men, two steps short of middle age and some horrible illness he would never be able to afford: or so it would seem in those moments of despair that his compulsive boasts triggered.

"What do you write?" they would ask.

"Oh, you know, detective stories. Science fiction. Stories for men's magazines. Several paperback novels. True crime." With a deprecatory laugh, he would add: "Whatever I can sell."

The last part, of course, was true. If he wanted to be honest — but who did? — he would answer, "I've written a hundred pornographic novels, plus thirty or forty obscene short stories for magazines like *Pussy*, which features pictures of women with their legs spread wide apart and glycerine smeared on their cunts to make them look excited. Actually, the only thing on their minds is whether their unemployment checks have come and whether they'll have time to cash them, which is more than I worry about, because I can't even collect unemployment. I write true crime stories, too, some of which I make up, but I can't always sell them. I keep writing stories for mystery and science fiction magazines, and even for the high-class jerkoff magazines like *Playboy*, but they always get rejected. Plus I'm working on a heroic fantasy novel, *Swords of Winbourne*, which might earn me a couple of thousand dollars from a paperback publisher, except that it's probably too good to be appreciated. I make a living out of writing, which is more than most people could do, but most people wouldn't call it a living."

This was terrible. Even though he had resisted his compulsion and not told the pump jockey he was a writer, he had still succeeded in depressing himself. He felt like finding a congenial bar and disappearing into it forever, but he forced himself to park near the police station.

He lowered the mirror to check his appearance. He wore short hair and a suit and tie because he often had to deal with people who considered such things important, but the strategy was spoiled today by his need of a haircut and a shave. His suit had needed cleaning, pressing, and mending even before he had undertaken a long drive on a warm June morning in a dirty car. He tried to wipe off a smudge of grease near his eye, but he only succeeded in spreading it.

"Fuck it," he muttered, getting out to shake his rumpled clothing loose from his sweating skin.

After a long wait on a hard bench, he was directed into the office of Maurice Donovan, the chief of police, a puffy and oversized gingerbread man. He was holding the letter Martin had written him and studying it as if he had never seen a letter before.

"How do you do, chief."

"How are you, Mr. Paige. You know, your name is familiar."

Ice touched Martin's heart. Could this man be holding a warrant from his ex-wife, the IRS, or the supermarkets or liquor stores where he'd bounced checks? Or even a contract on him from "Crazy Jerry" DeGenerato, who had advanced him money on a stroke-book he had never delivered?

"What do you write?"

"Oh, you know, detective stories. Science fiction. Stories for men's magazines. Several paperback novels. And of course true crime, as I say in my letter." With a deprecatory laugh, he added: "Whatever I can sell."

"*True Murder Facts?*" That was the name Martin had mentioned in his letter, although the sale was not assured.

"Yes."

"Ever write for *Detective Secrets?*"

"Oh, yes."

"Well, that must be it, we had some copies laying around the shop." He put down the letter, still reluctant to draw his eyes away from so marvelous an artifact. "What can I do you for?"

"As I said, the facts in the Laughlin case. Pictures of the bodies, if you have any."

"No pictures." The chief laughed. "No bodies. Just some bones and teeth and clothing, a truss from Frank Laughlin, barely enough to identify the victims. Laughlin was a commercial artist, lived in an old mill he'd restored —"

"Rocco's Ranch?"

"No, this was a different one, the Glendower Mill on Pine Hollow Road. Supposed to be haunted even before they moved into it, and it's still vacant. His wife, Rose, thought he was messing around with a neighbor, so she killed him and the neighbor and her son, who apparently got in her way, and then dissolved all their bodies in acid. She died in a fire at the booby hatch a couple years back. Poetic justice, you could say — they found less of her than we did of her victims. Case closed. Of course, I wasn't the chief then, Philip Marlowe was. What's funny?"

"He was a famous private eye, Philip Marlowe."

"Well, this couldn't've been the same one, this was our police chief. Anyway, he was always hinting that he could tell a strange story, if he was of a mind to, but he was the kind of guy who hated to tell anybody the right time of day, and he could make a federal case out of a speeding citation. So I never took him too seriously. There was some weird stuff, though, I'll admit that."

"What weird stuff?"

"Like the tar on the stairs. Some people claimed it was shit. Only I figure, it's easier to come by a half dozen barrels of tar, which is what it would've needed, than a half dozen barrels of shit. Smelled sort of like tar, I thought, only it was dry. Most of all like rotten eggs, when you come right down to it, only it was black."

"And where was this stuff?"

"It went from the third floor, where Laughlin's studio was — that's where they found his remains — down into the basement, where they found the neighbor lady and the son. There was a whole mess of it in a room below the basement that was full of torn-up books and furniture."

"Didn't anybody analyze it?"

"What for?" Donovan seemed amazed at this suggestion. "It was just some more of Mrs. Laughlin's craziness, it didn't have nothing to do with the murders."

"What other crazy things did she do?" Martin asked, making a few desultory notes. *Check haunted angle,* he wrote.

"The door to the cellar and the front door were all busted up, like she'd tried to enlarge them with an ax or a crowbar. Or maybe dynamite. She was just a skinny little thing, but you know what they say about crazy people having surprising strength. And somebody had drove a bulldozer through the woods in front of the house, knocking down all the trees, only they never found the bulldozer. Or its tracks, either." He paused, as if struck for the first time by this anomaly, but he quickly recovered. "What it must've been, it must've been the wind. We did have a real rouser of a thunderstorm along about that time."

"What do you think happened?"

"Like I said, she murdered her husband and his girlfriend, plus her own son, then tried to dissolve all their bodies in acid. The few bones we found were transparent and rubbery. Disgusting."

Rubber bones, Martin wrote, then asked: "But all the other stuff —"

"I don't even bother to think about that. If you investigate a motor vehicle accident in front of a pizza parlor, you don't go in and ask how pizzas are made. All that other stuff, either Mrs. Laughlin did it because she was crazy, or somebody else did it for a practical joke, or just to confuse the issue."

"The guy who found the bodies, George Spencer —"

"He's the last person, believe me, who would have fooled around like that. If you told George Spencer it was raining, he would make you put it in writing and get two witnesses to swear to it. A fussbudget lawyer of the old school. He took off kind of sudden, and some people thought that was odd, but he did it later, after his wife died — that was cancer, nothing suspicious there. Plus around the time of the murders, his son, who was thirty or so, took off with a fifteen-year-old cheerleader, caused quite a scandal. So, what with one thing and another, it was understandable that he wanted a change of scenery."

"Where did he go?"

"No idea. They might know at the bank. I hear he dumped everything in their lap — no, I'm a liar. A month or so after he left, his house was broke into and messed up. I tried to contact him, but the bank had no forwarding address."

"Now, about the acid. What did she use, a bathtub or —"

"We never did get into all that. Her confession was kind of incoherent, to say the least. She did most of her talking in a homemade language. When she spoke in English, it was mostly to tell us to watch out, 'cause she was God's daughter." The chief looked momentarily uncomfortable, as if struggling against an atavistic urge to cross himself. "Her father was a cult leader on the West Coast who said he was God, so it was easy to see where her craziness came from. She had freaked out at a wild party they had at the mill a few days before, a Hallowe'en party, so she was floating along on pills when she croaked everybody. Quite a party. A kid threw a fit and has been in a coma ever since. Good kid, our high school's star quarterback, and that shot the shit out of the Thanksgiving Day game with Mansfield that year. Rose Laughlin had a lot to answer for. Plus Frank Laughlin raped and beat up some faggot from New York City, who filed a complaint against him. They weren't our kind of people at all. Four, five years ago, the Laughlins were just about our only weirdos, not counting all the damn loonies from the college." He snickered. "Except for the Doctor and his Devil-worshippers, but they're like a respectable local industry, selling dried toads and bats' blood by mail order."

Donovan's manner suggested he wouldn't need much prodding to talk at length about the local Satanists. The leader of the group had been extensively written up a few years ago, and now it was old news.

Martin looked back through his notes. He had learned little more than what he already knew from the newspapers. Without pictures of bodies — it was stupid of him, unforgivably so, but it hadn't occurred to him that there could be no pictures — the story would be hard to sell. *True Murder Facts* wouldn't be grabbed by a picture of an empty house, or a picture of Chief Donovan staring in horror at Laughlin's empty truss. His only hope would be to sell it on the basis of an offbeat angle.

"What was that about the mill being haunted?"

"I wouldn't know about that. George Spencer would have been the man to ask, he was our local history expert."

Donovan folded his hands and looked up alertly, a bright pupil awaiting his next question. Martin couldn't think of one. He couldn't fault the chief for lack of cooperation, but he had seldom encountered such slovenly police work. Apparently they had found a raving lunatic at the scene of the crimes, asked her if she'd killed them, and closed the case when she'd said yes. Since it would have been impossible to bring her to trial, they hadn't even bothered to look for evidence. The real murderer

— George Spencer or his cradle-robbing son? — might still be running around loose. By steering a careful course past the libel laws, he might make that the angle of his story.

"You send me a copy of this when it's published, okay?" Donovan urged as Martin took his leave. "And I'll be looking for your name in *Detective Secrets.*"

Martin considered going next to the office of the local weekly newspaper. It might save time, but experience had taught him that it might also cost money. Besides, the appearance of the office indicated a one-man show, and that one man had probably made an unsuccessful attempt at selling the Mt. Tabor Massacre to some magazine. He wouldn't look kindly on an outsider coming along to rub it in.

He went instead to the library, formerly the town's one-room schoolhouse, where a chipper lady in octagonal bifocals steered him to a book of local history, *Rambles Through Historic Mt. Tabor,* where he found this:

> Before the Great War, children of Mt. Tabor who refused to eat their vegetables or otherwise comport themselves as perfect little ladies and gentlemen were sternly advised that Mordred would surely get them if they didn't mend their ways. Who or what Mordred was, the children didn't know, and it is unlikely that many of their elders did, either. The story of this hobgoblin's origin represents a blot on the escutcheon of our fair town, and indeed on the progress of intellectual enlightenment in nineteenth-century New England.
>
> Mordred Glendower was probably a native of Wales, although information about his early life is sketchy. He came here from North Berwick, Maine, in 1810 and built the mill that still stands on Pine Hollow Road, and a dwelling on the north shore of the millpond. A proud, solitary and sardonic man, he did not ingratiate himself with the local gallants when he made the foremost belle of the town, Purity Jennings, his bride. He was reputed to give short measure at his mill, and he was constantly engaged in litigation over real and fancied encroachments on his privacy and property. His business did not thrive, but he never seemed to want for cash, which gave rise to a rumor that he had realized the alchemists' dream of turning lead into gold.
>
> Resentment against Mordred intensified when his wife, who had not been seen in public since her marriage but who had reputedly been reduced to a pitiable condition by her husband's cruelty, died shortly after giving birth to a daughter, Mirdath, in 1812. Poisoning was widely suspected but was never proved.
>
> To her father's pride, unsociability, and intellectual acidity, Mirdath added in herself a streak of willful viciousness that not even her stunning beauty could mitigate. When she was barely fourteen,

but to appearance a full-grown woman, a horse splashed mud on her dress in Main Street. To the utter horror of the momentarily paralyzed onlookers, she seized an ax from a display in front of LeFanu's General Store and buried it in the poor brute's skull. A year later, when Enos Forker hanged himself in a fit of despair at Mirdath's cruelty, she laughed merrily and made several observations that may not be decently committed to print. He was only the first of several young men to take his life on the fiery-haired hellion's account, and her eipitaphs on these unfortunate suitors became progressively more unkind and unprintable. Although many of them are probably spurious, Mirdath's comments on her departed swains were circulated through the latter part of the nineteenth century as a local form of bawdry.

In 1830, Mirdath began to style herself "Mrs. Hodgson," although no Mr. Hodgson had ever been known in or around Mt. Tabor, and in that year she gave birth to a son whose parentage was a source of the most unsavory sort of speculation. Which townsman the boy would favor as he grew older, or whether he would favor the Devil himself, became the object of many wagers; but the lad developed, by all accounts, into the very image of his grandfather.

The popularity of this grandfather continued to decline over the years. In 1847, when three infants were stolen from their cradles in as many weeks, Mordred was blamed. Whether the mob that attacked his house found evidence of his guilt is not clear, but the house was burned with Mordred in it. Mirdath was taken to the old oak tree which still stands at the intersection of Brookside Lane with the main highway and hanged. She was then decapitated, and a stake was driven through her heart. She was buried at the crossroads with her head facing downward and her mouth stuffed with garlic, in the manner of witches or vampires.

Martin watched the dust drift through the bookish sunlight and brooded over this passage for a long time. *Swords of Winbourne,* his interminable work-in-progress, boasted more wizards, thaumaturges, and oneiromancers than you could shake an aspergoire at, but he didn't believe in any of that stuff for a minute. Even though he was also a writer of pornography, the ultimate science-fiction, where a single fact of physiology no more complex than the corking of a bottle is extrapolated into a whole new cosmos of sensation, he believed in nothing that he couldn't touch, and not even in all (for example, the dollar, the automobile, and the handshake) that he could. Challenged once in a bar to sum up his beliefs, he had meditated a long time, and answered: "You can never have too much toilet paper."

But he wanted to believe. Although he mocked them relentlessly, he was gnawed by a certain envy of those who held a passionate belief in flying saucers, assassination conspiracies, God, communism, astrology, or the Bermuda Triangle. They didn't have to (or so it seemed to him, peering in from the outside) think up a fresh reason for getting out of bed each morning, and another for not cutting their throats when they did. They didn't have to puzzle over the answers for life's incessant multiple-choice quiz, knowing in advance that no answers would earn a passing grade.

So he wrote of worlds where all the riddles had answers, just as they did in *Detective Secrets*. For his living, he conjured a world with no riddles at all, where every woman would do it and every man could. In his spare time, he ruled a world peopled by chaste princesses, righteous heroes, and practitioners of pure evil.

The people who had lynched Mordred and his daughter, however, had believed in the sorcery he only played with — or had they? Perhaps witchcraft had been a flimsy excuse to get them for the miller's short weights, his daughter's snotty remarks, and the suspicion of their incest. Whatever the reason, it had nothing to do with the Mt. Tabor Massacre of four years ago, but he copied almost the whole passage into his notebook, needing something — anything — to fill out the sparse facts of the case. He wiped his fountain pen (he didn't believe in ballpoints, either) on his trouser leg and returned the book to the librarian, hoping she wouldn't look inside and discover his inky fingerprints.

"The old oak tree, the one where the miller's daughter was hanged — is that still standing?"

"What a delight it is to hear someone use correct English!" the librarian cried, beaming at him.

"I beg your pardon?"

"Washing is hung. People are hanged."

Unless they happen to be the heroes of my stories for Spread, Martin thought, but he said, "Is it still there?"

"Why, no. The tree was struck by lightning when I was a girl, and later the highway was rerouted and the town dump laid out on the site. That caused quite a stir, because it came out only after the dump had been in use for a few years that the site had been a potter's field until the early part of the nineteenth century. None of the graves had ever been marked or recorded, so no attempt was made to relocate them. And no one said a word about it when those tacky little apartments were built on the same ground."

So much for pictures of the haunted oak. "The book doesn't say what became of Mirdath's son. Would you happen to know?"

"He changed his name to Glenn, went out west, and made a fortune cheating the Forty-niners out of their claims. The mill remained in the family, I guess, but no one used it until his great-granddaughter returned and converted it into a house. Ugly thing!"

"Mrs. Laughlin was his great-granddaughter? Did you know her?"

She sniffed. "Our library wasn't quite good enough for her, I'm afraid. Possibly because of our policy of selecting literature in preference to popular garbage — nothing personal, of course, young man. I'm sure that any author who knows enough to say 'hanged' would find a welcome on our shelves. If we had shelves for paperbacks, that is."

"Do you have a copy of *Behold Now Behemoth,* by Hogarth Zurer?"

"Yes. It had a brief vogue, but —"

"I wrote it."

"Did you," she murmured, averting her eyes nervously. She didn't believe him, she might even have thought he was crazy, and he couldn't imagine why he'd raised such an unpleasant subject. He quickly changed it: "Do you believe that Rose Laughlin murdered her husband and son?"

"Oh, yes, of course I do. She wasn't a nice person at all."

She opened the book he had returned, and Martin bade her a hasty farewell before she could discover his fingerprints.

Hogarth Zurer was an apocalyptic novelist. Fire ants, wayward comets, mutant nutrias, and sewer-spawned alligators frolicked in the lucrative chambers of his imagination. His novels were routinely made into movies and would sometimes cling to the bottom rung of the bestseller lists for weeks.

One of Martin's friends was a slightly more successful hack than he, Rod Usher, who even had a marginally respectable literary agent. Zurer's big-time agent drew Usher's small-time agent aside at a cocktail party and confided that his client was looking for someone to ghostwrite the novelization of a screenplay (which had already been written by at least three other people, cronies of an erratic Italian film mogul) called *Behold Now Behemoth,* about a fisherman's duel with a brainy sea-monster.

The hardcover book by Zurer, published by the ancient and prestigious New York firm of Wittol & Ingle, or at least by the international cartel that had bought their name, would appear first. The fact that it was a novelization would be kept secret; it would thus attract the attention of book-reviewers (some of whom had already been lined up to hail the masterpiece) who normally ignore pre-chewed literature, and earn public-ity for the movie. The release of the film would coincide with the book's paperback publication and the marketing of action-figures and a com-puter game.

Usher was offered six thousand dollars for the job. He would receive no royalties, retain no rights, and get no credit for the work: in fact his contract bound him never to reveal himself as the true author. He accepted the project and tinkered with it until his deadline loomed only two weeks away, and then he panicked and hired Martin to write two-thirds of the book for half the money. Martin did so, drawing heavily on *Moby-Dick, Jaws,* and all the old Godzilla movies he'd ever seen to flesh out the incoherent screenplay. The book was reviewed favorably in *The New York Times* and elsewhere, as had been arranged, became a brief bestseller, and could still be found in places like the Mt. Tabor Public Library. The movie, starring a British actor with a brilliant future behind him, made only a few million less than expected.

While working on the book, Martin hatched a diabolical plot. He copied, word for word, five or six clean passages from his published dirty books and stuck them into *Behold Now Behemoth*. When the book was published, he would threaten Zurer with a suit for plagiarism. The famous author, who had trumpeted the novel on national chat-shows, would either have to admit that it had been written by a ghostwriter's ghost or else defend himself from the charge that he stole from the most odious sort of garbage (*Nice Girls Come First*, by Tanya Hyde, and *Play With It Again, Sam*, by Dick Standing, published by the Split Beaver Press). Zurer would undoubtedly opt to buy Martin's silence for a princely sum.

One day Martin stood in his seam-sprung sneakers and gazed for a long time through the Barnes & Noble window at the gaudy heaps of *Behold Now Behemoth*, with Zurer brooding like a thoughtful toad in a blond wig on the rear dust jacket, and he found that he had no stomach for his plot. He had sworn no oath of secrecy, but Usher, who had, and who had thrown him a bone when he'd needed it, would suffer. If he pursued the extortion, his own name would become anathema to every publisher. No matter how good *Swords of Winbourne* might turn out, it would never know print. He was again tempted to press his claim — but he resisted — when he caught the movie on television and heard the expensive actors speaking lines that had originated in his ancient Underwood. Like a dowdy mother who filches her daughter's sprightly new dress, the final screenplay had absorbed the brighter parts of his novelization.

Recently turning to a radio talk show one night, Martin happened upon an interview with Hogarth Zurer. Asked what he was now working on, the author had answered, with what might have sounded like graceful self-effacement to most listeners, "Well, I have two novels being written now."

When he got back to his car, Martin took out his notebook and wrote: *Check further into Mirdath for some feminist pub.: Sadistic murder of intelligent, independent girl* — he crossed out *girl* — *woman who rejects suicidal bumpkins.*

He thought another moment and wrote: *For* Pussy: *Nympho librarian who forces overdue borrowers to her will.*

It might turn out to be a productive day, after all.

Chapter Three

*H*aving somehow managed to sleep, Amy woke in bright sunshine to find that the bulb in her bedside lamp had burned out. She switched it off. It startled her by coming on. She crawled out of bed and crept cautiously through the kitchen. All of the other lights, which she clearly remembered having left on, were now off. The tray on which she had carried her snack stood in the drainer by the sink, and all of her bone china cups hung from their proper hooks.

In the living room, the chest was closed and securely locked. The photo album presumably lay within it, but she was reluctant to look. The mirror was unbroken, and Bozo stood firm and erect in his place. Remembering how her blood had dripped onto his jaws, the ghastly way his stone lips had seemed to absorb it, she pushed back her sleeve. There was no cut on her wrist.

She was profoundly relieved. She had begun to fear that her visitors had returned to clean up the mess, even to the point of gluing Bozo together again, but she took the pale, unbroken skin of her wrist as absolute evidence that she had only dreamed of finding the pictures disturbed and of breaking the statue. The earlier part must have been a dream, too.

But what a strange dream! To dream that she was awake in her own bed, unable to move — and the memory of her paralysis and terror were as real as any remembered events of her life — and even to dream a perfectly plausible conversation of her downstairs neighbors. . . . Well, that part of it could have been real.

She breakfasted hastily on an English muffin and tea — she couldn't bear the idea of making cocoa, as she usually did — thinking only of fleeing the apartment for someplace with plenty of air and sunlight. Only when she had reached it would she give serious thought to the question nagging her: should she call her psychiatrist at college?

As she collected her mail from the box at the bottom of the steps, Toni Farmer (although she had never introduced herself by her full name, Amy thought of her that way, since the man she lived with was called Todd Farmer) sauntered from her apartment. *Sashayed* from her apartment, her mother would have said. She was the sort of blond that Amy wasn't: rosy and full-figured, healthy and tan, with a spray of freckles across her cute nose and more than enough regular white teeth to make her a television star.

"Hi, there, sexpot! Collecting all your love letters?"

Amy went to pieces when people teased her like that, even though she knew that was why they did it. Her cheeks burned as she giggled and sputtered and hid her face in her letters.

"Bills," she finally managed to say.

"Well, you ain't the only one." Toni leafed through her own letters. She did it clumsily because of a bandage on her left hand. "Last notice. Final notice. Last warning before final notice. Final notice before last warning. Comes the revolution, we'll line all these bloodsuckers up against the wall, and we won't even give them a final notice."

"What happened to your hand?"

Toni studied the bandage as if puzzled herself why she wore it, as if an answer might come to her if she gave it a close look. Amy wondered if her question, prompted by a sudden burst of sympathy, hadn't been rudely intrusive.

"It was the damnedest thing! I put my hand down on the electric stove — I guess I was reaching for something in the cabinet above it — and I didn't realize, maybe for five seconds or more, that the burner was on. I must've really been in a daze, not to feel it. I feel it now. I've got these three rings burned right across my palm, and it hurts like a son of a bitch."

"How awful!"

"I wasn't even drunk. You know how it is when you been really pissed to the gills, and you wake up with some real mother of a bruise that you don't even remember how you got it?" Amy nodded gravely, as if this happened to her all the time. "Only I was wide awake and cold sober. You're hitting the bricks kind of late, aren't you? Another big night?"

Amy was again thrown into convulsions of embarrassment while Toni watched her with detached amusement. She hadn't noticed the time until now, but it was indeed the unconscionably late hour of ten a.m. She forced herself to ask: "You didn't hear anything last night, did you? Out of the ordinary? From —" she ran out of breath unexpectedly and choked on the words, destroying her effort to seem casual — "my apartment?"

"No. Should I have? You weren't throwing another one of your orgies, were you? Next time, invite me."

"I had a nightmare. I thought maybe I might have been screaming in my sleep."

"I didn't hear a thing. Growing up in the city, you learn how to automatically shut things out."

Toni never missed a chance to mention her urban upbringing, nor did it ever fail to make Amy feel like a rube. She switched back to an earlier subject, one that would ever so gently assert her own claim to superiority: "I can start as late as I want to, nowadays. I don't have all that much to do since I sold my house. You never did come to look at it."

"Well, you know, one thing and another. And it was really kind of out of the question, Todd's plans being up in the air like they are."

Amy would have liked to prolong the conversation, but Toni's bare feet kept inching steadily backward on the concrete of their mutual entryway, as if her apartment exerted a magnetic influence on them. Her toenails bore a coat of bright polish the exact color of the blood that had dripped on Bozo's lips.

"I have other houses, though. I mean, when I get the people out of them. Even if you don't have any plans. It would be fun."

"Sure. We'll do it. Really. I have to run."

"So do I."

Amy got into the old red Porsche that was part of her new image as a fun-loving young person and started it with the usual inept roaring and gear-grinding that was the despair of the car-buffs of Brooksprite Gardens. She had nowhere to go, but her last words to Toni obliged her to simulate purpose and dispatch.

She knew perfectly well that Todd and Toni were unlikely subjects for her fantasies. Todd was big and rough-looking and sarcastic, his arms adorned with tattooed skulls and daggers and serpents; in the flesh, he reduced her to twitches and stutters, and he seldom removed his sleepy-looking eyes from her crotch or her breasts. Toni was rather coarse, and their friendship went not one bit deeper than the casual exchange of pleasantries in the entryway. Todd and Toni weren't married, had no intention of getting married, and the last thing on earth they wanted was one of the big old houses that Amy's mother had left her.

But in her favorite fantasy, Todd and Toni were an ideal young couple, and she was their very best friend; more than a friend, an older sister or very young aunt (even though she was actually two years younger than Toni and seven or eight years younger than Todd) whose advice and approval they sought for every little decision in their lives.

Big and vulnerable and stupid — and with all those nasty tattoos missing — Todd would gaze at her appealingly and say, "I don't know what it is, Amy, but Toni seems so distant lately."

"You should bring her flowers once in a while, Todd, and help out more often with the housework."

"Todd doesn't love me anymore!" Toni would sob into her shoulder.

"Nonsense, dear, you know how men are. He's just preoccupied with one of his cases." (Fantasy-Todd was a lawyer, for no other reasons than that it was respectable and lucrative. The real Todd had an unguessable job that involved late and irregular hours, while the real Toni collected disability payments for some unknown ailment.)

Todd and Toni would buy a house from her — she knew just the house, just the colors it would be painted inside and out; which room would be Todd's book-lined study, which the nursery — and she would be like another member of the family, with preemptive rights to the guest room overlooking the rose garden. Their three tow-headed children — Amy, Peter, and Jane — would call her "Aunt Amy" and she would take them to movies and museums. She would teach young Amy how to dance (she didn't know how, herself) and beam palely on her triumph at the Senior Prom.

The only encouragement her fantasies ever got was from Toni's geraniums: leggy, incipient trees, very nearly horticultural eyesores, they sprawled in three pots that Toni kept in the mouth of the entryway. Sometimes Amy would catch her talking to them ("You call *that* a flower, you little son of a bitch?") while she watered them, and it seemed to indicate a latent domesticity in her neighbor.

She hadn't always idealized them. When she had moved into her apartment, she had been haunted by the belief that Todd beat Toni. Amy's mother may have subjected her to a relentless psychological bludgeoning, but she had never once raised a hand to her. She had never so much as seen one person strike another, outside of a schoolboy fight or a movie, and in both situations, she'd always covered her eyes when she'd seen it coming. And she usually skimmed or skipped (as she did the sex) the violence in novels.

But she knew about men ("They're all bullies, Amy, taking advantage of their size and strength to abuse women," her mother would say), and although she wasn't surprised, she would be terrorized, and would sit up trembling for hours with the memory of Toni's pitiful cries ringing in her ears. Although she knew it was unreasonable, she couldn't help feeling that Todd was coming for her next.

It happened almost every night, just after she went to bed, and it would go on for an hour. Todd always chose the bedroom, directly beneath hers, as the setting for these vicious assaults. More than once her hand had been on the phone to call the police, but she had always held back. A man, another member of the conspiracy whose nature had been revealed by her mother, would answer. And if Toni hadn't reported him, it wasn't her business to do so; she might bring down worse punishments on the poor girl's head.

But after she had been in residence a week, it became more than she could stand. "Stop it, you animal! Stop it, stop it!" she had whispered at the floor, stamping her foot with all her force — which force she would cancel at the last moment, so that her heel made no more noise than a falling pillow, inaudible above Toni's wails of pain and despair.

She had run lightly down the open stairway, meaning to ring the bell and complain — or, possibly, to ring it and run, which might effectively stop the beating. But, as she did in everything, she wanted absolute confirmation of her opinion before she would act on it, and she crept to the front of the building and slipped in among the shrubbery beneath their bedroom window.

Never in a life spent hurtling from one embarrassment into another had she been so embarrassed as she was by what she learned at the window. She wished she could have dissolved into the mist and melted into the ground. She wished she could have turned into one of the evergreen shrubs that pricked her with its wet twigs and stood there in silence forever, rather than having to turn back and run the risk of being seen creeping up the stairs. She had come out with no thought for the figure she must have cut in her nightgown.

Inside the screen and not two feet from where she crouched, to a rhythmic accompaniment of squeaking bedsprings, Toni hissed insistently, "Faster faster faster *faster!* Yes yes yes *yes!*" And then her voice broke into one of the pitiable screams that had nightly troubled Amy's rest.

At first she felt deceived and betrayed. She hated that animal, Toni, far more than she had ever hated the brutal, belching, farting, scratching, beer-swilling, hairy, smelly *man* that Toni had permitted to touch her like that, for whose swinish attentions she had abjectly pleaded.

As calm prevailed, she rose above such immature and unworldly emotions. Toni and Todd were adults, doing what adults did. She was a baby; worse, a fool confronted with her own folly. What Toni was doing — what, even now, Toni was doing — was, by all reliable accounts, fun. Just because she couldn't break through the locked ice of her repressions and allow a man to touch her without screaming, that was no reason to condemn the practice or hate Toni.

Some day she would grow up. Some day she would meet a man — a man not at all like Todd, someone gentle and fatherly and artistic — who would ever so carefully strip her cocoon, strand by strand, permitting the sensuous butterfly within her to dance naked in the sunlight.

She suddenly realized that her hand, unnoticed, had for some time now been lingeringly caressing Bozo's buttocks, and she tore it away in distress.

"Todd *isn't* coming for you next!" she spat at her haggard image in the pier glass as she turned and stomped off to bed.

*S*he discovered with alarm that her car had carried her to Pine Hollow Road, and that after she rounded the next curve she would be at the entrance to the Laughlins' driveway. She braked before reaching the curve and pulled onto the shoulder, where she shut off the engine and became aware of singing birds and the endless muttered monologue of the millstream that here capered beside the road.

The subconscious logic that had steered her here was obvious and unpleasant. She had loved Patrick Laughlin, and he had loved her. Sensitive and artistic and gentle, he would have been the one to lead her into those pleasures now forever forbidden. It was because she had encouraged his advances that her mother —

She ripped her mind out of that track and seized the unopened mail on the seat beside her as a convenient distraction. She opened the bills and advertisements and read them with close attention. She found a letter from college asking whether she was returning in the fall. She didn't plan to, but she hadn't been able to bring herself to make the irrevocable move of notifying the registrar.

No one ever wrote her a personal letter, but that was what the last envelope seemed to contain. The address — merely "Miss Amy Miniter, Mt. Tabor, CT" — had been erratically typed on a manual machine whose keys badly wanted cleaning. The stamp had been affixed with a dirty thumb, and so had the flap. She opened it two find the following, dated two weeks ago:

> *Dear Miss Miniter:*
> *I have been commissioned by a major crime magazine to investigate and write the story of the so-called Mt. Tabor Massacre.*
> *I will be in Mt. Tabor on June 23, and I look forward to meeting you. I earnestly appeal for your cooperation in answering a few questions. Please tell me when and where we might meet.*
> *I have enclosed a self-addressed postcard to facilitate your reply. I can, if necessary, change the date of my visit for your convenience.*
> *I understand that it may be painful for you to recall the details of this unfortunate tragedy. But since you were the only eyewitness, and since your mother was one of the victims, it would be unfair to publish the story without hearing your side of it.*
> *Perhaps we could talk over lunch.*
> *Very truly yours,*
> *Martin Paige*

As it was to so many things in her life, Amy's reaction to this letter was one of confusion and panic. She was thrilled by the prospect of meeting a writer, appalled by that of talking about the death of her mother, and she wondered where she go for the rest of the day to hide: for today was June 23. Despite the date on the letter, the postmark indicated that it had been mailed the day before yesterday.

She held the paper up to the light. It was cheap, with no watermark, and the same dirty fingers had folded it. The enclosed postcard gave a

New York City address on Great Jones Street, a name that suggested both eccentricity and elegance to Amy, who was unfamiliar with that city. Even the grubby fingerprints and the black dots that served for *o*'s and *e*'s could be excused as the oversights of a raffish intellectual.

As for the text itself, not even William Empson, confronted with a hitherto unknown sonnet of Shakespeare's, would have given each word a more rigorous scrutiny. Seven *I*'s, for instance, had never obtruded themselves in any five-paragraph letter that Amy had ever written; but she supposed that one didn't become a writer for a major crime magazine by hiding his light under a bushel. But what was a "major crime magazine?" She had never heard of such a thing. The image of the intellectual faded to be replaced by a brash, pushy reporter, for whose dirty fingers there could be no excuse.

"Earnestly" set her teeth on edge at first, suggesting false sincerity, but then she saw that he used the word honestly: his desire to pry into her life, if nothing else about him, was in earnest. "Cooperation in answering" was very suspicious. It suggested that her answers would be the result of a collaborative effort designed to suit his needs. "Cooperation *by* answering" would have been better.

"Tragedy" was tacky; that was the language of an insurance man or an undertaker. President Kennedy's death may have been a tragedy, but not even Eugene O'Neill could have raised her mother's death above the level of a misfortune. And to modify "tragedy" with "unfortunate," in the absence of any fortunate tragedies, was simply stupid.

Having unburdened himself of such false sentiments — it was neither tragedy nor misfortune to him, just a job he would be paid for — he revealed the mailed fist: if you don't cooperate, I *will* be unfair. After the stick came, as an afterthought, her carrot, an insultingly vague invitation to lunch.

She refolded the letter carefully and put it in her purse — dirty and insulting it might be, but it was still a personal letter — and tried to face the questions that all her nit-picking had permitted her to defer. She was no eyewitness. She had been there — she was told she had been there — but she hadn't seen anything. She'd heard. . . .

She snatched off her seatbelt and fled the confining car, not knowing whether to face the memory of what she'd heard or to suppress it. It scared her, but it elated her, too, that something should be emerging from the tight curtain her mind had drawn over the event. But facing it did no good. She had heard . . . what? It was like one of those faint stars that can be seen only with peripheral vision.

She found herself at the Laughlins' iron gate, which was chained and locked and bore a *No Trespassing* sign. Despite the lock, one had merely to walk around the gate through the thick underbrush to get in, and she did so. The house was unusual, and it had previously occurred to her that she might track down Rose Laughlin's California relatives and sound them out about buying it. She went forward more confidently, a businesswoman inspecting a prospect. That was all she was doing here.

It was big and imposing, an industrial building imperfectly converted into a home. Blocky, modern additions, like Frank's studio with its huge skylight, didn't harmonize with its original lines. "Baronial," she was sure, would appear in the advertisement — or prospectus? — she might eventually write.

She walked across the graveled apron where all of their dogs, hers and her mother's — including the original Bozo — had been found dead. She and her mother had come here at Patrick's invitation, and they always took the dogs on any excursion. Patrick had gotten fresh

with her on the telephone, deliciously so, altogether unlike him. It was hard to believe now, but if he had said just the right words, done just the right things at that particular stage in her life, she would have let him do anything with her. What a silly little idiot she had been!

She turned to look behind her at the strangely regular swath the wind had cut through the trees. It could still be marked, although it was now so overgrown that the road couldn't be seen beyond it.

The ruined front door had been boarded over, and so had all the downstairs windows. She made a slow circuit around the mill until she came to the pond, which lay still under a mat of algae in the hot, flat sunlight. She heard no birds now, only the sullen slap of water against stone, the louder splashing of the stream as it spurted through a pipe that had replaced the long-gone millwheel.

Why had they come here? Rose was ill, but that wasn't the reason. Patrick had wanted to show them something, or have them meet someone: his grandmother. It was hard to sort out what she had previously known from what she had read in the newspapers or been told, but she was almost certain that this was an entirely new memory.

The kitchen door, facing the pond, hadn't been boarded over. When she tried it, it opened.

An old, empty house on a sunny day — what could have been more harmless, or more congenial to her nature? But this particular house. . . . She tiptoed inside. Whatever had killed them, it wasn't here anymore. Everyone thought Rose had done it, and Rose was dead.

It was dark as. . . . Not wanting to think what it was dark as, she snapped on the penlight she carried with her key-ring and searched the kitchen cabinets until she found candles and matches. Some pots and pans and dishes were still here, even some rusty cans of food, but all the furniture and appliances had been taken by the new heirs, or by looters. She remembered the massive kitchen table where she had sat out the Hallowe'en party a few days before the murders. Patrick had been especially nice to her that night. So had that man who claimed to be a Satanist.

He had invited her to his Sabbat, and Patrick warned her that Satanists needed virgins for their ceremonies. So she had — oh, my. She blushed even now, remembering that she had actually — how could she have done it, where had she found the nerve? — she had actually invited him to insure her against that fate.

What was far more embarrassing, he had declined.

The cellar door stood open, but she wasn't ready for that yet. She toured the empty house all the way up to Frank's studio. It had been cleaned, but the ghost of an odor lingered, a sulphurous smell that threatened to evoke more memories than she wanted to deal with. She kept her mind strictly on the details of the work she would have to do — a still-unfinished bathroom, the many broken treads and splintered railing of the staircase, the lack of windows in the huge central room the Laughlins had called the Great Hall. Then there was that damned, smelly pond, but that could probably be set right with chemicals. It would all be an enormous project, but if she did it right, she might be able to get a million-five for a home like this.

At last there was nothing left but the cellar, and she descended with a brisk and businesslike stride that faltered only on the last few steps. Her candle flickered, and the light was lost in the gloom of the huge, low-ceilinged cellar, confounded by the shadows of many brick pillars.

She was drawn to the wall facing the pond, where she knew it had happened, to the door leading down into the sub-basement from which . . . from which. . . . She looked down into that empty room, where the nauseous odor of brimstone and rotting meat was no longer a ghost but an overpowering presence, and a gust of foul air extinguished her candle.

She couldn't move. But she had to move, because in the next instant she would faint and fall forward into the room where the horror had come from. She broke out of her trance and raced on tiptoe to the stairs. She tried not to scream as she heard something that was no memory, but the sound of real footsteps on the floor above her; footsteps that now began to descend the stairs.

Chapter Four

*T*oni Sloane waited for the last receding clash of Amy's much-abused gearbox before she drifted out into the warm sunlight again. She hadn't wanted to prolong her conversation with the Droop, as they called their upstairs neighbor, but even less had she wanted to return to the dank apartment, redolent of Todd and dirty sheets; where Todd himself was now snoring amid those dirty sheets but would shortly wake up and seek release for his morning hard-on.

She wished that, like the Droop, she had someplace to go in the mornings, but that was one of the disadvantages of not being a Lady of Property with a snazzy kraut sports car. Talk about unfair! She couldn't even drive the damned thing, and nobody else would be able to, either, when she got through with it. The Droop was living proof of the adage so relentlessly drummed into her by her mother — even though their many landlords had never bought it — that property was theft.

Todd kept nagging her to *cultivate* Amy in the hope that some of her property would rub off. A lonely neurotic like the Droop, he said, would beg to take them places and buy them things if they just went a little bit out of their way to pretend that they liked her. He just wanted to recruit her for a threesome, and maybe borrow her Porsche.

She tested the soil in her geranium pots with a fingertip. They didn't need water, but they sure as hell needed pruning. She had too much imagination: cutting into any living thing was almost as bad as cutting herself, and she dreaded that above all else. She loathed knives. Once she had tried to overcome her fear and cook something fancier than steaks or hamburgers, and Todd had jumped all over her for misusing one of his precious knives. He hadn't known what it had cost her even to touch the damned thing, so that had ended her efforts to be a gourmet cook.

A beat-up car with New York plates pulled into the space Amy had just vacated, and a seedy-looking man, a lookalike for the young Don Knotts, twitched his way out of it. He couldn't be selling anything or collecting bills, not in a thrift-shop suit and torn sneakers. Just for the hell of it she leaned back against the wall, stretching out her long legs, and fixed him with an up-from-under look. He stumbled straight for her, grinning like a hound at dinnertime.

"Miss Miniter?" he asked eagerly.

"Aw, shit. No, I am not Miss Miniter. Miss Miniter hauled ass not ten minutes ago. What did you do, find her name written in a john?"

He laughed as if she were making fun of someone else and tugged at his sweaty clothes. She saw with sudden interest that he was wearing something she'd never seen before: a dickey with an attached necktie. He wore nothing under it beneath his frayed jacket, she could see as he tried to get some air moving near his body.

"Where did you get that?"

"What?" he searched himself in confusion, even surreptitiously brushing a hand over his fly.

"That dickey."

"Oh." He turned red, but he answered with seeming honesty: "They made me wear it in a snotty restaurant once, so I got even by stealing it."

Toni whooped with laughter. "You're a real pistol!"

"It comes in handy when you don't happen to have a clean shirt."

His words seemed less defensive than they did pathetically anxious to enlist her to his point of view. He didn't realize that he had made a good impression already, as someone who had stolen something from a snotty restaurant. The most she had ever managed was silverware.

She took enough pity on him to refrain from pointing out that the dickey was dirty, too.

"You're not a bill collector or a process server."

"No. I'm a writer."

"Oh? What do you write?"

"Oh, you know, detective stories. Science fiction. Stories for men's magazines. Several paperback novels. *True Crime* —"

"That's why you want the Droop," she interrupted, but he pushed on like a priest who could hear nothing but his own litany: "Whatever I can sell."

"Don't we all."

"I beg your pardon?"

"Sell whatever we can," she said with another mock-sexy look that disconcerted him almost as much as it would have the Droop. "It's a shame you don't write jerkoff books. My old man would want your autograph."

"I —" he began, and he bit something back as he looked away. "Do you know where I could find Miss Miniter?"

She shrugged, and he got so much covert enjoyment out of it that she did it again, then drew her shoulders back to give him a better look. "She's a regular little gadabout, I don't know where you'd find her. You can't miss her, though, not in this town, a prissy little milk-and-water blonde in a go-to-hell red sports car."

"I suppose I could leave a note."

"I suppose you could."

It reminded her of a magician's routine, the amount of wadded paper, Kleenex, and crumpled Camel packs he was able to pull from his various pockets and, after he had found his notebook, stuff back in again. He bent to retrieve the surplus littering the ground, giving her another amusing glimpse of his bare torso. She discovered that there was something sexy about a man wearing a suit with no shirt, even a man like this.

"My name's Toni Sloane," she said.

"You have a very lovely name. I'm Martin Paige." She hesitated only an instant before accepting his knobby and somewhat dirty hand.

His handshake was firm without being aggressive and unexpectedly dry, increasing his perverse sexiness. She guessed he was about thirty-five, and he really did have more chin than Don Knotts. The chief points of resemblance were his receding, curly hair, his inconsequential build, and most of all, his crazy eyes. She saw insecurity and timid lust in them, but they held a deeper terror. It was as if he could see, far off on the horizon, his death loping eagerly to meet him. She shivered and jerked her hand away.

"Someone walked on my grave," she said when he looked hurt.

He waved his note to dry it. "You've hurt your hand," he said.

She was sick of hearing about it. "Electric stove."

"I guess I could just push this under her door?"

"I guess you could." She didn't want to start taking messages for Miss Minnie Mouse, much as Todd, if he'd known, would have liked her to.

He clattered up the stairs. She readjusted her unbuttoned blouse, tied loosely under her breasts, to show a little more. Todd had really gotten off on watching her make love to other men. She wondered if she could sell him this one. But that other time had been a special case, prescribed by his guru, so probably not. He would fold this one up like a paperclip if he caught them.

As he started down the stairs, he noted the changes she had made and nearly fell the rest of the way. "Are you a friend of Miss Miniter's?"

"We're bosom buddies."

He reddened. "The murders — her mother, and all —"

"I wasn't here then, I come from Bridgeport. I only know what I heard, which ain't all that much. Her mother was about as sexy as a truck, Todd says — that's my old man — which makes the whole story kind of funny, but there's no accounting for tastes. Are you going to write up the murders for some magazine?"

"Yes." Even though she could see that he liked her, he wanted to leave. She had no sympathy for people who put business ahead of more important things. "It was nice meeting you —"

"With pictures?" she interrupted.

"If possible."

"You can take my picture if you want to." He was at his car now. "I don't even mind posing in the nude. I've done it before."

"That's very nice of you, we'll have to talk about it," he said as he climbed into his car and started the engine.

"Fuck you, faggot," she muttered under her breath as she glowered at him. She called out: "Come back again real soon."

"*Toni!*" That was Todd, but she ignored him. She drifted back into the shadows, waiting for Martin Paige to drive off so she could run upstairs and read his note. She had decided to please Todd by retrieving it and delivering it personally to Amy.

Martin kept one eye on her as he backed out, so she smiled and waved. Then old man Gertner, from across the way, drove in. Eyes fixed straight ahead, Mr. Gertner breezed right past his parking space. Instead of slowing down to stop for Martin — she was sure of this — he accelerated. She screamed a warning just as the cars collided with a screaming crunch of metal.

Martin's car spun around in a half-circle, its rear end banging into Todd's parked car.

"Son of a bitch!" Todd yelled from the bedroom.

Toni ran first to Mr. Gertner's stalled car. A starburst on the windshield marked where his forehead had hit. He was slumped over the wheel, moaning, with blood running from his forehead and nose.

"I couldn't stop," he groaned.

"You mean your brakes failed?"

He turned scared eyes on her. "I couldn't *stop!* I couldn't step on the brake. My foot just kept pushing down on the gas."

"It's all right," Martin said as he came up to the other driver's window, apparently unhurt. "There's no real damage done, let's forget about it."

Toni laughed out loud. The door of Martin's car had been stove in, the side window shattered. She was sure he was taking this line because he had none of the insurance required by law. He might not even have a driver's license.

"You're not really hurt, are you?" Martin asked.

"Son of a bitch!" Todd howled. He had come out in just his trousers, his incipient pot bulging slightly over his belt. She thought that was cute now, but in a year or so it wouldn't be, she knew. He stared at a brand new dent, no worse than the others, in the side of his Firebird.

"Which one of you cocksuckers did this?"

"That one did," Martin said, pointing at Gertner as he sidled to his car.

"Hold it, pal." Todd gripped him by the arm. "Just hold it. Let me see your license and registration."

Martin tried to shake himself loose and started a new rip in his jacket. "I think I left them in my other suit. Look, this wasn't my fault! That guy ran right into me as I was backing out."

"It was my fault," Gertner agreed, approaching them with a bloody handkerchief over his nose.

"He ran into you, so you ran into me, motherfucker. Look at that!" He dragged Martin closer to his car, pointing at what was really no more than a negligible ding. "That means a new paint job, pal."

"Leave him alone, Todd! Let him go. You'll only get him in trouble with the fucking cops. If they get into it, they might just decide to take a peek inside *your* car."

"I don't want to cause anybody trouble," Mr. Gertner said. "I'll say I ran into you, Todd, and you can make your claim against my insurance. We'll leave this fellow out of it."

"Stupid old bastard," Todd growled. "They shouldn't let you assholes loose on the road." He turned to Toni. "Why are you standing around here with your bare tits hanging out? Go make some coffee, for Christ's sake, make some breakfast."

Released, Martin hurried to his car. Todd strutted and scowled after him, flexing his muscles and throwing out his hairy chest. He sucked his gut in so far that his pants started falling down, and Toni giggled.

"It's all right," Mr. Gertner said to Martin. "It was my fault."

"It's all right," Martin agreed.

Toni had thought that Gertner was being generous at first, but now she realized what was going on. "Wait a minute! Stop!" She stepped in the way of Martin's car, which he hadn't yet been able to start. "You ought to pay him something, Mr. Gertner. If he made a claim against you, you'd lose your insurance. And your license, too, probably. You've wrecked his car."

"Oh, mind your own business," Todd said. "They probably ran into each other because you were bending over your lousy flowers with your shirt half off."

"He won't make a claim against me," Gertner said, smug and sly.

"I will!" Toni cried. "I'll call the cops right now, if you don't pay him something for what you did."

"It wasn't my fault! I don't know what came over me, it was like something forced me to speed up."

"Crazy old asshole."

"Exactly," Toni said. "That's just what the cops are going to say. They'll probably make you take your driver's test all over again."

"They ought to take you to the old folks' home and gas you," Todd said.

Mr. Gertner had several times complained about Todd's loud, late-night habits. Finding an even better victim than Martin, he grabbed Gertner by the elbow and marched him to Martin's car. "Look at that, you crazy old bastard! You think you can get away with that?"

"It's all right, really," Martin said, seething with impatience to get away.

"How about fifty dollars?" Gertner asked Martin.

"Ha!" Todd shouted in his ear, shaking him. "Five hundred, that's more like it. You think this is still 1949, you fool? Write him a check for five hundred dollars, or I'll get Toni to call the cops. Thought you could pull one over on us, huh?"

Toni was thrilled. She knew Todd was a moron and a bully, but she had always loved to push him in the right direction and watch him go. His sleepy gray eyes had caught fire, his white teeth were clenched, he was the picture of a champion of the downtrodden in action.

"A hundred."

They haggled and threatened while Martin pounded his head against the wheel and all but danced in his seat with frustration. A small crowd had gathered, and people were beginning to ask if anyone had called the police. Toni tried to squelch that talk.

Gertner was parking his car. Todd was reaching through Martin's window with a clumsy paw to slap him on the back and shake his hand. He had gotten Gertner up to $250, probably not much less than Martin's car was worth, and he beamed with pride as Martin roared off in a cloud of blue-black exhaust smoke.

"Son of a bitch thought he could pull something," he said, jerking his chin truculently at Gertner, who gave him the finger and ran into his apartment when Todd took a menacing step forward. "Why were you messing with that wimp? I heard you, nude pictures."

"He wanted the Droop."

She remembered the note and ran upstairs, where it lay protruding from Amy's door.

> *Dear Miss Miniter:*
> *I am in town, as per previous letter. I will try to call or visit later.*
> *Yours,*
> *Martin Paige (10:30 a.m.)*

It was a disappointment, but it would serve its purpose. She folded it neatly and took it into her apartment. She handed it to Todd as he sat on the toilet with the door open, one of his less appealing but unbreakable habits.

"What's this?"

She went into the kitchen and made coffee, keeping one eye nervously on the stove as she plugged in the coffeemaker. The stove couldn't attack her. She thought of Gertner as she had seen him, staring straight ahead while he accelerated.

"He's a writer," she called. "He wants to write up those murders."

After the usual irksome noises, Todd heaved his usual profound sigh and rattled the paper roll.

"Him and some other guy."

"Who?"

"A friend of the Doctor. I think he's a fairy. He's even more of a jerk than that guy was."

Toni stared at the stove. Ever since she was a child, she had been subject to mild seizures. They had peaked during her adolescence and then stopped altogether. When she had mentioned this to Todd, he coached her on just what to tell a physician, who had certified her for disability payments as an epileptic. A fringe benefit was a prescription for phenobarbital; Todd had told her to ask for that, and he would trade it for other things.

Her aura had always been a winking light that had led her down a long, dark tunnel. That hadn't happened yesterday. She'd been standing at the stove. She'd turned the burner on, intending next to open a can of cream-of-chicken soup. But she had just stood there while the electric ring turned red.

A voice behind her ear had said: *What are you doing?*

"I'm —" Toni had started to answer, but another voice had cut in: *Observing the effect of hot iron on its flesh.*

The first voice said, laughing: *I know that effect.*

Toni had looked down. Her hand lay flat, the fingers spread, on the glowing electric ring. White smoke or steam hissed up between her fingers. She smelled it. Then at last she felt it and screamed, but seconds passed in a paralyzed frenzy before she had been able to lift it. Then she fell screaming and writhing in agony to the floor. Now it throbbed like a remembered toothache, even though she was floating on a cushion of codein.

The toilet flushed and Todd came out of the bathroom without his pants, his swollen cock at half-mast. "Maybe we can make some money out of it," he said.

"Out of what?"

"Your boyfriend, Martin. Amy. This other guy at the Doctor's, he kept talking about *The Pittsfield Ghouls* and how much money that made. Zillions. He knows what he's talking about, he had diamond rings every place but his nose."

She batted his hand away when he made a lazy grope for the button of her shorts. "Martin didn't. Does he look like money to you?"

"The Droop does."

"You just want the Droop because she looks and acts like she's about fourteen. It would be just like child-molesting, only without the penalty, that's what appeals to you."

It amused her to note that his penis stiffened slightly after she said that. Like pushing buttons. It was a kick. Had someone done that to her yesterday? To Mr. Gertner, today? Who?

"What's eating you today?" Todd asked.

"My hand hurts."

He laughed. "Use your other one." He pulled her right hand down. She fondled him briefly, then slipped away.

"You think she's a virgin?" he asked. It was a question he had asked before.

"How the hell should I know? They don't wear signs."

"You know, you're a woman. If you don't, ask her."

"For Christ's sake, ask her yourself!" she screamed. "You're the one who wants the Droop, I don't!"

She stamped into the living room and flung herself into a chair. She picked up *TV Guide* and pretended to study it.

"I don't really want the Droop all that much. Honest. But the Doctor could use a virgin. Big night tonight."

"The Doctor could use a shrink." If she had known Todd planned to go to one of the Doctor's crazy parties tonight, she would have given a definite invitation to that cute twerp in the dickey. "Are you serious?"

He shrugged, grinned, and drifted around the edges of the room, unabashedly playing with himself. She peeked while still pretending to read.

She'd been into astrology when she'd met Todd, and he had made a profound impression on her, right at the start, by displaying more knowledge of the subject than anyone she had ever known. He had asked for her birth date and hour, then pulled out a book of tables and told her how her Sun Sign (Cancer), her Moon Sign (Leo), and her Rising Sign (Sagittarius) all worked together to make her just the kind of person she was.

Toni eventually lost interest in the subject. Todd was a Virgo, and so was Amy, and that should have proved what astrology was worth, but Todd said it was because of the different planets they had in different houses, and he explained it at greater length than she wanted to hear.

He didn't put any real faith in astrology, either. It was just a minor tool, he said, in the equipment of a Wise Man. That would have sounded like a funny thing for Todd to want to be, moron and bully that he was, except that he always gave the words a subtle inflection, with implied capitals, that altered it from the everyday meaning. He would also refer to his coveted goal as *Adept*. He sometimes called the Doctor, his guru, the Adept. (Guru was Toni's word, and Todd didn't like it one bit.)

The Doctor — who wasn't a medical doctor, Todd said, but who had degrees from Harvard and Oxford — had been charging him every penny he could scrape up for the past two or three years in return for teaching him how to become a Wise Man. When that happened, and she suspected the Doctor wouldn't tell him it had happened until Todd was irreversibly tapped out, unable to scrounge the price of a single further lesson, Todd would be able to make everybody do what he wanted, to get any woman he desired, to give up his job as short-order cook at Pepe's all-night diner and coast through the rest of his life. Todd didn't express his ambitions in those terms, of course, he made them seem noble and self-sacrificing, but she knew that was what they boiled down to.

She wanted nothing to do with the Doctor and his gang. She knew he was a fraud, a dirty old man (although he was in his 40's and dressed impeccably), and she resented his dishonest manipulation of her boy-friend But against her better judgment, she had last year been persuaded to go to a "Christmas party" at the guru's place.

It was held at noon on Christmas Day. Toni was never a churchgoer, but she almost turned right around and walked out when she saw the manger inside the front door, with the figures of the Holy Family and the Shepherds and the Three Wise Men (was that where they stole the idea, she wondered?) intertangled with the barnyard animals in a confusion of unnatural acts. Other, similar decorations, either repulsive or silly, further reviled the Christmas theme. Some of the guests were naked, and some were snorting or smoking or shooting up, but she'd known in advance it would be that kind of party.

The guests were unemployed schoolbus drivers, retired beauticians and bagboys; postal clerks and prison matrons and unpromotable army captains; flashers and bike-seat sniffers on probation; cripples and dimwits and losers of every conceivable stripe: all of them with a slick line of patter about the "old" or "natural" religion of their Aryan forefathers, too long driven underground by that ultimate Jewish plot, Christianity, and how its practice would release their infinite potential and make them all whole and beautiful. Among them slithered their guru, exchanging gifts and pushing eggnog, kissing them under the mistletoe (which one woman, who turned out to be a high school teacher named Brenda Willy, wore on her navel), his salt-and-pepper Van Dyke wagging constantly as he suavely reassured each misfit that he or she was the fairest of them all.

All of these people had one thing in common with Todd: they were all smart enough to read a lot of books, but not smart enough to evaluate them. Besides the porno novels, detective stories and science fiction that Todd devoured like peanuts, he read widely in history, anthropology, psychology and mysticism, and he believed every word of the last book he'd read. If you told him that the earth went around the sun, chances are he would suspect you were lying or misinformed; but if he read it in a book, any book, he would believe it until he read another one that said it didn't.

Toni was different. She seldom read anything more profound than *TV Guide,* but she had the sense to question everything in it. Inspired by her the teachings of her mother, a dedicated but selective Marxist, she had even gone to the trouble of finding out who owned it and what else they owned, and she always interpreted the magazine in the light of that knowledge.

The problem with the Doctor's religion, she believed, was that there was no such thing as Evil with a capital *E.* It was no dark Presence on a basalt throne, it was a case of the crabs; it was drowned kittens, starving children, it was flunkies from the power company who froze old people to death for not paying their bills. It was everybody who was "just doing his job." It was rain on Sunday and cars programmed to fall apart as soon as the warranties ran out. Evil lived only in specific instances, as when Gertner had just tried to cheat that poor slob. (Or in making someone put her hand down on a hot stove, just for kicks? But she didn't want to think about that.) How could you worship evils like those?

At the party she soon tired of drinking eggnog and chatting with fruitcakes, and she was actually relieved when the Doctor clapped his hands and announced that it was time to get naked. She even enjoyed the next part, when everybody helped one another get covered — or *anointed* — with a pleasantly herb-scented grease from a big stone crock, with much horseplay and groping. Everyone was especially eager to anoint her, and by the time about six different people had done it, she was shocked by a tremendous, disorienting rush. The grease apparently contained some drug that filtered through the skin to the bloodstream. Her head expanded to fill the room, then floated up above the house until she could look down on all the tiny Satanists like people in the wrong end of a telescope. They were no more than dolls in a dollhouse, and she was the Birthday Girl who had been given this marvelous gift.

By that time, she believed, it would have sounded like fun if the Doctor had told her to cut her own throat, so he had no trouble cajoling her into being the altar for his ceremony. She crouched on knees and elbows before an inverted crucifix, her bare bottom facing the congregation, whose members sang and danced and would periodically chant, *"Evoë! Evoë! Saboi!"* The Head Loon used her body and his own to do distasteful things with communion wafers and got her to piss into a chalice that had probably been stolen from a local church.

The worshippers then lined up to kneel behind her and take communion, a ritual that included kissing her anus. She already had a bad case of the giggles, and it got worse when some of them used an inordinate amount of tongue. Holding her in place when she was about to squirm away reflexively, the Doctor assured her that there was nothing wrong with laughter, that pranks and high spirits distinguished their religion from all others. He got her to drink from a chalice. She believed it was the same one she had pissed into, but she didn't give a damn at this point, and now it was filled with slimy green stuff, which Todd later told her was mashed peyote and grain alcohol. The Doctor presented his own ass to be kissed, which she did with giggly fervor, then climbed on from behind and sodomized her. Just about everybody else took her in one way or another, and that ended the formal part of the ceremony.

Later they all wound up in a dark room, floored with mattresses, where no distinctions of sex were observed. She even kissed Brenda Willy under her mistletoe. She had fun, even if she was a bit sick and sore, but part of her mind was free to stand aside and observe disdainfully how sad and shabby and dated this party was. The strobe-lights, incense, Op-art posters, the hard-charging rock on the bone-buzzing music system, the group sex, even the idea of Satanism itself, suggested that all these outsiders, having caught one of the Roger Corman hippie-movies that Todd liked to watch, were at last daring to experiment with the possibilities of the Sixties.

Still later, stoned out of her mind, she became enraptured with a huge black statue in a dim, remote room. It reminded her of a Greek god, except that it had female breasts and hips, but impressive male equipment, too, and the kind of face that would give them nightmares in the lion-house at the zoo. An endless serpet slid sinuously and hypnotically around his legs and his genitals and his belly. She knew that sculptured serpents didn't move, but the unafflicted part of her mind made allowances for the drugs.

In one hand he held a scroll that contained the whole story of the world. He gave her a peek. It wasn't in writing, nor was it exactly in pictures, but in an unheard-of medium that enabled her to comprehend what a king or prime minister was saying, what his advisers were thinking, what a worm beneath the foundations of the palace was up to, what a moron shoveling shit in the street outside had eaten for breakfast, in a simultaneous instant. It was fascinating, even though it tended to give her a headache, but he wouldn't let her see it all. Then he unrolled the scroll he held in his other hand, which showed her own life and death — and more, too much more — in a glimpse, and she began to scream in terror.

The next thing she knew she was throwing up in the sink, while Todd and his guru and others were hugging her and making sympathetic noises.

They were terribly excited, for it seemed that the Doctor had no such statue in his house, and not a little jealous, for she had been granted a personal vision of an even bigger deal than the Devil himself. This entity was mentioned in the unspeakable *Book of Dead Names* under the cabalistic acronym of TWI(N): That Which Is (Not). The form which He/She had assumed for her was that worshipped by the ancient Persians under the name of — here the Doctor paused to look over his shoulder and lower his voice to a whisper — *Zurvan*. Brooding beyond such man-made constructs as space and time, He/She contained all opposites and would one day bring an end to all the contradictions of the physical universe, making whole the now-broken egg on which He/She traditionally stood.

Although she humored them in their fantasy for as long as it took her to get out of the house, Toni knew a bad trip when she had one. She fiercely resisted all their attempts to get her back into the cult. The Doctor promised to make her his equal in the organization and proclaim her as the avatar of Hecate, Goddess of the Night — the old letch wanted her to go and play house with him, that was what that was all about — with Todd's eager acquiescence. Eventually they gave up their efforts to convert her as they went on to some new mania, or some likelier sucker. Toni stuck to ordinary drugs, rationed her consumption of alcohol, and had no more audiences with Zurvan.

*T*odd now stood behind her, stroking her hair, while she pretended complete absorption in a story about David Duchovny. She shivered at his touch. Troubled by her vision, she hadn't let him touch her for a week after the Christmas Party, and she'd seriously considered splitting for good. But she liked being where she was, more or less. She liked Todd, more or less. She couldn't think of any better place to be or any person she'd rather be with, except possibly David Duchovny, and the final horror revealed in the scroll of her life had at last faded from her memory. Todd rubbed his phallus against her cheek, and she turned to accept it into her mouth.

Chapter Five

Martin fled Brooksprite Gardens in a dull rage. He had resented Toni's coming on to him — pose nude, indeed! — secure in the knowledge that her pet ape snored in the bedroom. Girls like her, embodiments of the Great American Wet Dream, could intimidate him without even trying, and she had tried. Their attraction seemed a frightening form of aggression that he could only deal with in his imagination, where he mastered them by transforming them into thrill-crazed automatons in the works of Dick Standing.

In real life he had never so much as touched a girl like that — well, once, but she'd been crazy: Margo Slye, who had picked him up in a bar and taken him home to bed with her. As a consequence, Martin fell madly in love with her. She was an aspiring actress, involved in a theater group in the East Village. Against his better judgment, she nagged him into writing a play for her — he was a writer, wasn't he? — that suffered through three or four off-off-Broadway performances before sinking out of sight.

She would come over to his place to walk the dog he used to have (Bing, named for his extensive repertoire of amiable groans) and to drink jug-wine with him in the afternoon, when he should have been working. She would kiss him and sometimes let him take off her shirt, and she seemed to like him (of course the real attraction could have been Bing), but she wouldn't sleep with him after the first time, claiming that she only fucked men she didn't know.

That episode taught Martin the uncomfortable truth that he was capable of rape and murder, and of deriving great enjoyment from both, but she dropped him completely before it could go that far. For the past two or three years, his sex life had consisted solely of jerking off on the pictures in the magazines he wrote for. He was in danger of becoming — if he hadn't already — one of the innumerable and interchangeable host of middle-aged masturbators who hang out in bars and bitch about the turpitude of women.

He resented Toni Sloane for helping him in the quarrel with the old man, for helping him get the check in his pocket (and he knew it would never clear the bank); but mostly he resented having needed her help because his license had lapsed and he had no insurance. It never failed: he couldn't even hate anyone properly, because all his porcupine quills turned inward to prick at the sores of his failure and ineptitude.

He ought to pretend that the check would not be stopped and go home, calling it clear profit. He didn't have to spend it on his car. The window wouldn't have to be fixed until wintertime. When he got home, why didn't he devote a month to writing a dumb, sprawly novel like *Behold Now Behemoth*, with a gray-eyed, shirtless hero who took immediate charge of situations, and a beautiful blond heroine who posed nude? Because he wasn't Hogarth Zurer, that's why, because he didn't know any Italian film moguls and couldn't subvert a reviewer for New York's premier suburban cookbook, and therefore no publisher would buy it.

The prospect of selling the Mt. Tabor Massacre to *True Murder Facts* began to look equally dim. He had written his letter to Miss Miniter in plenty of time, but then he had forgotten it and mailed it only two days ago. Assuming her answer would be *no*, he had decided not to wait for it but to come as planned and try to persuade her in person.

With no pictures of bodies, no George Spencer, no clever police work, and no Miss Miniter, there was just no story. Spencer had come to the mill to look for his missing son, the one who had run off with a high school girl, as it turned out. In the basement he'd found Amy with what was left of two of the bodies. Upstairs he'd found Frank's remains. Then he'd come upon Rose, mad as a hatter, in her bedroom. Spencer or Amy or even the missing son — and what had ever become of him and his cheerleader? — could have done it just as easily as Rose, but Martin would never know the truth.

He began writing in his head: *Does the ghost of Mirdath Glendower, willful and tempestuous beauty from Victorian days, still stalk the night in search of victims? That is a question which residents of Mt. Tabor, Connecticut,* bullshit bullshit *bullshit!*

The dead can't talk, and the living won't, and only the picturesque mill rising beside the bullshit bullshit *bullshit!*

Bluff, hearty Burgomeister Maurice Donovan says that Frau Laughlin murdered her husband, the mad artist, but then he pauses and listens as if waiting to hear the strains of the demonic pipe of Ygor, hulking henchman of the diabolical Prof. Gertner. . . .

Maybe he would get lucky after all. He parked behind the red sports car that sat unattended on a wooded road. It was easy to guess the owner: his own letter was sitting among some bills on the passenger's seat. He scanned the woods on either side of the road. He peered over the roadside fence to check the banks of the stream below.

"Miss Miniter!" His voice startled a flock of birds. They exploded above the stream on drumming wings. "Amy!"

He leaned back on the hot metal of his own car and opened his coat to fan himself. He resented Toni Sloane, too, for spotting his dickey. He had been certain that no one could have told he wasn't wearing a real shirt and tie. Nobody had ever mentioned it before, anyway. He had thought he could get away with the sneakers — who ever looked at a person's feet? — but maybe they were noticeable as well. You used to be able to buy a wardrobe for $250, with enough left over to wear it someplace, but God only knew nowadays. He would pick up sneakers every so often from the bargain-bins on Fourteenth street and hadn't priced a real pair of shoes in ten years.

"Miss Miniter!" That might be the wrong approach. She had probably dashed into the woods to take a leak and was now lying low and only wishing that he would go away.

He didn't care if she answered. He was beginning to enjoy the bright day. The sunlight and shadow of innumerable leaves presented a fascinating confusion to eyes dulled by granite and concrete symmetry. He threw his jacket and dickey in the back seat and set off down the country lane with a rolling, barrel-chested gait, pretending he was Toni's ape. "Pose naked for that little fucker, will you? Take that, bitch!" *Pow!*

Often asked — by himself — why he had become a writer, Martin would reply that he had done it so he could smoke a pipe, wear a tweed jacket with suede elbow-patches, and take long walks in the country when other people were shut up in stuffy cubicles. He had never gotten the knack of smoking a pipe; he still had the elbow-patches in a bottom drawer, but the jacket had disintegrated away from them; and he hadn't taken a walk in the country since . . . since. . . . He took a deep breath of the healthy country air, but it made him cough and he had to light a cigarette.

He suspected he had really become a writer to impress girls, but they remained unimpressed. He had all but abandoned the search for a quiet, intelligent young woman whose idea of fun was a long walk in the rain or a good book, one as pretty as Toni or Margo Slye, but in a low-keyed, unassertive way that most men might overlook.

He had been driving in Pine Hollow Road with the intention of taking a look at the Laughlins' mill, but it surprised him when he rounded the bend and came upon its gate. The red walls of the building rose far off through the trees. He walked around the gate and continued up the driveway.

Trusting in precise words and in nothing beyond his five senses, Martin was unnerved whenever he was confronted with a feeling or an atmosphere that he could neither define nor account for, and he walked into a wall of it here. The mill and its additions were ungainly but pleasant, its setting was lovely, but it gave him the creeps. He stopped dead in his tracks on the gravel apron as the hair rose on the back of his neck. Someone, as

Toni had said, was walking on his grave — marching over it with drums and bagpipes.

*T*he green pond behind the mill had been made for the disposal of murdered men. He could all but see gray hands emerge from the slimy blanket of muck to clutch blindly at the mossy stones, and he gave the nominal water as wide a berth as possible when he went to the gaping back door. Confusing glimmers, reflections from the pond, danced within the stone-walled kitchen but did nothing to light it. He took the matches from his trouser pocket and lit one as he walked in, but it dispelled neither the darkness nor the rippling water-lights. He regretted having left his jacket in the car when the temperature dropped twenty degrees as he stepped beyond the threshold.

Finding candles scattered on a counter, he lit several and placed them around the room until he could gauge its gloomy volume. It would have made — it one day undoubtedly would make — an ideal setting for one of Tanya Hyde's S&M books. Rose Laughlin, ghost, flitted about domestically, calculating if she had acquired enough acid to dissolve all her victims. He wondered what woman, apart from Ilse Koch or one of Dracula's brides, would feel at home sipping her coffee or eating her Wheaties in a place like this. He carried a candle to the door at the head of the cellar stairs and began to descend.

Down in the gloom at the foot of the staircase stood a white wraith with terrified eyes. Long, straight hair as pale as her face hung below her slim shoulders. Her sudden appearance should have scared the hell out of him, but it didn't, because he knew her: as Tenniel's *Alice* and as Katy Marsden, the girl he'd loved when he was ten; as Rhiannon MacLear, the pale enchantress for whose love the world is well lost in *Swords of Winbourne*; as translucent china and chintz curtains billowed with sunlight, as hectic leaves awhirl past autumn skirts, as *Claire de Lune* and the *Moonlight Sonata*, as everything fair and fragile and elfin and evanescent in the race of females. He knew that this instant would be burned forever in his memory, destroying as it did at a blow his long-held scorn of such a thing as love at first sight, of such a thing, for one grown sour in the frictionary service of sprawled jades' shadows, as love itself. *I will become pure and good and true and deserve her,* he thought; and then he thought, *Fat chance.*

"Miss Miniter? Is that you?"

A shaky penlight danced on him. "Who are you?" He might not be scared, but she was in a transport of terror.

"I'm nobody. I'm harmless. I'm not here to hurt you. Honest. It's all right. Really."

He must have said something right. She galloped gracelessly up the stairs and flung herself on him, squeezing him so hard it hurt. "Help!" she sobbed. *"Mother!"*

"It's all right. Really, everything's okay. What were you doing down there? Isn't that the last place. . . ?"

"Amy took some goodies to her Grandma," she half-sang in a wispy, little-girl voice that made him shiver to match her shaking, "but she had big eyes. And big teeth. And big, bloody claws. I told Patrick to feed my mother to the thing he kept in the cellar, and he did, but then it said it was still hungry, so it ate him. And then it was *still* hungry, and it looked for me. It looked and it looked, but it still couldn't find me, because I stayed as quiet as a mouse while it squinched . . . and it sucked . . . and it crunched . . . all around and around the cellar. 'Come out, little girl,' it said. 'I won't hurt you.'"

Martin thought of slapping her, as men used to do in the movies to bring hysterical women to their senses, but he could no more have slapped her than he could have slipped a knife into his own heart. The most he could do was give her a tentative, gentle shake as he led her toward the sunlight, which he hoped would have a beneficial effect. He could have kicked himself for not bringing his camera from the car. Here was the only eyewitness at the scene of the crime, in the grip of a horror that no one could have faked. In the next instant he snarled at himself for entertaining such a cheap idea. It upset him almost as much as did the suspicion that she was crazy.

"My mother told me never to let a boy touch me, and then I let Patrick touch me, and she died. God punished me. It was all my fault. Everything!"

She struggled to free herself, but he hung on, and he dragged her outside to the edge of the pond. It was not at all menacing now, not after the interior of the mill, just mouldy and unpleasant. He tried to decide whether her pale eyes should be called green or blue. As he studied them, they sharpened with sudden awareness of her surroundings, and of him. He was relieved to see her prompt recovery, but her scrutiny began to make him nervous. He released her at last, and she made no move to run away.

"Who are you?"

"Martin Paige. I —"

"Where's your shirt?"

"It was such a nice day. . . ." He folded his arms over his narrow chest. "You are Amy Miniter, aren't you?"

"Yes. Your letter must have been delayed. I only got it today, and I'm afraid —"

"What were you doing down there?"

"I was thinking about buying the mill. Fixing it up." She laughed unconvincingly. "It was getting on my nerves — and then your foot-steps. . . . Forget whatever I might have said. You'll have to forgive me for being such a goose."

"I think it was awfully brave of you to go down in the cellar alone, considering. I want to take a look myself, but of course it doesn't hold any special meaning for me. Would you wait here while —"

"No, I have to go."

She started to do just that. Martin turned from the door and hurried after her.

"It doesn't matter. I'm not going to write the story anyway. I don't think I will."

She was almost as tall as he was, and her posture was regal. He felt like some clownish executioner in a peasant revolt, tagging along after a doomed queen.

"Why on earth shouldn't you? Isn't that why you came here?"

"I couldn't sell your name, your troubles, to *True Murder Facts.* It would be obscene, sacrilegious. You're the prettiest girl I've ever met. And that's the stupidest adjective I've ever used. You look like Alice in Wonderland, you look like the girl I was always certain I was going to meet, when I was a dumb kid planning the life I never had."

She lowered her face to hide it with her hair and walked faster. "Stop that! I don't enjoy being made fun of."

Martin ran in front of her and kept back-pedaling as she walked straight ahead. He waved his hands, groping for his words, false friends that had abandoned him the one time in his life they were needed. "I'm thirty-six years old," he said in desperation. "Is that too old for you?"

"Go away! You're crazy. Or drunk."

"No, I'm not, I've just been going through the motions of living for years now without purpose or reason, and now I've suddenly, unexpect-edly found it, and it's you. I know this is not the way to talk to a girl. I don't know how to talk to girls. The only people I ever talk to are bill-collectors and bartenders. But I want to impress upon you that I'm serious. I mean what I say, I'm not making fun of you. Would you like to go to a movie tonight?"

He collided painfully with the gate while she ducked around it and dashed down the road.

He lost one of his sneakers but didn't stop for it as he hopped after her, the blacktop searing his sockless foot.

"Wait! You can't go like this. I take back everything I said. Pretend that I said nothing but clever, charming, fascinating things, and from now on, I swear, that's all I'll ever say to you. Can we have dinner together?"

She stood by her car, staring at him through fingers pressed to her flushed face. "Are you really a writer? I don't believe it."

"Yes," he hissed as he hopped forward. "I am! I'm the best writer in the world, only I have nothing to say. I thought that life was a joke, that there was nothing at all worthwhile in it, and I know that some people get away with writing novels to prove just that, but they can't really believe it or they wouldn't do it. I can't, anyway. And now I've found you, and you're worthwhile, you're no joke, and maybe you can inspire me. I promise to try, at least. If not, I'll get a job washing dishes or selling encyclopedias right here in Mt. Tabor so I can be near you."

She turned away from him and giggled. He took this as an encouraging sign. She said, "What do you write about, besides *unfortunate tragedies?*"

He didn't detect the sneer in her voice, nor did he recognize the quotation from his own letter, which he had deliberately written to appeal to the sort of dunce he had thought she would be. He took a deep breath and said, "I've written a hundred pornographic novels, plus thirty or forty obscene short stories for magazines like *Pussy,* which features pictures of naked women with their legs spread out and . . . so forth. I write true crime stories, too, some of which I make up, but I can't always sell them. I keep writing short stories for mystery and science fiction magazines and even for the higher-class men's magazines, but they always get rejected. I wrote one really rotten play that was actually produced, although it didn't last long, called *The Wild Hunt.* Plus I'm working on a heroic fantasy novel, *Swords of Winbourne,* which might earn me a couple of thousand dollars from a paperback publisher, except that it's probably too good to be appreciated. I make a living out of writing, which is more than most people could do; but on the other hand, most people wouldn't call this a living."

"That's disgusting!" She got into her car and slammed the door. "What you are, is, you're a *bum!*"

"I know, but I'm honest. With you. I've never been honest about it with anyone else."

"And you're cynical and unpleasant and you're *dirty!*" She started her car and tortured the gears. *"Ugh,* you make me *sick!*"

That, Martin reflected as her red car sped away down the wooded lane, was exactly how great romances got started in the movies, but he had no illusions about the relation of such fantasies to real life. Within fifteen minutes of finding the one girl in the universe whom he had given up hope of meeting, his heart had been returned with a rejection slip. Suppose he had been clean and reasonably attired, suppose he had spoken or acted differently; or just as easily, suppose he were Errol Flynn. It was just no use.

He limped back to his abandoned sneaker and stared at it for a long time without bending to retrieve it, like one envisioning a shrine on the site of a miracle: *When I stood in that spot, in that sneaker, she stood before me in the flesh, and now she is gone.* It seemed impossible that such an inconsequential span of time should separate them as effectivelty as light-years of space, yet it did, and no amount of willing it different could change it. He put on his sneaker and walked back to the mill. No longer baleful, it was the Mecca of his new religion, the Place where he had met Her.

He was still interested in the mystery it hid, not only because it was a part of Amy's life, but for professional reasons. His unwillingness to peddle her name to a cheap rag, his resolve to become worthy of her by becoming rich and famous, and his earlier impulse to write a dumb novel like *Behold Now Behemoth* had all come together to trigger a brainstorm: he would write a whole book about the Mt. Tabor Massacre, a supernatural horror-story purporting to be based on fact. Surely the things Chief Donovan had told him, together with Amy's hysterical rant about some version of the Big Bad Wolf, contained the seeds of a nightmare at least as scary as *The Pittsfield Ghouls,* by Merry Treece, who had been a hack like himself, even selling to the same markets until she hit the jackpot. Although he didn't believe in an occult interpretation of the local events, he hadn't believed in that book, either, but that hadn't stopped it from outselling even *Behemoth* by a factor of a thousand.

Any hope of earning another sort of living than by writing as a freelance was futile. After five years of freedom, he could no more have held an ordinary job than a dog who has run wild with a pack can come home to romp harmlessly with children. He would quit the first time someone told him what to do, he would smash the alarm clock when it rang. The only work he was fit for was the work he did, and the best chance – the only chance – of making it pay seemed to be the story of the massacre.

His daydream rolled on with musical accompaniment (the Beatles singing *Paperback Writer)* as he entered the kitchen, took up one of the candles he had left burning, and descended the dank stairs to the cellar. He would write an electrifying letter of inquiry – *Dear Sir or Madam . . .* – this very day to an agent, stressing the occult-horror angle, reminding them of its current vogue, and hinting that he knew far more about the Massacre than he could commit to a letter. He would emphasize his close, personal friendship with the only surviving witness, a qualification no other hack could boast. The agent would plead for an outline and a couple of sample chapters and then secure Martin a six, five, well, certainly no less than a four-figure advance from somebody like Wittol & Ingle, and then he could afford to spend long, delightful hours interviewing Amy. Talking to him would heal her wounded psyche and she would find herself falling in love with him, her combination confessor, physican, and champion.

What if she had a boyfriend? A fiancé? Some kid her own age who had done all the right things with his life and who even knew enough to wear a shirt and a pair of socks in public? He suspected that she didn't. Her hysterical speech, the way she had of hiding her face with her hair or her hands, even her proper walk suggested an emotional ten-year-old who was even less at ease with men than he was with women. What had she called herself? A *goose*. It suggested that she didn't do much talking with her contemporaries. Her deepest fear, already confessed to him, that the storm of her pubescence had brought on her mother's death, seemed to clinch his profile. His only rival would be her neurosis.

*H*e toured the cellar, carefully guarding the feeble flicker of the candle with one hand. It was a big place, but not as big, he estimated, as the mill above it. Passages began only to end abruptly, and certain niches had the look of bricked-up doorways. He wondered if Mordred's fabled gold — not transmuted from lead, of course, but earned by smuggling or slave-trading or bootlegging — could still lie hidden here.

To win Amy, he decided, he would need to be uncharacteristically aggressive and persistent. Missing her mother, whom she had instinctively called on in her moment of panic, she would respond to someone who moved confidently into her life and took charge. He would phone her, knock on her door, bring her flowers, write her — by all means, write her, that was something he *could* do. He wondered if he could still write poetry; not that he ever could, but he had once thought he could.

> *How to begin it? Her*
> *Head I shall spin it, her*
> *Hand I will win it, sir,*
> *Darling Miss Miniter!*

He came at last to a door and stairs leading downward into the sub-cellar room that Donovan had told him about. It had been thoroughly cleansed. He smelled nothing but a very faint, residual odor of some powerful disinfectant underlaid by a pervasive mustiness.

Descending, he saw that shelves had once lined the wall, although only their gouged and splintered frames remained. Had the Laughlins really kept something down here in this room, something that could eat people? A bear, perhaps, or a tiger?

In a pile of fragmented wood that had been shoved into a corner he found scraps of paper and leather that suggested very old books. One yellow, crumpled sheet proved to be a title-page: *Unaussprechlichen Kulten,* by Friedrich Wilhelm von Junzt, published in Düsseldorf in 1839. Although he knew nothing of German and even less of rare books, this particular title rang a faint bell.

The page, like the splintered wood, had been smeared with some black stuff, now dry, that had no smell whatever. He scratched a bit of black dust from it, but he could make nothing of that, either. He folded the page in quarters and stuck it in his wallet with the thought of having it analyzed.

Chapter Six

*M*eeting Martin Paige had given Amy Miniter a compelling urge to hurry home and do her neglected laundry. She had wanted to meet an interesting person like a writer, and Martin filled the bill: interesting as a centipede in the bathtub is interesting, it holds your interest long after it slithers away to its home in the pipes; and every bit as much a writer as those horrible boys who like to scrawl graffiti on vacant houses.

The Greeks said that you must never ask the gods for anything, because they just might give it to you. Perhaps Bozo (she really had to look him up in the library and call him by his proper name, if he had one) could grant wishes in the same spirit. He stood on top of the case that held her favorite books, and she had surely made the vague wish in that very spot. She'd had a writer in mind like John Irving, but she'd wound up with one who not only wrote dirty books, but a *hundred* of them! What on earth could he have possibly written after the second page of the first book? And he boasted of it. Women with their legs spread out. *Ugh!* She would take a shower, too, and put on crisp, clean clothes and pretend the day had never begun. Then she would find a nice, empty house somewhere and hide in it, giving him plenty of time to leave town in his dirty, dented, disgusting car.

Empty house. What had she told him? She couldn't remember now exactly what she'd said to him when she'd fled the cellar of the mill, but she knew she had bared shameful secrets to that horrid little man. She had not just remembered the day when her mother died, she had relived it in all its horror, and she had run to him with the foulness of it still clogging her sight, her smell, her hearing. She had wanted Patrick, she had wanted her mother dead, and those two obscene desires had taken form and walked the earth.

Mr. Gertner, a white bandage adorning his bald head, peered at her from the edge of his curtain as she parked in her slot. He was the sort of man who permitted Martin to make a living: he undoubtedly possessed *The Complete Works of Martin Paige.* She hated wearing jeans, they made her feel like a tomboy, but lately she'd had no choice, because Mr. Gertner would often lurk beneath her open staircase in the morning, waiting for the chance to peek up her dress when she came down. She had tried varying the time of her departure, but Mr. Gertner, retired and a widower, had all the time in the world to lurk. Todd Farmer spotted him once, knew immediately what he was up to, and threw a pot of water on him. But Todd didn't normally get up early enough to protect her.

She wondered why he was wearing a bandage. Brooksprite Gardens seemed to be having a high casualty rate today. Curious though she was, she had no intention of giving him time to dodder across and talk to her, to paw her arm and breathe gin and tobacco-smoke in her face. She bolted from her car and fled up the stairs without a backward look, pretending not to hear when he opened his door and croaked her name.

She shed her clothes and jammed them into the laundry bag. She was about to strip the bed and do the same with her sheets until she realized how inviting the bed looked. She lay on top of the bedspread, but only to compose her mind and rest her eyes.

She felt quite refreshed when she opened her eyes — and no wonder, the clock said *two*. It couldn't have been much later than noon when she lay down. She snapped off the bedside lamp, unable to remember when or why she'd turned it on. She took off her underwear and put it in the laundry bag, then stripped the bed and balled in the sheets and pillow cases.

Avoiding the windows (for not even the heavy brocade drapes could assure her that she was safe from Mr. Gertner's rheumy and unblinking leer) she went to her dresser and opened the lingerie drawer. There she found a dilemma. She wanted to take a shower — she *needed* to take a shower, after that filthy cellar and that filthy man — but she didn't want to do that until she had dealt with her dirty laundry. If she put on clean underwear now, she wouldn't want to put the same things on again when she came newly scrubbed and tingling from the shower. Clean though they still might be, they wouldn't be *absolutely* fresh, and that mattered. But to put on a second set of clean underwear after she showered would be wasteful. Worse, after all the drudgery of doing the laundry, she would be nagged by the knowledge that every last bit of her clothing was not clean, that in the bottom of the bathroom hamper still festered, despite all her trouble, the unwashed bra and panties she had worn while doing the laundry. She could take two showers, of course — one now, before she put on clean things, and another one after she did the laundry — but that struck her as almost neurotically fastidious. And even though her underwear would be cleaner, she would have worn it before, if only for half an hour. She could retrieve the things she'd recently worn from the laundry bag and wear them while she did the wash, but that seemed the worst possible alternative. She thought of the bag as a dank and fecund womb of germs that were even now swarming and spawning on her undies.

She hit upon a drastic and daring solution: she would wear no underthings while she did the laundry. She had never once in her life stepped outside the door without her underwear, but it now seemed the only sensible thing to do. (Some people, of course, never gave a thought to stepping outside the door without even a shirt, for heaven's sake!)

Sensible or not, it gave her a delicious little *frisson* of mingled fear and naughtiness that she stifled as she rolled deodorant on her armpits — she would shave, too — and went to the closet to select a pearl-gray, belted dress. Slipping into pale blue sneakers without socks recalled the image of that man's corpse-white foot with its dirty, yellow, overgrown, crooked toenails, but she erased it from her mind.

She pinned her hair back and struck a variety of poses before the full-length mirror. The bodice of her dress was loose, even baggy, and only when she stretched her arms high over her head and leaned backward slightly — and there was no reason why she should do that while washing her clothes — could she detect the outlines of her nipples, which had become annoyingly hard and sensitive from the moment she had conceived her bold plan.

She snapped off the bathroom light — she didn't remember turning that on, either, it was unlike her to be so careless and wasteful — and went to the kitchen, where she kept her washday supplies under the sink. It was a bright day, and only when she had entered the kitchen did she realize that the overhead light, the light in the hood of the stove, and the lamp on the table were all burning.

She turned deliberately to the stove, where a pot sat scummed with milk. Above the sink, one of her bone china cups was missing from its proper hook. The serving tray, which had rested in the drainer this morning — she *knew* that! — was missing.

Fully prepared now, she didn't scream when she entered the living room and found the chest forced open and her treasures strewn about the Anatolian carpet. On the coffee table lay her mother's photograph album, the pictures beside it in a clumsy pile. On the opposite side of the room, Bozo, the mirror, the cup and the saucer lay broken near the tray and the scattered cookies. She looked down at her bare forearm and found the pale skin marred by a recent cut.

"*Shit!*" she spat.

She went to the locks of the front door, all secured, and touched their cold, reassuring steel. Had she only dreamed of going out this morning, talking to Toni, visiting the mill and meeting Martin Paige? She looked at her watch. It was twenty after two. Enough time had passed for all of that, and for her nap, too.

She carefully picked over her first memories of the morning, when this mess had not existed. Those memories were as clear as — well, they were at least as clear as her memories of last night, when she had woken to find exactly the same evidence of intruders.

She had taken psychology classes at college, hoping such knowledge might enhance her acting, and so she could explain what had happened: unwilling to acknowledge the existence of the mess this morning, she had simply refused to see it. Perfectly healthy minds are capable of playing even more elaborate tricks than that. One of her professors had once pulled the classic experiment of staging an unexpected event in the classroom, a disruptive intrusion by a student from another class, to prove that each of the eyewitnesses would give a different account of the event, that they would see no more nor less than they were predisposed to see.

Of course, that was beside the point. It didn't explain how someone had penetrated her securely locked apartment to create the disorder.

The answer to that was even more unnerving, but it could be the only answer: she herself had made the mess. In her sleep, unremembered, she had forced the chest and removed the pictures from the album. Then she had returned to bed and dreamed an elaborate dream to explain what she had done. Her paralysis and the unpleasant things she had been "forced" to do — all were products of her subconscious, and they were the ultimate fruit of that evil vine whose roots lay in the fetid sub-cellar of the Laughlins' mill.

All this went far deeper than playing innocent mind-games on herself, she now admitted. She would call her psychiatrist at college. Today. Now. But first she would put the pictures back in their sleeves, return the album to its place, and clean up the living room.

Up until now she had been calm. She was worried by what she was doing to herself, very worried, but she still felt in control of the situation and competent to rectify it. Then she looked down at the top picture on the pile, and it was like looking through a little window into hell.

It was a picture her father had taken when she was eight years old, the year he had died, the year he had given her the pony. Gentle and mildly ironic, always dim through a haze of pipe-smoke, her father would simply vanish altogether when her mother asserted herself with more than usual force. Things were done only one way in her family, her mother's way.

Amy had wanted a pony. Her father had said, "We'll see," her mother had said, "No," and Amy had known that was the end of it, but she had nevertheless kept bringing up the subject. The pony was waiting for her in the barn with a big red ribbon around his neck on her birthday. Her mother hated it, the dogs hated it, but there it would stay, hers, and she loved it. Later, when she would hear her mother and father — hear only her mother, actually, while her father smoked his pipe and murmured — arguing about the pony late into the night, when they thought she was fast asleep, she would sometimes wish that she had never asked for it. She would feel guilty and ashamed for having desired such an extravagant and impractical and controversial gift, a gift that had divided her dear mother and father. When, three months later, her father died of a heart attack, it had seemed like one of God's relentless and innumerable punishments, clearly invoked by her greed. It had seemed only just when, promptly after the funeral, her mother had sold the pony.

But in those three golden months when Scrapple had been hers, her father had taught her how to ride him and how to care for him, and he had spent hours walking beside her with a firm hand on his bridle as she rode around her grounds and in the neighboring country lanes. ("The poor man knew his heart couldn't stand such exertion, but he couldn't say no when you pestered him to go tramping around with you in all weathers on that loathsome, dwarfish animal," her mother used to say.) He had squandered roll upon roll of color film on her and on Scrapple, too, and the prints lay here. It was as if, before his departure, he had tried to fix her in time forever in his memory and in his grave.

But time had perversely refused to stay fixed. In the top print, Scrapple gazed shyly into the camera as he had always gazed, head lowered and slightly averted ("I didn't mean to cause all this trouble," he seemed to say), but the girl on his back wasn't eight-year-old Amy in her pinafore, it was Amy as she was now, wearing nothing at all.

Her pose was lewd, brazen: legs spread and stretched out like a model from one of Martin's magazines, hands resting back on the pony's rump, breasts thrust forward; but not even those adjectives fit the utter depravity, the wicked, cynical knowingness of her smile. Amy glanced up at the cracked mirror across the room and knew that she had never smiled, could never smile, in just such a way.

She sat on the couch by the coffee table and closed her eyes while she took several deep, steady breaths. This is only one more hallucination, she told herself, and when I open my eyes it will be gone. She opened her eyes. It was still there.

She picked up the photo in shaking fingers. She stroked its cool, satiny surface. She turned it over and studied the name of the manufacturer and the processor's symbols. She read the appropriate date, written by her father in faded ink. When she turned it over — and there could be *no question about this* — it would show eight-year-old Amy in her pale green pinafore. She turned it over. It showed wanton, naked, grown-up Amy.

She dashed into the bedroom, snatched up her laundry bag, and flew out the front door, remembering only when she was halfway down the stairs to return and lock it, and remembering only then to check beneath her for Mr. Gertner, whose hours of patient lurking would at last have earned him the ultimate reward. But he wasn't there.

Each entry in Brooksprite Gardens normally served four apartments, two up and two down. In Amy's entry, however, the space next to Todd and Toni's apartment held the laundry room and, beyond it, the storage room for their building. In the laundry room were two washers and two dryers. She could hear one of the washers chugging away as she approached the door. She didn't want to see anyone, but she wanted even less to return to her apartment, and just getting into her car and driving off without any underwear was unthinkable. If she stood outside much longer, Mr. Gertner would spot her and corner her, so she hurried into the laundry room.

She thought at first that the room was empty, but then Todd said, "Hi," behind her back, and she choked out an aborted scream. She backed tightly against the idle washer. Todd wore only a pair of cut-off jeans, not even shoes. Hadn't this inconsiderate man ever heard of athlete's foot? His feet were strong and brown, the toes regular, the nails clipped, not at all like Martin Paige's feet. Gold hair glittered on his dark ankles.

"Don't mind me," he said, smiling sarcastically and confidently. "Just another housewife." He emphasized his lack of consideration by blowing cigarette smoke at her.

"I won't." She turned her back on him and pulled out her dark blue sheets and her jeans and put them in the washer. She rummaged guardedly in the bag as she searched for other colored things, fearful of letting him see some embarrassing garment.

"I've got a message for you," he said at her ear.

She squeezed around to face him, loathing the thought of actually touching his naked body — although he proved to be at least two feet away when she had turned. That was still far too close. He seemed to be stealing her air. He sensed her fear and took a step — a mocking step — backward, extending a piece of paper in his fingertips. She accepted Martin's note, scanned it, and ripped it jerkily to shreds.

"You're very welcome, I'm sure."

"I'm sorry. Thank you for giving it to me. It was from a tiresome, wretched pest."

"We have the same taste in people. I bet we have a lot in common."

She ignored him once more as she turned to the washer. She would put in her colored things, start the machine, and go outside to wait. Mr. Gertner in the open air would be preferable to Todd in these cramped quarters. Todd might even chase him; and Todd in the open air would be preferable to Mr. Gertner.

"What's really interesting, of course, is our differences."

She ignored his words until she heard him shoot the bolt of the door, and only then did their suggestive significance register.

She spun around. "Unlock that door this *instant!*"

He shrugged against the door, grinning. "They put the lock there because you girls were worried about getting raped." He hitched up his shorts more snugly against the big, tubular, and unmistakably hard outline at his crotch. "You don't want to get raped, do you?"

Freezing her face in its grimmest lines, she squared her shoulders and marched briskly toward him. She reached for the bolt. With no apparent effort at all, but with the sure speed of a striking cobra, his big hand shot out to engulf her wrist. He tugged, and she collided with his naked chest.

"Let me go!" she shouted, and when she started to draw in more breath for a proper scream, he gripped her hair and wrenched her head back to plant his scratchy, tobacco-reeking mouth on hers.

Almost every single day of her life, it seemed, her mother had told her exactly what to do in a situation like this. She had the power to stop him cold, just as if she held a revolver in her hand. But, just as she would have if it had been a revolver, she hesitated to use the power. The idea of seriously hurting another human being held no appeal at all. She had, however, no choice: he was kissing her, suffocating her, twisting her arm and pulling her hair painfully, and she had no doubt at all that he meant to rape her. Squeezing her eyes shut, she shot her knee up between his legs and felt it driving a soft mass of flesh hard against unyielding bone.

He stopped kissing her. He sucked in his breath. His face drained of color. But he didn't let her go. She had time for one scream before splinters of bright pain burst inside her skull and the pure white wall of the washing machine rushed forward to smash her face.

"You —" he spoke slowly, precisely, and in a weak but fearfully earnest voice — "are *really* going to get it now."

He bent over her as she lay sobbing on the floor and ripped the pearl gray dress from her back. Angry and in pain though he might be, he could still laugh and make vile observations about her lack of underwear. She wept all the harder when he told her she had a *great ass.* Nobody had ever said anything like that to her before, and she might have secretly revelled in the crude compliment, but to hear it in this situation, from this man, was unbearably painful.

He ground her face down into the rancid duckboards as he fumbled at her crotch, and she passionately willed herself to faint, but no amount of willing could wipe clean the utter filth of consciousness.

She exulted when she heard the first voice, but only for an instant. These were not the voices of timely rescuers, they were those of her intruders from last night.

The Cold Voice: *Is this their method of procreation? It seems needlessly violent.*

The Female Voice: *The woman is unwilling. Make her more receptive.*

"I knew all along this was what you wanted," Todd said. "Why did you have to make such a God-damned fuss about it?"

Against her will — against her caged and frenziedly struggling will — Amy spread her legs and arched her back, presenting herself as shamelessly as a bitch in heat, lifting herself to receive him. She couldn't move then, she couldn't even flinch from the rupturing thrust of his hard flesh. She dug her claws into the pillow beneath her face and discovered at last that she could scream.

The echo of the scream rang in her ears, rang from the walls of her bedroom. She could feel Todd's warm sweat, feel the stain of his hands on her breasts, feel him tearing through the occluding membrane and stuffing her with his phallus; but he was gone, she was alone, lying face-down on her own bed and wearing her bra and panties. She twisted the damp hair from her face and saw that the bedside clock said *one.*

She rinsed her face with cold water in the bathroom before touring the apartment. Everything was exactly as she had left it this morning. There was no sign of the intruders. She stared for a while at the closed chest, wondering if she had the courage to take out the album and see if the pictures were just as they should be. She didn't.

Clean and whole, the pearl gray dress that Todd had torn and defiled hung in her closet. This time she selected a pale blue one, and she didn't remove her underthings before putting it on. She paused to study her face in the mirror. In her dream, she had known her nose was broken when she hit the washing machine, but her face was now unmarked. There was no cut on her forearm, either.

Never in her life, not even last night, had she experienced such a vivid and horrifying nightmare. Sights and sounds, smells and tastes and textures, had been just as they are in the waking world, and at no time had her thoughts or her reactions differed from what they would have been in real life. Instead of leaving her terrified or doubting her sanity, the dreams had acted as a catharsis for all her current fears and discontents. She had only been *dreaming!* She sang as she ran lightly down the stairs with her laundry bag.

She enjoyed this mood only until she entered the laundry room to find one of the washers running and heard Todd Farmer say, "Hi," behind her back.

She turned to face him. She held the bag ready to swing it, although it weighed nothing. He was dressed just as he had been in the dream.

"Don't mind me. Just another housewife." The smile, the cigarette smoke, they were the same, too.

When she headed back to the door, he stepped in her way. "I forgot —" and only now did she remember that she had forgotten to bring it in her dream, too — "my detergent."

It was ridiculous that her good manners should oblige her to make excuses to the man who, she knew for a fact, was going to beat her and rape her in just a few more minutes. She should kick him right now, or at least start screaming, but she couldn't muster the nerve to act on a conviction that the rest of the world would think insane.

"I've got a message for you." He pulled the folded paper from his pocket. The motion drew her eyes. They skittered past the bulge of his erection.

"Don't give it to me," she ordered. "It's from someone named Martin Paige. He was here at ten-thirty, and he'll call me. Is that right?"

His surprise was obvious, but his sly nature made him unfold the note and read it, pretending he hadn't done so already. "I'll be damned. Are you psychic?"

"I met him. He was a —" She cut off the words from her dream, but it made no difference, because his response was exactly the same: "We have the same taste in people. I bet we have a lot in common."

"Would you get out of my way, please? I'm in a hurry."

"What's really interesting, of course —"

The door, hitting him in the back as it opened, interrupted the nightmare sequence of words and events. Amy clutched at the edge of the washer that had broken her nose in the dream, feeling dizzy from an overwhelming rush of relief and gratitude. If it was Mr. Gertner, she would run to him and kiss him.

"For Christ's sake!" Todd snarled.

"My, my, Todd, what kind of talk is that? You'll never amount to anything that way," said the bearded stranger who entered. "You're Amy Miniter aren't you? I knocked at your door just now, and when I heard voices here. . . ."

"I'm sorry," Todd said. She hadn't believed him capable of expressing the servile humility of his words and attitude.

The man ignored him, his bright eyes — black and cunning, the eyes of some harmless forest creature that wouldn't be considered at all cute if it could grow to a greater size — on Amy, who cried, "*Yes!* Yes, I certainly am. May we go outside and talk? I feel a little faint."

The man took her arm solicitously and opened the door for her. She was unused to that kind of treatment. He was as far removed from Todd as would Louis XIV have been from a stableboy; nor would that stableboy have assumed a more deferential attitude to his king.

"You certainly have grown into a lovely young woman," he said. "I wasn't at all sure I recognized you."

"I'm sorry. . . ?"

"Howard Ashcroft. We met several years ago at the Laughlins'. Their Hallowe'en party?"

"Of course! It's unforgivable that I didn't now you. You were the only person there who was nice to me, outside of Patrick."

"I wouldn't be at all pleased if you did recognize me. I'm not still dressed up as the Scarecrow of Oz, after all."

"You invited me to your Hallowe'en party, I remember. I'm sorry I couldn't come."

"Not at all surprising under the circumstances," he said dryly, and it only occurred to her now that her mother had died on the night of his party. She couldn't imagine anyone else having the nerve to speak of it ironically; she admired him for it. "The invitation is still open, for any of my parties."

"I'd love to," she said. She cast a guarded glance at Todd to see if he was taking a lesson in gentlemanly behavior. Some of the contemptuousness had returned to his manner as he lounged against the outside of the door and listened to them chat.

"The reason I called on you, Amy — may I not call you Amy? — is that I'm thinking seriously of selling my house. I saw what a marvelous job you did on your own place, and I'd like you to take a look at mine and give me the benefit of your experience and good taste. I'd pay you — what would be fair? A couple of hundred? — just to look it over, and perhaps we could later arrive at some mutually profitable arrangement for sprucing it up and selling it."

Unready for such an offer, she twitched and shrugged and blushed. He took this for agreement and pressed her: "Would you come with me now?"

"Well, I don't know," she said, although she was eager to accept. To flee Todd and Mr. Gertner — who was surely watching them behind his curtain — and the shifting quicksand of her apartment with this charming gentleman and distract herself with the details of business would be like an answered prayer, but her shyness held her back. "My laundry. . . ."

"Don't worry about that, Todd will do it." He grinned at Todd. "He'll be happy to. Won't you, Todd?"

She flung her hands to her face. Even so, a snatch of her giggle sputtered free. She turned her back, but not before she had seen the black look Todd gave her, and that intensified her attack. She heard him say meekly, "Of course I will, Doctor."

"I knew you would," Ashcroft said as he led Amy to his big black car.

Chapter Seven

*F*or Martin to separate himself from Amy with a tangle of turnpikes and a waste of meaningless towns full of people he didn't even want to know would have been impossible. She was in Mt. Tabor, and there he must abide. But he had twenty dollars in his wallet and a negative balance in his checking account. He went directly from the mill to Gertner's bank, where his dream of Amy spurred him to an excess of persistence he hadn't known himself capable of.

The unsympathetic manager was even less impressed than the police would have been by his lapsed driver's license, and not at all moved by his New York Public Library card or his membership — even though Martin produced that card with the panache of a gambler nailing down a royal flush — in the Smithsonian Institution (an honor accorded all subscribers to its magazine).

While the manager interjected grunts of boredom, embarrassment, and disgust, Martin unleashed a torrent of words. Of course he had no account in this bank! He was a penniless traveler in the wilds of New England, he was without food or gasoline or a place to stay, his car — he dragged the manager to the window to view the wreck — had been all but destroyed. His only asset in the world was this check, written by one of their most respected citizens and valued customers — who probably wouldn't remain one for long, not after he heard about this outrage — and accepted by himself in good faith as the equivalent of hard cash. Since he had nowhere else to go, he would remain forever in the bank, right here where he sat on the floor. Call the police? Splendid idea! Ask to speak to the chief, his old friend and boon companion, Maurice Donovan, who would vouch for his identity. Fortunately the manager didn't call his bluff, since it might have provoked questions about his failure to report an accident, but he decided that it was worth $250 to get rid of Martin.

He went to a cut-rate store and bought two turtleneck jerseys, chino pants, white tube socks, a blue sport jacket and loafers: the last made of plastic in Taiwan. He wore his new clothes out of the store and took his suit to a cleaner. On the way, with some regrets, he stuffed his dickey into someone's garbage can, burying it well in the hope that the garbage men wouldn't find it and get a laugh out of it. He went to a barber who treated him like a long-lost leper and indulged in the luxury of a shave and shampoo as well as a haircut; which latter, he suspected, in conjunction with his bright blue jacket, loafers, and white socks, made him look like one of Buddy Holly's Crickets. But what the hell, it was an improvement, he thought. After going to a drug store, where he bought a razor and various products guaranteed by television commercials to turn women into Pavlovian dogs, he had $120 left. What next? Dancing lessons? A Charles Atlas course?

A reaction set in, and he began to grumble at himself for wasting money and acting like a fool, but that didn't stop him from renting a furnished room for $60 a week in a stuccoed house that wanted only Ida Lupino in peasant blouse and Gypsy earrings as landlady to give it the *coup de grâce* of steamy sleeze and despair. Having taken a lukewarm shower in rusty water, he left his typewriter and toiletries there with some misgivings and drove to Brooksprite Gardens.

Amy's car sat in its slot, but no one answered his rings and knocks at her door. He circled the building and looked up at her balcony, but the glass doors behind it were tightly curtained. He saw a flurry of motion behind the imperfectly drawn drapes of Toni Sloane's downstairs apartment, but he averted his eyes and hurried away, fearful that her boyfriend might suspect him of peeking.

He returned to the entry, where he heard the sound of machinery from the laundry room. He looked in. The machines were running, but the room was empty. A door in the far wall probably led to a storage room, but he resisted the temptation to investigate. Amy might be in there, but cornering the shy creature in a blind alley twice in one day would not get the romance off to an auspicious start.

He went to Toni's door to ask her where Amy was; and to thank her for her help in getting him the check, which he now believed he had accepted with a bad grace. (Showing off his new image had something to do with it, too.) But as he reached for the bell, he heard a rumpus inside: a loud television set, furniture being pushed around, and a woman shrieking, *"Again! Again!"* It was feeding time — or mating season — in the ape house. He withdrew his hand and backed away.

Checking the time — one-forty — he left another note under Amy's door, simple and businesslike as the first, promising to return later. On the way out of the complex he checked the swimming pool and the tennis court, but both lay unused. He would have to buy a swimsuit, too.

He found that it was impossible to picture Amy in a swimsuit. It was even difficult to call up her image in the sweater and jeans she'd actually worn today. Like Rhiannon MacLear in *Swords of Winbourne* — and there was no longer a discrete image of Rhiannon in his mind, she was Amy — he could picture her only in a white gown appropriate to a sorceress or in nothing at all. In the white gown her image was clearest, even down to such details as the scab of the recent cut he had noticed on her left forearm.

*G*eorge Spencer's house stood on a knoll that set it apart from its neighbors in the town's most expensive street. A Victorian building of three stories, plus a high attic under a mansard roof, it might have served as an ideal setting for Gothic horrors if it had been permitted to run down, but it had been maintained or restored with the loving care that might have been accorded an old man's dollhouse. The newish paint was robin's-egg blue, the closed shutters bone-white; all the gingerbread and frilly grillwork sparkled. The lawn and high hedges had been kept neatly trimmed in the owner's absence.

In the rear, behind a three-car garage with cupola and weathervane, probably a former stable, the property abutted on a cemetery, which Martin chose as the best avenue of approach. He parked well beyond the cemetery and strolled back through it, trying to look the picture of bereavement in his electric-blue sport coat.

He had never broken into a house, not even as a child. He had been a well-behaved, even a rather sanctimonious child, the sort that might reasonably be expected to grow into a bookkeeper or a minister, and he sometimes wondered where he had gone wrong. The prospect of breaking and entering scared him, but he had to start his investigation somewhere, and Spencer, a central and mysterious figure in the events surrounding the Mt. Tabor Massacre, wasn't around to answer questions.

He climbed the high iron fence with only minor difficulty — he felt a seam part at the shoulder of his new coat — and approached the rear of the house by the side of the garage. He was sure no neighbors could observe him. The doors and the shuttered windows of the house looked secure, but under the back porch he found a crawlspace that ended at an unshuttered cellar window. He wished he could have taken off at least his jacket and left it on the steps, but he knew that would have been like leaving a bright blue ensign — Burglar in Residence — for the gardener or a patrolling cop. He left it on as he wormed his way through the dusty, cobwebby darkness.

The window was locked, but he broke it with his plastic shoe after two flinching tries and reached in to unhook it. He tried not to breathe as he lay still and listened for the hue and cry. He heard only the far-off drone of a power mower and, farther still, a dog's random barking. He squeezed through and hung in darkness for a moment before dropping into the unexpectedly deep basement, where he stumbled over some noisy junk.

He toured the cellar, lighting matches. He didn't know exactly what he was looking for, but he suspected that it wouldn't be found here, among the ordinary accumulation of old furniture, trunks and suitcases, broken bicycles and rusted bedsprings. He found no carboys of acid or suggestive vats, anyway.

The door at the top of the stairs was unlocked. It opened on a big, modern kitchen that was neat and, except for a film of dust, clean. Bright spears probing through the shutters diffused to bathe the room in a still twilight, so he didn't even try the light switch; but when, from idle curiosity or force of habit, he opened the refrigerator — full, untidy, and evil-smelling — the light came on. Someone was paying the electric bill. Either Spencer intended to come back, or he had arranged before fleeing to make it look as if he did.

He passed through the butler's pantry into the dining room. Over the fireplace hung a snowy farm by Andrew Wyeth that looked like an original. It might have tempted either thieves or vandals, but the house-breakers Donovan had mentioned hadn't touched it. In the sideboard a massive silver service lay undisturbed.

The dark-paneled central hall was hung with eighteenth-century architectural engravings that were also probably valuable. Doors gave onto several rooms, and one of the doors was marked by rusty splotches that looked like blood. The marks had not been made at random, he saw on closer inspection, but were ideographs of some sort: a circle and a double loop, both symbols of eternity, and a third that might have been the yin-yang symbol except that it was oval in shape and the line through it was jagged, like an SS lightning bolt; or like a crack in an egg. He opened the door.

He hadn't liked the house until now. It was too formal, neat, and tasteful. He saw his ghostly hosts as rich and self-satisfied and proper and boring. The study he now entered revealed the unbuttoned George Spencer at home, with books meant to be read and pictures — a Vargas calendar, for instance — meant to be looked at. George had sometimes even missed the ashtray with his cigars, and there were burns in the oriental carpet under his roll-top desk. A broken leg of that desk was propped up with an old Manhattan telephone directory. The Harris tweed jacket that hung on the coat rack was in worse shape than the jacket Martin had left to be cleaned.

The study showed the first signs of vandalism. The locks on the desk had been broken, the drawers pulled out, dumped on the floor, and flung aside. The books from the shelves all lay on the floor, and much of the paneling behind the shelves had been ripped out, as with a crowbar. Some of the floorboards had been pried up.

It seemed obvious that George Spencer's house hadn't been invaded by vandals, despite the grafitti on the door, but by someone who had been looking for something; a highly specialized thief who had ignored silver and art to look for — what? Money? Jewels? An incriminating document? Even though he could adduce no logical basis for it, he felt that the burglar had been seeking some vital piece of evidence relevant to the massacre. That someone had already gone over this ground, someone who'd had the advantage of knowing what he was looking for, made his own task seem hopeless.

He rummaged among the books. Whatever warmth he had begun to feel toward his reconstruction of George diminished as he came upon a skull that had apparently rested in one of the bookcases. Scorning superstition as he did, Martin had no special feelings about skulls, except to feel, from some sense of taste or fitness, that they belonged in the ground, not on people's bookshelves. Only an effete poseur would use them for decoration. That this was the skull of a small child, maybe even an infant, compounded his distaste.

Instead of law books or volumes appropriate to the local historian Donovan had described, they were books of fantasy and supernatural horror by H.P. Lovecraft, Arthur Machen, Lord Dunsany, Ramsey Campbell, and Thomas Ligotti. Lovecraft was the most heavily represented. In addition to his fiction, there were volumes of his letters, books about him, and original manuscripts. He leafed idly through a long one called *The Legacy of Winfield Hazard*. He couldn't recall reading it or even hearing of it before, but the author's atrocious handwriting didn't tell him much.

Although he knew nothing of most rare books, popular literature of this sort was his chosen field. He knew that first editions of Lovecraft's *The Outsider and Others* and *Beyond the Wall of Sleep* would fetch many hundreds of dollars each from collectors. He had been thinking of selling his car in order to pay his expenses in Mt. Tabor until his next $400 check came in from *Pussy*. His car would bring (and here he knew he was being optimistic indeed) $200, while the book in his hand — *The Outsider* — might bring five times that amount. Because he had respect for what he would be stealing, because he would probably even read the book and enjoy it before he sold it, it didn't seem quite the same thing as pilfering silverware.

He returned the volume decisively to the shelf and wondered why a man with no religion and no trust in organized systems of ethics should choose, in every moral question, to act like a proper Boy Scout. He could no more steal the book than he could have raped and murdered his exasperating former friend, Margo Slye. He took out his notebook and made an entry: *For sht. sty., scrupulous thief who steals only what he respects,* accidentally spattering some drops of ink on the original Lovecraft manuscript at his feet.

Rare books — specifically, Lovecraft's rare books — sparked a connection in his mind. To make their horror stories seem more real, Lovecraft and his circle dreamed up the names of a number of fictitious books purportedly containing magical spells and forbidden knowledge. In a typical Lovecraft story, a feckles hero meddles with the secrets of the books without realizing how horribly dangerous they can be, and suffers the consequences. The most famous of those imaginary volumes was *The Necronomicon*. Another was the *Unaussprechlichen Kulten*, by Friedrich Wilhelm von Junzt.

He took the title-page he had found at the mill from his wallet and unfolded it. Such a vile stench rose from the folds of the old paper that he had to throw it down, turning aside to retch and gasp. Spencer's icebox was a rose garden compared with this stinging, suffocating stink. He could only conclude that the black stuff on the page had released the odor after contact with the warmth of his body. It seemed odd that he shouldn't have noticed it when he'd taken money from his wallet to pay for his various purchases. Perhaps its unknown chemistry required full exposure to the air. One prone to occult interpretations might have believed that the cabalistic signs on the door of this room had activated it, but Martin was prone to no such interpretations, and he chuckled fondly at the readiness of his creative imagination.

Wiping the tears from his eyes and holding his breath, he spread out the page on the floor with the toe of his shoe. The title and author were just as he remembered. Of course this proved only that the name of a real book had been slipped in among the imaginary ones in the horror stories he'd read, either as a joke or to make the other titles seem authentic, and he hadn't known the difference. The black stain on the page was gone, as if it had vaporized completely; or as if it had flaked off in his wallet. He took it out and sniffed cautiously, but now he smelled nothing at all out of the ordinary, either in his wallet or in the room at large.

"Yog-Sothoth will get you, if you don't watch out," he said in a portentous voice, adding a diabolical chuckle for good measure.

He stepped from the study and George Spencer's world of adolescent fantasy, Vargas and Lovecraft and Vincent-Pricey skulls, into the world of his public image as a rich and respectable attorney. He found no evidence at all of a desperate search in the realm of the Wyeths and Hoppers, the Chippendale furniture, the Bösendorfer piano.

Everything upstairs was in order, too. He found neither whips nor rubber sheets under the canopied bed in the master bedroom. In the room he took to be Rupert's, the wayward son, he found an expensive computer, and again he was sorely tempted — even more so, this time, because he would be stealing it for the worthwhile purpose of writing stories for *Spread* — but again he resisted. He learned from the printouts in Rupert's desk that he had written non-fiction articles on such lame subjects as picturesque churches and scenic hiking trails for regional New England magazines. He had been working on a novel, too, about the Gulf War. It wasn't bad, judging from a couple of random pages. Also in his desk were love letters and pictures (some of both were torridly explicit) from more than one girl. Martin didn't like Rupert Spencer very much.

On the third floor were guest rooms and storage rooms, also undisturbed. All that he had seen confirmed his belief that someone had broken in to look for something he had known would be in George's study, and that he had probably found it. Then he noticed the same markings he had seen on the door of that study, on another forced door that led up to the attic. Had they really been drawn in blood? He scraped some with his fingernail and touched it to his tongue, but he still couldn't say for sure; though it didn't taste like paint, nor had it dried to a smooth surface like paint or ink.

What he found in the attic amazed him. A prominent lawyer might not have wanted his fondness for weird fiction to become generally known, but it wouldn't have been considered a disabling eccentricity. Greater men than George Spencer have had sillier hobbies. But in the attic Martin found evidence that George not only liked to read about demonic forces, but to play games with them, as well.

Pentagrams and less recognizable symbols had been drawn on the floor in colored chalks, erased, and drawn again, many times over, among stubs of candles and lumps of wax where candles had burned. Even more surprising, fires had been built on the bare floorboards and had charred them deeply — unless, of course, the demons had done that as a side-effect of their materializations. There was indeed a vat here that looked big enough to accomodate corpses, and the empty acid-carboys that he had expected to find in the cellar stood near it One quarter of the vast, undivided attic was devoted to gadgetry that Martin, from his knowledge of alchemical instruments (acquired merely to decorate *Swords of Winbourne,* and extending not far beyond their names) took to be athanors, serpents, crosslets, and double pelicans.

Books, thousands of them, had been strewn around the room as if in fury. Had the intruder been looking for a book, or for something that might easily be concealed in a book? For the books, all pulled from their shelves and lying hip-deep in places, were the only things that had been disturbed.

These were not works of fiction, supposedly, but books on demonology that had been written by and for believers: the writings of the notorious Aleister Crowley, fancied by the gullible of his day to have been the Great Beast of the Apocalypse; those of Montague Summers, the screwball priest who had longed for a reconvening of the Inquisition to root out witchcraft and diabolism. Martin saw books on spiritism, astral projection, autohypnosis, metaphysics, mysticism, astrology, numerology, phrenology, *I Ching* — the whole ragbag of systems that people have devised to put themselves in touch with Higher Powers, to make themselves the masters of Hidden Wisdom. Never had he found a less discriminating collection of books under one roof, not even in second-hand bookstores: paperback packets of mental chewing gum like Edgar Cayce and *The Chariots of the Gods* lay cheek by jowl with a five-hundred year old copy of *De Artibus Magicis,* with a 1565 edition of *Strategemata Satanae.* Nor had George, in his lust for the Wisdom of the Ancients, stinted at scrawling all over the very old and presumably valuable books in the blue ink and spidery hand that Martin recognized from papers in his study. The biggest puzzle here, Martin concluded, was how the poor old booby had found the time to practice law.

In such a library, the most ordinary sort of book seemed a curiosity, and Martin was impelled to pick up a slim red vinyl volume, stamped in imitation gold, *My Diary,* the common sort of ruled and dated book every schoolgirl has, to find out what use George had put it to. Nothing odd about its use: it was his diary. Martin had read halfway through the first entry, dated a month before the murders, before the significance of his discovery fully registered:

> *I have found persuasive evidence that Mordred Glendower, the "miller" who established residence in Mt. Tabor in 1810, was that very wizard who fled Salem to North Berwick, one step ahead of the rope, in 1692. It remains to be seen whether this was the same Mordred Glendower who was born near Cardiff in 1560 and who later served as secretary to Dr. John Dee when he was working on his translation of the (fictitious?) Necronomicon.*

Here was nothing less than the solution to the mystery. Anyone who believed such nonsense was crazy enough to imagine he would be doing the world a favor by wiping out Mordred's descendants and anybody else who got in his way. And he would have been just the sort of man to smear that tarry substance in the mill and do the other queer things that Charles Manson — another notable student of the occult — called "witchy stuff."

The rest of that entry, and all the entries for several pages following, were in cipher, except for the dates, which Spencer had written himself, having crossed out those printed in the book. The entry for October 30, the day before the massacre, began in English, however:

> *Patrick believes himself to be the avatar of Mordred Glendower, and he may well be just that. I have received confirmation that N. was no figment of Lovecraft's imagination. In his loathing of the modern world, Lovecraft gave sardonic hints of secrets that could destroy it. Although officials there are most reluctant to admit its existence, the Voynich Manuscript lies under lock and key at the University of Pennsylvania. Things at the mill have gone too far, much too far!*

Much more followed in cipher. The next clear entry was for November

1, the day Spencer supposedly discovered the bodies:

> *Rupert is gone; the guilt is mine. He asked me about the old Hanging
> Tree on Brookside Lane, and like a fool I told him what I knew. I was
> preoccupied with my plan to steal the* Necronomicon *from the mill.
> Now I fear that Mirdath got him, and probably killed that missing girl
> as well. I must go to the mill and find out the truth.*
> *(Later.) O horror! Horror! Horror! Tongue nor heart cannot conceive nor
> name thee! But I have the Book!*

On the last word of that page, George's pen had torn the paper in the
apparent heat of his excitement. The final twenty pages, unhappily, were
encoded.

Up until now, Martin had assumed that the burglar who had ransacked
the house and made the symbols on the doors had overlooked the diary
in his obsession to find one other, specific book. But beneath the last
entry, in a much surer, neater hand, and in the same rust-brown fluid,
were the symbols from the doors. The smugness of this last piece of lunacy
— the mad intruder putting his idiosyncratic period to the other mad-
man's diary — made his flesh crawl. The symbols looked like evil little
worms that might presently uncoil, and the fancy grew so strong that he
slammed the book shut, uncertain whether he had done so from annoyance with himself or fear.

Both feelings receded before a wave of self-congratulation. He had done
a damned good day's work. He had learned that George Spencer, the
upright citizen Donovan considered above suspicion, had been crazy as
a bedbug; and that his mania had centered on the Laughlins' mill, where
— in what he read as a statement of murderous intent — "things had gone
too far." George believed that Mirdath had killed his son and Shana
Jennings, and if they really were dead (AUTHOR UNCOVERS NEW VICTIMS OF
MT. TABOR MASSACRE! REVEALS ALL IN SMASH BESTSELLER SOON TO BE A MAJOR
MOTION PICTURE!), then George had killed them. He had no doubt that it
was George — "Come out, little girl, I won't hurt you" — whom Amy had
heard mucking about in the cellar that day, imagining himself to be
Mirdath Glendower, or the Instrument of the Lord's Vengeance, or the
Creature from the Black Lagoon.

He had no qualms about stealing this book, for it held the key to his
future, but whether the theft would do him any good was questionable.
Surrounded by tons of rare and quirky books, Spencer had probably used
a book-code for his cipher, the easiest to conceive and the toughest
(without knowing what book had been used for a key) to crack. Martin
would have to spend a year in this house looking for the right book, or
else come back with a moving van. He put the diary in his pocket and
decided to worry later about solving the code.

The attic, he had noticed in entering, was abuzz with flies. Nasty little creatures, he thought: not as picturesquely ominous as vultures, but hanging around us all the time for a similarly ghoulish purpose. *Hurry up and die, Big Guy, so I can eat your rotting corpse and lay eggs in it!* Why worry about malignant spirits in a world where no pentagram could guard against such real devils and their arsenal of invisible diseases; a world where neither George's breeding, education, nor money had been able to protect him from madness; where the Laughlins had never suspected, until it was too late, that they needed protection from the crazy ideas stewing behind the kindly eyes of their fussy old family lawyer? Martin was delighted that his book already seemed to be writing itself.

In a corner he found the presumptive source of attraction for the flies. Near one of the deeply burned spots in the floor lay a heap of broken and apparently gnawed bones and a long-dried, leathery mass of organic material. It looked as if something had been roasted on the spot and eaten, a lamb or a piglet, perhaps. He was unable to identify the animal, since he could find no skull.

He came upon a ladder leading to a door in the steep lower slope of the mansard roof. The door looked as if it had been installed by someone with a minimal knowledge of carpentry, and he assumed that had been George. He guessed that the would-be wizard had used it to check on the constellations, or perhaps, after one of his barbecues or alchemical experiments, to catch a breath of dephlogisticated air. On the other hand, the door might lead to a hidden compartment in the ceiling. He climbed to investigate.

The door was not locked, but it was stuck. Throwing his weight against it made him stumble off the ladder as the door flew open. He found himself clinging to the knob as it swung out into empty air, four stories above the flagstones of a patio.

Chapter Eight

*A*fter he had picked over all of Amy Miniter's panties for her damnably colorless and elusive pubic hairs, then wrapped the collection in a relatively clean tissue from his pocket, Todd Farmer activated the washer with a quarter, dumped in her laundry and his own soap as the machine began to fill, and banged down the lid. He derived only brief satisfaction from contemplating the mess this would make of her clothes. Soon he opened the lid, fished out the wet mass and thumped it down on the washer containing his own laundry, and sorted it. The Doctor had ordered him to do this humiliating job, and it went without question that it had to be done right. Todd knew of people who had come down with very unpleasant ailments after incurring the Doctor's displeasure; he had even participated in the ceremonies that brought on the ailments. David McAllister, who had left the coven last year after exchanging angry words with the Doctor, was now a resident of a state hospital, his hands bound in padded mittens to keep him from tearing his flesh as he tried to scratch off the lice that nobody else could see.

It was all psychological, of course, but pinning a name on the curses didn't make them go away. In order to be admitted to the Inner Circle of Thirteen, you had to demonstrate both a total faith in Natural Wisdom and a reflexive obedience to *Adepti* such as Ashcroft. Each suppliant was given a personal — and horrible — test to prove himself, and Todd had passed his two years ago. Ashcroft had driven him to an isolated house in a well-to-do suburb of Hartford. They were admitted by a distinguished, gray-haired man in a dressing gown and ascot. He exchanged small talk with them about the weather, and about a crucial Red Sox game that had been played that afternoon. Todd followed Ashcroft's lead in refusing a drink as the man guided them to his study, where he requested them to turn their backs on him for a moment. While Ashcroft smiled and hummed softly, while Todd wondered what was going on, their host blew his head apart with a cap-and-ball six-shooter, a .44 calibre Colt Dragoon. Ashcroft stepped quickly to the twitching body, picked up the gun, and cocked it with a heart-stopping click. He handed the gun to Todd, who knew that this ancient, heavy weapon was every bit as powerful as Dirty Harry's magnum. Assuring him that he wouldn't be hurt, he ordered Todd to shoot himself. Todd's dedication to the Natural Religion of his Aryan forefathers was absolute, and he had prepared himself thoroughly for this test, whatever form it might take. To have hesitated or shown fear, to have allowed a doubt to form in his own mind, he knew, would have been fatal. He stuck the long barrel in his mouth and pulled the trigger. The hammer snapped on a defective round.

Just as he hadn't questioned the order, so he never afterward questioned the proposition that his unwavering faith had made the pistol misfire. His test could have been rigged, he knew, but other members of the Inner Circle told stories of thrusting their hands into heaps of blazing coals, drinking substances that were unquestionably poison, or flinging themselves from high places. Brenda Willy had cut her own throat with a razor, died, and woken up next morning without so much as a scar. Todd couldn't doubt that one, since he had actually fucked her dead, bloody body with its gaping throat-wound, like a horrible grinning mouth below her chin. After her miraculous resurrection, she teased him for coming too soon.

Of course they all knew of suppliants who had failed their tests. Places in the Inner Circle were not easily filled.

The sort of faith that Todd had willed himself to develop couldn't be turned off like a faucet, merely to shirk a distasteful or humiliating assignment, a job fit only for a human housewife or a nigger maid. Calling it *psychological* wouldn't save him from madness or suicide, or even from some lesser punishment the Doctor might inflict, like hives or boils, for failing to make a good job of Amy's laundry. So he grudgingly proceeded to do it right, returning only dark-colored items as the machine began to agitate.

He saw no harm in grumbling about it, though, and he resolved to take his full revenge on Amy at the celebration tonight of the Eve of St. John the Baptist, one of the most important festivals in the Liturgy of Wisdom, where he had no doubt the Doctor would succeed in luring her or coercing her. He could just see her smug, superior, my-shit-don't-stink expression twisted into a mask of horror, her porcelain skin smeared with pungent semen, with blood flowing from every one of her holes, with. . . .

He flung down the jersey that he was balling and twisting in his trembling fists before he could, in a trance of lust and anger, rip it in pieces.

Having to do his own laundry was bad enough, but if he didn't, nobody else would. He had long ago given up his efforts to move Toni off her lazy ass when she didn't want to be moved. He hadn't fully appreciated the image of words "going in one ear and out the other" until he met

Toni and saw ninety per cent of his words taking just that route. She heard only what she wanted to and did only what she pleased, the idle cunt, and it would be a waste of breath to bitch about the dirty laundry while she was sitting, as she was now, with all her sensory input-jacks plugged into some fucking soap opera on TV. So he did his laundry. And hers. And Amy's.

People had always pushed him around or ignored him because he was smarter than they were, because they resented his use of correct English, because he read books they couldn't even begin to understand. Even when he cut them down to size by correcting their grammar or quoting some authority on an issue, they would get back at him in unfair ways. In school they used to call him names — "brain," "sissy," "brown-nose" — and beat him up. So he had developed a body to match his awesome mind (*Mens sana in corpore sano*, read the legend on the bloody dagger tattooed on his left bicep, and how many people have the brains or the class to get tattoos in Latin?) It hadn't really worked, though, and it taught him the first and most important fact of life: When Todd Farmer gets an edge, they change the rules. The teachers hadn't said a word about it when the kids would steal his hat or trip him or shove him in the corridors, but as soon as he got big and strong and started kicking the living shit out of his long-time tormenters, the pussy and faggot teachers all jumped on *him!*

He finally got his own back — or thought he had — in high school, when he dragged the Head Fag, the principal, into a supply closet. It was the happiest day of his life. The prissy little cocksucker had already banned him from athletics (he was too big and tough for the wimps, that was the problem, not that he had injured all that many of them) and now he was going to expel him for arguing with a teacher (being smarter than the teacher, that was the real reason); and Todd, wielding a length of lead pipe with a will, saw in him all the unfair, hypocritical persecutors of his life, all rolled into one detestable insect that dared to call itself a human being.

He would have loved to hear Mr. Satterthwaite scream and beg for mercy, and do a bit of groveling and boot-licking, but you can't have it all in this unfair world, and so he had silenced him at the outset with a tap on the skull. He had then proceeded, with the painstaking thoroughness that only a Virgo can bring to any task, to break each and every separate bone in his body. It took more than an hour to do it just right, and Mr. Satterthwaite regained consciousness a few times, but not enough to do any really satisfying screaming or groveling. Todd finished by giving his head a thorough pounding and leaving him for dead.

Unfortunately, that hadn't been good enough. The principal regained consciousness after a couple of months and accused Todd, and that was the end of his formal education, unless you counted cooking classes in the reformatory, and he didn't. He had to take what small satisfaction he could from the fact that Mr. Satterthwaite remained bedridden until his death the following year — of pneumonia, unfairly denying Todd full satisfaction, but of course it was unfairly ascribed to the beating, made his unfair sentence even longer, and resulted in his most unfair transfer to an adult prison to serve out his time.

Prison was a constant battle with snitches, sodomites, guards, all scum who resented his racial or intellectual superiority, so he spent less time in the prison kitchen than he did in solitary confinement, but he managed to whack four so-called *people* without getting caught. It was in The Hole that his true powers were revealed to him, powers that made his brains and strength and will-power, however extraordinary, seem puny.

Todd had modeled his early life and opinions on Conan, the all-conquering barbarian of Robert E. Howard's heroic fantasies; and it wasn't just the fact that Conan didn't take any shit from anybody that appealed to Todd about these stories. He was fascinated by the atmosphere of wizardry and wonder, the dark colors of supernatural evil with which Howard had painted his canvas. A man with the strength, courage, and inflexible will of Conan the Cimmerian, coupled with the demonic powers of his wizardly opponents, would indeed be a man to reckon with.

All his life he had received teasing little hints of his paranormal powers — but just hints, really, nothing more. When the phone rang, he almost invariably knew who the caller would be, even if it was the unlikeliest possible person. He could set a mental alarm clock and wake within five minutes of the desired time — usually, right on the dot. Such tricks were a far cry from real power, but his efforts to achieve clairvoyance, astral projection, or telekinesis (he once concentrated on a feather for three straight hours, trying unsuccessfully to levitate it) always ended in failure.

But he kept trying. In prison he read *From Here to Eternity,* by James Jones, and he was profoundly impressed by Maggio's ability, when in solitary confinement, to dig a hole in time and bury himself in it. Since he had plenty of opportunity, he decided to try it, and he was astounded and exhilarated when it worked. They would lock him up, he would induce an autohypnotic trance, and the next thing he knew, it would be time to leave the narrow cell with its perpetually stopped drain, no matter whether three days or three weeks had intervened.

Despite his youth, he had earned a reputation as the hardest rock in the prison by the time he left, and he could have capitalized on that to gain the introductions that would have launched him on a profitable career in crime; but he prided himself on his honesty, and he detested criminals. His only quarrel with society stemmed from its unfairness; in trying to keep him on parole, for instance, after he had paid an exorbitant price for a justifiable act of resistance against the unfair actions of the high school principal. He freed himself by assuming a new identity (he wanted to rename himself Conan, or Merlin, or Harmgard Hammerfist, but he had to make his choice from the genuine birth certificates of deceased infants) and leaving his home state of New Jersey.

He then began an intensive course of self-education in the occult sciences that led, after many exasperating detours, to Dr. Howard Ashcroft and the Natural Religion that had been practiced by his Aryan ancestors. He knew — the incident of the misfiring pistol confirmed it — that he had found the true path to power, the doorway to a world where Todd Farmer, enthroned in gold, would take no shit from nobody.

As he transferred the first load of his own wash to a dryer and began to wash a second load of his own and Toni's things, he reflected that he still had a long way to go. But the day would come when, with a word or a gesture, he might get Toni to do the washing, the cooking, and the cleaning, and smile while she did it.

Or he might have replaced her by then with a younger and prettier girl, if not several of them. He had got Toni with a spell. He had seen her around town and had tried coming on to her without success, so he had crept into her room one night while she slept and stolen a lock of her hair with which to work magic. He knew it had only worked because it hadn't run directly counter to her will. To make her do something she didn't want to do — like the laundry — would require powers like the Doctor's. Pubic hairs would have worked better, of course, and he would have had no trouble getting those now, but a second attempt at casting a spell on someone usually had the unfortunate effect of neutralizing the first. He had high hopes for the hairs he had collected from Amy's underpants, however. Once she had recovered from the Sabbat, if she ever did, she would be eager to join Toni in his bed.

He liked Toni well enough. Sometimes he even believed that he loved her. She was placid and even-tempered, and she would go along with him in most things: like the disability scam, that meant the difference between steak and mackerel casserole; or like the Doctor's Christmas Party, where she had made him proud of her not only by being the most beautiful girl there, but by throwing herself so wholeheartedly into the spirt of the season. He never failed to get an erection when he summoned up his remembered image of Toni taking on three men at once while masturbating two other girls.

He had no idea what to make of her vision at that party. At first he'd thought she was kidding, or stoned, but her answers to the Doctor's questions had convinced him otherwise. He didn't know whether to be proud of her gift or jealous of it, since he himself had never experienced direct contact with such a power . . . or whether to be terrified. The Doctor himself had been unnerved, and he hadn't pressed his plan to recruit her very vigorously.

Toni, in fact, was full of surprises. She might be a dumbbell — and he hadn't really made up his mind on that question, although he knew that she wasn't nearly so stupid as he'd thought at first — but she could come up with startlingly acute insights into people and their motivations. She knew that he wanted the Droop, for instance, no matter how cleverly he thought he had hidden his desire, and she knew exactly why: because Amy's awkwardness and innocence acted on him like an aphrodisiac. Amy's appeal was even stronger, now that he'd had her . . . or thought he'd had her . . . or dreamed of it. . . .

What had happened, he now believed, was that his mind had slipped out of gear while he was talking with Amy. She'd been startled to find him in the laundry room, even frightened. Her fear had provoked him to scare her more with some sexual banter. While they talked, while she cringed against the washer, he drifted into a daydream of what it would be like to shoot the bolt, kiss her, rip her clothes off when she resisted, knock her down and fuck her. Then, in the midst of that daydream, a voice had cried in alarm:

Save her for me! Summon the Adept and begin again!

And he had found himself starting awake in the middle of the conversation, struggling with the unshakable belief that they were saying things they had said already. Before he could sort out this experience, the door hit him in the back — and who should it be but the Adept himself, as if in answer to the "summons?" That part of the experience, thinking of Ashcroft's title just before his appearance, seemed like his clairvoyance about telephones. But the rest of it. . . . The voice had said, *Save her for me!*, at the precise moment he had busted her cherry. He woke from his vision with the sharp pain of that thrust still stinging his prick, with the queasiness of remembered agony from the bitch's knee in his balls. It didn't matter. Tonight she would get what she'd escaped, and then some.

He loaded the second installment of Toni's wash and strolled next door, where Toni was touching up the crimson polish on her toenails and watching an imbecile game show.

"They got this girl here, I'm sure she'll win the car today," she said.

He studied the screen with contempt. A blond Barbie in a bright red dress, who had apparently just done something right, leaped and bounced in the arms of a smarmy chorus boy, the emcee, who winked and mugged for the camera over her shoulder.

"You ought to go on one of those shows," he said, "and show them what a real pair of tits looks like."

"You gotta be in Los Angeles."

"So, go to Los Angeles. Win me a car to replace the one your boyfriend smashed up. Why didn't I think to take that check for myself? *Abattoir*," he added, answering the next multiple-choice question before the emcee had finished reading it.

"You were right! Why don't *you* go on the show? You're the one who's always bragging about his pornographic memory."

"They want some sucker with enthusiasm, somebody who doesn't care what a jerk he makes of himself." Besides, his old parole officer might see him. *"Anthony Perkins."*

"Meaning, I don't? And I knew that one myself, so shut up and let me watch her win the car."

He went into the kitchen and carefully extricated the remains of a ham from the disarray of the refrigerator. He selected the butcher knife from the rack of carbon-steel knives that were his special responsibility and tested it on his thumb. Dissatisfied, he took the whetstone from the drawer where it was kept wrapped in a chamois, smeared it with a drop of oil, and proceeded to work on the edge with meticulous, reverent care. Iron is traditionally fancied to be the bane of those called witches by their ignorant persecutors, but it had special significance for the followers of the Natural Religion. Each and every knife, they believed, held an immanent spirit that could be a source of assistance or of fearful harm. Toni wasn't allowed to touch these knives, not since he'd caught her mangling one of them with a dime-store sharpening wheel.

"It's red, bright red, just like the Droop's."

"Seems like everything is red today," he grumbled. "Is that one of your political statements? What's red now?"

"The car, dummy. I bet she wins it."

He shaved a small patch of his wrist with the knife. He wondered why he had selected the butcher knife. A boning-knife would have been better for the mangled wreck of the ham. But he was content with the edge, and he shaved a number of translucently thin pieces and put them between rye bread lathered with butter and mustard. Munching, he went to the living room and stood behind Toni's chair as he had this morning. His dick was still hard from thoughts of Amy and memories of Toni at the Christmas party, and he pondered taking it out to massage her neck. How long would it take her to realize what he was up to?

She laughed, turning, the firm young cords of her throat standing out as she said, "Don't tell me you want —"

He passed his free hand across her throat as his teeth closed on the sandwich. Something warm and wet sluiced his right wrist. Only then did he realize that he still held the knife in his hand, and that he had just cut Toni's throat from ear to ear. She staggered to her feet, gurgling. Her severed windpipe whistled liquidly as she tried to breathe and began to drown in her own blood.

He found that he couldn't chew the mouthful he had taken, nor could he stop himself from walking deliberately after Toni in her erratic progress and jabbing clumsily downward with the bloody knife. He did it again and again, shredding her shirt and the breasts beneath it, lacerating her hands and wrists as she tried to fend him off.

It will not go in.
Her ribs are arranged to protect her vital organs. You must thrust upward.
Again! Again! Again!

Todd knew the second voice as the one he had heard in the laundry room during his confusing attack of déjà-vu. He also knew diabolic possession when he felt it. Toni was beyond saving, but at least he could teach these spirits a painful lesson: they weren't, after all, dealing with some common clod who didn't know the difference between Goety and Theurgy. He urgently formed in his mind — for he had no control over his lips, no more than he had over the knife that kept punching upward with machine-like regularity into Toni's belly as she sagged against the wall — the words prescribed by Hermes Trismegistus. He immediately wished he hadn't.

It knows something.
Not nearly enough.

If a thought could be a stream of acid, forced into the innermost recesses of his brain and spreading outward to flow through every vein and every nerve of his body, then that was the thought injected into Todd's brain with the precision of a dentist's drill-bit. He would have turned the knife on himself to end the pain if he could have done so, but his hand was beyond his control.

The pain stopped. But as if to demonstrate further its total control, the force within him drove the knife as no mortal man could have driven it. It was no longer visible as a knife. It shimmered before his eyes, weaving strange patterns in a flickering band of steel, not even slowed by collision with Toni's flesh and bones and teeth. It was the weaving band of steel that held her more or less erect, for she had been dead for minutes; and when at last she fell, leaving a wide red swath on the wall, it was to tumble as a heap of disconnected parts.

At the insistence of the second voice, the totally alien one, he took the limp bag that had been her lower torso, overflowing with bloody guts and malodorous excretions, and demonstrated how human beings performed sexual intercourse.

Chapter Nine

*T*he door swung out until it lay against the roof, which was very nearly vertical. Martin could not have stood on it, but he was able to ease some of the strain on his arms by lying against it. At the bottom of the slight slope, the frilly grillwork he had admired from a distance looked alarmingly sharp and sturdy. It wasn't strong enough to stop him, but it would give him a gratuitous impalement on his way down.

More ironwork decorated the top, where the mansard roof flattened. He might use it to haul himself up if he could scale the door, which seemed beyond his ability, and then balance himself on top of it, which seemed beyond his courage. Even if he succeeded, he would be stuck on top of the roof, where he would abide until he starved to death or the police came to take him away.

The thought of the police made him look over his shoulder at the picture-postcard view of Mt. Tabor, snuggling with its church steeple and iron bridge in a pocket of comfortably rounded green hills. Anyone in town who happened to look up would see him, the electric-blue cat-burglar, hanging in the wind. But he wouldn't hang for long. His arms were beginning to tremble from the exertion of suspending himself.

He tried to brace his feet and swing the door back the way it had come, but his Taiwanese shoes slid on the slates like glass slippers. He could brace them against the door — and he did — while gripping the doorknob less securely, but that ended his hope of swinging the door back. He wanted more than anything else to scream, but he knew that for a symptom of panic that could lead nowhere but to the unyielding flagstones below.

He took a tentative step toward the doorway on his right. Lying at the angle it did, the inconsequential molding of the door-panel seemed a secure toehold. It encouraged him to take another step, still clinging to the doorknob on his left — but what if that came loose, as doorknobs often did?

He knew that he had come as close to the doorway as he possibly could by that method. It was now up to him to release the knob, seize the jamb, and pull himself inward, diving headfirst. If he failed: thrashing, pinwheeling, screaming, it would take two seconds — and how long was two seconds? *One Mississippi, two Mississipi. God!* — to hit the patio.

His task seemed impossible, but he told himself that the doorknob was a bomb that could kill him, that he must let it go. Some dim ancestor that had lived through a tight spot by clinging for dear life to its mother's fur rejected his logic. He himself would leave no descendants smart enough to know when to let go. Thinking of his descendants made him think of their other ancestor, Amy. He had to get out of this for her sake. He had a compelling reason to act bravely and live. He let go of the knob and stretched.

He clutched the frame of the doorway, just barely, and dived. He made it. He wound up head-down on the ladder inside the attic. This seemed infinitely preferable to his last position, for the floor of the attic wasn't nearly so far down as the patio. Rather than proceed like Dracula, he let go again and swung downward and upright, wrenching his wrist painfully and putting another rip in his new jacket. He tried the Tarzan-yell he had failed to perfect as a child and found that it didn't sound any better now. Perhaps the most difficult thing he made himself do came now, when he climbed the top rungs and reached back out to close the door; but some alert neighbor would be sure to spot that opened door, even if his own antics hadn't already been remarked.

He saw no point in running now. Either the police were already on their way, or they weren't. He took the diary out of his pocket. If he heard them coming, he would put it aside, then come back and steal it later. He had no intention of handing it over to a cop who would in turn hand it over to some writer or journalist with a bankroll. Its possession qualified him uniquely to tell the story of the Mt. Tabor Massacre. He would mention that in his letter to an agent.

He believed he knew now what the thief had been looking for. George Spencer had believed that a copy of the *Necronomicon* existed at the mill, and his entry, "But I have the book!" could be given only one interpretation. Martin doubted that any such book existed, but George had believed in it, and the sort of loon who would make hex-signs in blood had believed in it, too. Perhaps George had babbled about his acquisition to the local Devil-worshippers.

One of his thoughts on first seeing the witchy stuff in the attic had been to go to those very people and learn more about George's hobby, if he could, without mentioning George by name. It now seemed a bad idea. Spencer's delusions might not have been self-generated. He could have been a member of that group; the burglar who had left the signs could have been another member. Martin had no desire to draw the attention of a gang of crazies who believed in the *Necronomicon*, who might have stood by and cheered — if not actively participated in — the massacre.

Five or ten years ago, Dr. Howard Ashcroft had been a minor celebrity. He had appeared on TV talk-shows and had been widely written up ("Saint — or Fiend?") in grocery-store tabloids. It went without saying that he'd had books to plug. His spiel was that he practiced the "natural" religion of European prehistory that had been persecuted as witchcraft and driven underground by those pesky Christians. The common image of the Devil was a slander on Pan, a horned and goat-footed deity that the so-called witches had worshipped.

He had a sense of humor about his religion, claiming that a lack of humor distinguished the established churches, and some of his publicity stunts had been amusing. He had tried unsuccessfully, for instance, to prosecute the proprietors of the Jolly Green Giant for blasphemy, on the grounds that their trademark was a caricature of the Green Man, an ancient god of fertility. It would have been no different, he said, to market sandals under the trade name "Jesus Christ."

Martin hadn't bought Ashcroft's pitch. The idea of a pagan religion that had survived through the Middle Ages and given rise to stories of Devil-worship was a nineteenth-century theory that had run out of steam before it was resurrected by the likes of Ashcroft and given a different twist by feminists. Martin believed that an organized religion of witchcraft had exsited only in the minds — or in the political needs — of the witch-hunters. Ashcroft was in it only for the money and the ego-gratification, practicing religion in the way that he himself (with notably less success) practiced literature.

But just as there were people who got off on the works of Tanya Hyde and Dick Standing, regardless of what Martin thought of them, so there were those who accepted Ashcroft as the demonic equivalent of Gospel: not witty con-men who could trade quips and plug their books with chat-show hosts, like their leader, but goons who cultivated their most antisocial instincts as virtues.

As he closed the door on the attic, having found no *Necronomicon,* a question struck him for the first time about those marks in blood: Whose? Perhaps George, condemned as over-zealous for his work at the mill, or unable to produce the book he claimed to have, had wound up in his own acid vat. As a reader as well as a writer of crime stories, Martin knew that such things as gallstones and false teeth resisted acid. He went back up and looked, but the vat was clean and empty.

In the bedrooms and then in the living room he checked beneath the dust jackets of the Book-of-the-Month-Club selections, but he finally decided he was wasting his time and returned to the study. He intended to call Rod Usher, whose work included paperback quickies on pyramidology and other screwball subjects, and pick his brains on Satanism. His hand was on the phone before it occurred to him that it might be dangerous. The *modus operandi* of the telephone company was unknown to him, and a call from an empty house — this one, especially — might be the equivalent of tripping a burglar alarm. The phone company's record of a call to someone Martin knew could be used as proof that he had broken in. He would wait until he got to a pay phone.

He jerked out the Manhattan directory that was holding up the desk — Usher had lived in the same place for at least ten years — and opened it, planning to save himself a call to Information. He read:

> *Whenas Aldebaran riseth to the Sixth House, and agreeth in all Ways with ye Conjunctions of Phutatorius as shall hereinafter be inscribed, then that is no Door which openeth on its Rising, but a Gate to ye Outside, through which All may pass but None may return save a Master of the Runes, or ye Host of Ekron.*

The book — he should have noticed that it was heavier than any phone book — had been stripped of its original cocover and rebound. He turned to the beginning and read:

NECRONOMICON
OR
YE BOOK OF DEAD NAMES

The title page stated that it had been rendered into English from the Latin translation of Olaus Wormius by Dr. John Dee, and printed in London in 1589. He bent down to check the leg of the desk it had supported. Instead of being broken off, the leg had been neatly sawed to accommodate the book.

He let the book fall open again, and it opened naturally to the passage he had read. The passage had been underlined in the same blue ink as that used in George's diary, and the facing page of astronomical tables had been enclosed in a box of the same ink. One line in the tables had also been underlined, and a nearby marginal note said, "Return(?)." It reminded him of a commuter's way with a timetable.

Leafing through the book (and picturing the thief as a sorcerer's dumb apprentice who had puzzled for hours over a telephone directory, bound as the *Necronomicon*, and wondered why his spells wouldn't work), he saw that George hadn't treated it any worse than previous owners. Nearly every line was circled, annotated, and underlined in inks of various shades and presumably various ages; words had been crossed out, others substituted; notes and commentaries twisted in and out among the lines and around the margins. Many pages were stained, torn, or missing entirely, and although this was supposed to be a translation, much of the text remained in Latin, Greek, Arabic, and some alphabet that Martin had never seen before.

His first thought was to put it back where he'd found it. Although it would make an amusing conversation piece (more amusing, certainly, than the soiled clothes, old newspapers, and festering cartons of Chinese takeout that highlighted the decor of his apartment); and although, even if it was a hoax, it had been brilliantly executed and was still probably valuable, it wasn't his, no more than the silverware or the paintings or *The Outsider* were. Taking it wouldn't be the same thing as taking the diary, which held the truth about an event of public concern, because truth (once Martin had repackaged and copyrighted it) belonged to everybody.

As for the book's value as a tool of wizardry, he gave that no weight at all. Finding a copy of the *Necronomicon* didn't prove George Spencer's delusions any more than finding a rabbit-hole in Lewis Carroll's garden would have proved the existence of Wonderland. He put it back where he had found it. .

But he had to admit that even he would have taken a second look at such a rabbit-hole. He pulled out the book and thumped it down on the desk, opening it again to the passage he had first read. Aldebaran was a star, and a door that "openeth on its rising" might logically be found in one's roof. Up until now, he hadn't given much thought to why that door was there, beyond assuming that George had put it there because he was crazy. Within the framework of his crazy premises, however, George had been able to think clearly enough. The way he had hidden the book indicated that much. He might have had a reason, discernable from this book, for putting the door where he had.

"A Gate to ye Outside" presumably referred not to the same sort of outside where Margo Slye used to walk Bing, but to some fancied other dimension or plane of existence. George hadn't actually stepped through that door in the roof, of course, because his broken body hadn't been found on the patio. But he might have persuaded some people – the Ashcroft crowd? – that he had intended to. He might be planning to stage a big comeback from "Outside" on whatever date was specified by the astrological symbols to proclaim himself Master of the Runes, or Host of Ekron, or Queen of the May.

Martin reached for the Mt. Tabor telephone directory, which held only ordinary listings. Turning to the yellow pages and "Astrologers," he found several entries. "R. Bamberger, Reader and Adviser," seemed to be the closest, with an address on Bridge Avenue. Also listed under that heading was "The Institute for Mithraic Studies, Howard Ashcroft, Ph.D, Director," but that was the last place he would take the book for an interpretation.

On the way out his eye fell on the small skull, which he had returned to the bookcase rather than the floor where he'd found it, and made a sickening deduction. He ought to take some of the bones from the attic and have a doctor look at them. He presumed that the police had entered the study to investigate the break-in and had, like him, considered the bleached and polished skull a legitimately-obtained curio. Perhaps they hadn't investigated the attic thoroughly enough to uncover the less presentable bones that might belong with it. He decided against calling anyone's attention to the bones until he had staked a clear claim to the story.

The picture of George Spencer that had emerged from this tour was an unpleasant one indeed, but Martin was exhilarated. He felt a proprietary fondness for his prime suspect. The ghastlier his crimes, the better it would be for the book. He hadn't just killed the three people in the mill, he'd killed his son, Rupert, too. Since Rupert hadn't eloped with the cheerleader, perhaps George had raped her and kept her chained in the attic until she delivered a baby, which he'd cooked and eaten. The mother — and how many more? — had been dissolved in the acid-vat upstairs.

He took out his notebook and flipped back to the entries he'd made in New York while reading the available newspaper accounts. The cheerleader's name had been Shana Jennings. He checked the note he'd made today at the library: Mordred Glendower's unhappy bride, Mirdath's mother, had been Purity Jennings. Everything fit, once the insane pattern was discerned.

As he thought about the book he would write, the shocking revelations he would make, the intricate historical roots and demonological branches he would trace, he walked straight out the back door and across the yard. Only when he had climbed to the top of the graveyard fence did he think to make a guilty survey of the terrain, but he spotted no one.

Caution directed him to a drugstore in Main Street with a self-service copying machine before he looked up R. Bamberger. Any occult practitioner in a town this size could be suspected of complicity with George Spencer. He spent a dime copying the page with the astrological tables. He tore the obviously ancient introductory passage from his copy, crossed out thoroughly the note in George's distinctive handwriting, and locked the book in his trunk before proceeding to Bridge Avenue.

Unlike the rest of the town, Bridge Avenue looked as if it hadn't yet bounced back from the Great Depression of 1873. The street dead-ended at the stream, where the eponymous bridge no longer stood. At its other end, lined with decayed cottages and trailers on cinderblock foundations, it meandered off into the hills as a rutted dirt road. In between, a handful of vacant or unsavory stores ("Pepe — Eat — Drink" in crayon on a cardboard sign) cringed among the hulking, brick shells of ancient mills.

He supposed that R. Bamberger would live in one of the trailers with her many children, and that her knowledge of astrology wouldn't go as far as the bigger words in her monthly horoscope magazine, but he found the name neatly painted, instead, on the window of one of the scruffy stores. The place looked vacant. The main window was obscured by a coat of something like spray Bon-Ami on the inside, and a tattered green shade was drawn inside the glass of the door. But as he approached the door he heard the sound of someone typing. This always irked him — whether from guilt, jealousy, or contempt, he didn't know. He peeked into the bare room through a rip in the shade. On the far side, at a formica-topped kitchen table, a beefy, red-faced man sat pounding a typewriter as old as Martin's with surprising deftness, as astonishing a sight as an elephant dancing.

Martin tried the door, but it was locked. When he rattled the knob, the typist leaped to his feet in confusion, like a man caught masturbating, and jammed a plastic hood over the machine and his unfinished page. As Martin knocked, keeping his eye to the rip, the man turned the top sheet on the thick manuscript beside the typewriter face down and looked around for other incriminating evidence before trying to button the top button of his black pajama-top and coming to the door.

"What do you want?" he asked through a chain on the door.

"Mr. Bamberger? My name is Martin Paige. I'd like to get your opinion on something. An astrological chart?"

His surly expression softened without quite becoming a welcome as he undid the chain and gestured impatiently for Martin to enter. These weren't exactly pajamas, Martin saw, but possibly something from a Viet Cong surplus sale. His rope sandals would have reinforced this impression if he hadn't worn them with white socks like Martin's own, probably bought at the same cheap store. Perhaps he was trying to suggest his connection with the Wisdom of the East,

or merely trying to make local muggers think that he was a karate expert.

"What are you writing?" Martin asked, knowing it would fluster him. When it did, he said, "I'm a writer myself."

Bamberger was unimpressed. "I used to teach English. I hated the job. I thought it was their fault, the little bastards, not buying the garbage I was shoving at them, but they knew more about it than I did. 'I wandered lonely as a cloud.' Bullshit! Will that make you rich? 'It was the best of times, it was the worst of times.' Will that make you healthy? 'Call me Ishmael.' Will that get you a piece of ass? Books are lies, writers are liars, money talks. As to what I was doing, that's my business. I have to bring my personal affairs to the office. What is it you want?"

The office to which he brought his personal affairs held a ratty old couch with an R. Bamberger-shaped trench in its soiled cushions. Between it and a rusty radiator, the bedding had been wadded. The table, two unmatched kitchen chairs, a bookcase made of bricks and planks, and some zodiac charts and posters on the walls completed the furnishings. Besides the typewriter, the table held an electric percolator and a hotplate.

Martin supposed he took his more formal meals at Pepe's, where he would filch the packets of sugar and non-dairy creamer that were littered around the coffee-pot.

He unfolded the sheet he had copied from the *Necronomicon* and passed it to the self-styled astrologer. "This line indicates a date, I believe. What is it? And I'd also like the time, on that date, when Aldebaran will rise to the Sixth House."

The request was one that wouldn't come his way in his usual practice, Martin knew, and it interested him. "Why?"

Martin disliked him too much (he hadn't even asked what Martin wrote) to use tact. "That's my business."

"It will cost you twenty-five dollars," Bamberger said promptly. "In advance."

Martin couldn't get him below twenty, and he paid it, rather than spread the word of his quest more widely by going elsewhere in town. Bamberger went to his bookcase and withdrew a battered paperback, a slim pamphlet, and a more substantial book. He consulted all three, taking rapid notes in pencil as he studied the chart at his table. He seemed to run into a snag. He threw down his pencil in disgust.

"What is this? Where did you get this thing?"

"From an old book."

"That's just the point, how old? Do you know what year it was printed? Or in what country?"

"Fifteen-eighty-nine," Martin answered without thinking; but even though this date provoked no visible reaction in Bamberger, he was seized with caution. "What difference does it make, what country?"

"Because the Julian Calendar was reformed at different times in different countries," Bamberger explained with the sarcastic patience he had probably used too often on his unfortunate students. "Do you want the date, or don't you?"

"England."

"Well, there you are. They changed in 1752." He went to the bookcase for another volume and hurried through his previous calculations as he consulted it. When he had finished, he looked at Martin sourly. "Is this a joke? Did someone send you?"

"No. Can't you do it?"

"Of course I can do it! It's today." He added slyly: "A big day," but he stopped smiling when he got no reaction. He leafed quickly through one of his books, then snapped it shut. "And the time you want is eleven p.m." He muttered to himself, "England, 1589," until it was obvious that he had made some connection. "What was the name of the book?"

"*Astrology Made Easy,*" Martin said as he went to the door. "Something like that."

Bamberger threatened to grow hospitable. "Martin Paige, eh? What do you write?"

Martin pretended not to hear as he hurried out to his car. George's bright red diary, he noticed only now, was sticking out of his coat pocket and had been plainly visible during his conversation with Bamberger. The title was hidden, however, so it could be any book at all. He decided that his pocket would be the safest place to keep it.

He was tempted to go back to the Spencer place and return the *Necronomicon,* since he'd got all he wanted from it. Although possession of the book might make him an object of interest to people like R. Bamberger (whose irascible temper, treasured grievances, and swinish living arrangments suggested a spree-killer who couldn't afford a gun), that seemed less of a risk than it would be to make another illegal entry of the house by daylight. He decided to return the book at 11 p.m., when he planned to be present for George's scheduled manifestation. In the meantime, he took it to his rooming house. He couldn't think of a better way to hide it than George had, so he unscrewed one of the short legs of his bed and replaced it with the spurious phone book. It fit nicely.

*A*t Brooksprite Gardens, he found his second note under Amy's door, just as he had left it. Any postscript he might add, he decided after a long debate with himself, might give her the impression, however true, that he was hounding her. She must be at work, whatever that was: file clerk, schoolteacher, librarian? Something very low-key and unobtrusive. He hadn't taken seriously her claim that she was thinking of buying the Laughlins' mill, even if she did drive a Porsche. After all, she lived in a dump like this. She probably had the car on loan from her boyfriend, a drug-smuggler named Raoul, with a pencil-line mustache and Vaselined hair, who preyed on New England maidens.

Whatever dumb job she had, she ought to be home soon, since it was after four. He decided to wait.

At the foot of the stairs, he again heard the hum of machinery from the laundry room. He looked in and found it empty. He was about to leave when he heard a scraping of metal on stone from the storage room beyond, and he went to investigate.

Halfway through the laundry room he stopped, catching a hint of a familiar and unpleasant odor clearly above the smell of bleach and soapy water. He took out his wallet and sniffed it gingerly, but that wasn't the source of the stench.

He listened at the door of the storage room, where the odor was definitely stronger. Despite the noise of the washers, he distinctly heard the sound of someone digging. He opened the door and walked in.

Chapter Ten

*T*he first surge of relief at having escaped Todd Farmer faded quickly, and Amy began to have second thoughts about driving off alone with Dr. Ashcroft, but he gave her little time to pursue them as he questioned her closely on the work she'd done at her mother's house. Even so, her mind kept drifting back to the night of the Hallowe'en party at the mill, but she could remember nothing threatening or unpleasant about his behavior then. He had been polite, that was all. The notion that he had been trying to lure her into some kind of orgy had originated in Patrick Laughlin's warped imagination.

His house was reassuring, too, expensive and well-kept. The only outside evidence of his weird preoccupation was a small sign at the foot of the driveway, *The Institute for Mithraic Studies.* It was a tasteful, unobtrusive sign, and any uninformed passerby would have taken the secluded stone house at the end of the drive for a religious retreat or scholarly foundation.

"What do you do here?"

"We help people."

"That's funny, coming from a —" The giggle that burst forth, instead of the word she was searching for — *witch, Satanist,* whatever — shocked her even more than it did him, and she was too embarrassed to continue.

He stopped in the carport before turning to give her his full attention. "Not at all. You see, there's a vital principle of energy in each of us, a creative urge to transcend our artificial selves and become one with nature. Society has been trying to beat it out of us for twenty centuries." His alert, ferrety eyes were fearfully earnest. "This creative energy poses a real danger to the powers that be, because it's the one thing that keeps us from being insipid clones of one another. That's what *they* want us to be, you know. It would make all their surveys and polls and market-research so much easier for them." Laughing, he jumped out of the car and trotted around to open her door. "But I didn't lure you here to convert you. You'll have to forgive my zeal."

"Not at all. No one ever explained to me what it is you. . . . How do you help people?"

"Simply by teaching them to use that energy, to respect it — to worship it, if you must — to release the creative force that has been stigmatized in various times as Satan, or sin, or the id. People come to us feeling left out of things, missing all the fun in life, troubled by fears and formless desires, by even the most frightful sorts of hallucinations and bad dreams." Amy thrust back the impulse to tell him that these very things were troubling her, but he might have guessed it from her determined avoidance of his eyes. He went on, "They are suffering because society has blocked up the energy within them. When it struggles to find a way out, it can hurt."

She didn't ask about the bars on some of the upstairs windows as they passed between ivy-grown pillars to the porch of the bg house. The wicker porch furniture had the look of stage props that would never be used. Even more than a religious or scholarly retreat, the place suggested an expensive private asylum.

"It sounds — if you'll pardon me — like psychiatry."

"We've been around a lot longer than Freud, and there are two signifi-cant differences. For one thing, psychiatry was nothing but *talk* until it began prescribing pale, synthesized imitations of some of the herbal remedies we have used for ages. Talk is nothing. As Wilhelm Reich dimly perceived, *action* is the key to mental health. If you feel bad, scream, and never mind what your dismal neighbor-clones think about it. Laugh, dance, strike, screw, as the spirit moves you!

"We also differ from the atheist Jews who dominate that profession — a great man once dismissed it as 'gutter science' — in acknowledging a power beyond ourselves, a limitless source of the energy that tries to express itself through us. A person who could make himself or —" in the manner of a patronizing afterthought — "*herself* an unresisting conduit for this great source could do literally *anything*"

Amy couldn't resist twitting him: "They could leap over tall buildings in a single bound?"

He refused to stay twitted. "*Anything*, I said. Anything. I have no compunctions about quoting the rabbi who said that faith can move mountains."

She had been tiptoeing toward the brink of taking him seriously until he had started on about *screwing*, which touched on her main concern about his "religion," and until he had started badmouthing the Jews, which had been one of her mother's unpleasant habits. He was probably a crackpot, and she resolved to keep her guard up against his considerable charm.

They entered a long hall that bisected the house. Nothing more sinister than tired, dusty rubber-plants lurked in the mahogany gloom. Beyond the glass doors at the end of the hall she saw a few people lounging around a swimming pool. None of them was wearing anything, but they all seemed to be behaving themselves.

In an open room to her left some others, not much older than she was, and quite respectable-looking in neat sweaters and slacks, engaged in quiet, earnest conversation. At a distance, she could hear someone giving Bach a very bad time of it on a piano. She wanted to feel reassured, but she couldn't quell a nagging suspicion that this wholesome atmosphere was a display deliberately structured for her benefit, an infomercial for the Famous Witches' School.

She planted her heels in the hallway. "This —" she jerked her hand at her surroundings —

"it's really not the sort of thing I could do anything with, or would want to try. You could sell a house like this to some institution, but I'm sure they'd fix it up just as they wanted it. It would be hopeless to spruce it up and try to sell it as a private home. I couldn't do that, anyway."

"Well, the fact is, I was lying." This admission amused him. "I have no intention of selling it. I just wanted to talk to you, that was all."

"About your religion? I really don't think. . . ."

"Oh, no, of course not! A friend of mine is engaged in a project that you might be able to assist him with. He wants it all kept secret, and that's why I didn't want to mention my real reason for bringing you here in front of Todd. I hope you don't mind."

He had started to walk, and she followed him warily. A young man in the room off the hall saw her as she passed and smiled amiably. She, having read about amiably smiling cultists and their methods, averted her eyes from this Satanic Moonie.

"How do you know *Todd?*" She hadn't meant it to sound like the name of a loathsome disease, but that was how it came out.

"He's attended some of our study-groups. He has a lot of rough edges, but he's very promising."

"This friend of yours —"

They had reached the music room at the rear of the house. Ashcroft hesitated at the threshold, and she looked over his shoulder to see the man who was giving Bach his lumps. The weatherbeaten but still handsome face, the gold hair waving back from the high forehead, the piercing light in his world-weary eyes — she knew him, and she couldn't completely stifle a squeak of excitement. He swiveled his leonine head toward the door, seeming more bored with the world than specifically annoyed by their intrusion.

"Amy, I'd like you to meet Hogarth Zurer. Hogarth, this is Miss Miniter."

Slowly — less from discourteous reluctance, it seemed, than from the effort required to move his body, which, like his books, was larger than life — he disengaged himself from the piano and stood up, big and rumpled and exuding a quality that Amy found hard to define, one that she didn't encounter in the people she saw every day: an individuality, a force of character that he was fully conscious of and used easily in social situations, the way other people might use a handshake.

She felt as if, as an anonymous member of the audience, she had been called upon to mount the stage and say hello to King Lear. In that situation, however, the magic would fade as she drew closer to observe the makeup, the effect of the lights, the sweating actor beneath the role. In this case the magic and the power of his celebrity got stronger as she got closer. She could hardly breathe by the time he had engulfed her hand in his huge, dry, fleeting grasp.

"Charmed," he said. "Do you mind if I record our conversation from the beginning? First impressions are terribly important, and you'll feel more at ease later, when we get down to business, if the recorder has been running from the start."

Without waiting for the reply she was unable to give, he went to a briefcase lying on the piano and withdrew a portable tape recorder. He set it up on a table in front of a settee and gestured for her to take a seat as he muttered, "First conversation with Amy Minister, two-fifteen p.m., June twenty-third."

"It's *Miniter*," Amy managed to squeeze out as she sat where she was told, "and I don't —"

"I haven't told her a thing," Ashcroft said. "She has no idea what this is all about."

"Oh. Well, young lady, my name is Hogarth Zurer, and I'm a writer —"

"Oh, yes, I know!" The power of speech came tumbling back. "I think your books are marvelous! The ones I've read, that is, although the other ones must be just as good. The one about the alligators in the sewer scared me so much when I was twelve I couldn't go to the bathroom for two days —" She blushed, having shocked herself with that admission, but she pushed on. "And *Behold Now Behemoth*, that kept me up until four in the morning, even though I had to go to school the next day, but I just couldn't put it down. It's such a pleasure to meet you. What a surprise! Dr. Ashcroft, you should have told me, I don't know what to say."

"Just call me Howard, please," the Doctor said, but Zurer overrode him with the rumbling, persuasive voice she had heard so often on television: "I'm very gratified that you think so, and it's helpful that you know of my work. You may be aware that one of my predecessors, Count Tolstoy, believed that there are groundswells of popular enthusiasm which arise independently of individual leaders and heroes. No man, however great, can lead the public in politics or in art, he can merely divine the shifting currents of popular interest or desire and attempt, as well as he is able, to satisfy them. To be a great artist and a successful one — and there is absolutely no distinction whatever between those two attributes, as Dickens, Shakespeare, and I so amply prove — to be a great artist, I say, one must completely submerge one's one ego, one's own desires, and surrender utterly to the will of the people, like a dutiful bride her bridegroom. I myself am the most humble of men. Whatever the readers want, I do my best to provide.

"But to determine what the people want, I must constantly keep my nose to the wind, my finger to the pulse, my ear to the ground. I devour newspapers, magazines, television, movies, books — you couldn't imagine all the trash I must wade through to keep abreast — in order to learn the public's will. When all the omens come together, when popular interest seems to have fixed on some subject, when some ephemeral novel or film seems to have captured the folk imagination, I move forward and stake out that ground for an enduring masterpiece."

She remembered that he had made pretty much this same speech to Larry King, defending himself against critics who said he was a rip-off artist who got his ideas from the headlines when he couldn't steal them from the latest best-seller. She hadn't entirely believed him then, even though she had liked his work when she was an impressionable teen-ager; but at this moment, with the man himself rumbling directly at her, leaning on her quivering knee with his diamond-studded hand, probing the deepest hiding-places of her doubt with his piercing eyes, she could only accept. Besides, even if he had stolen the idea from *Jaws* by way of *Jurassic Park, Behemoth* had been an exciting book, much better-written (if she recalled correctly) than most such stuff.

"What has all this got to do with me?" she asked.

She had been wondering how, politely and without giving offense, she could ask a celebrity like Hogarth Zurer to take his hand off her leg. Now he removed it spontaneously to slam his hands together, making her jump. He stood up and paced.

"The time is now. The omens have come together, the public has spoken, their need is clear, I must submit. And I beg — I beseech you to help me, Miss Miniver. That ephemeral piece of trash, *The Pittsfield Ghouls,* was like the patter of the first raindrops presaging the onrushing storm of my genius. The public demands a *true* horror story, a tale of ghoulies and ghosties and long-leggedy cheerleaders, of murder most foul and noble minds o'erthrown, of things that go *squelch* in the cellar. In word, my dear Emily — if I may — the story of your own unfortunate tragedy."

"Oh, yes! I'd love to help you, but. . . ."

"You will? Then what more is there to discuss? I told Howard to offer you two hundred dollars, but —"

"That's not it at all. The fact is, I don't have any story. I don't remember anything."

"You remember the evening we met at the mill," Ashcroft said.

"Yes, of course. But nothing happened."

"Well, something happened," Zurer said. "That Curtis boy has been a vegetable ever since."

"Oh, that. I don't see what it has to do with anything that happened later that week. We were sitting at a table, Patrick Laughlin and I, in his kitchen. Mr. Bamberger was there, too, our English teacher. Dressed as a bat. Bruce Curtis had crashed the party with his girlfriend, Shana Jennings — is that who you meant by the long-leggedy cheerleader?" She giggled. "She was pretty enough, I guess, but she was an awful person. She used to . . . well, never mind. Anyway, Bruce came in with her and some other boy and started mocking us and pushing us around. Even Mr. Bamberger, they said they were going to throw him out the window and see if he could fly. Since he was dressed as a bat, you see. So I told Bruce what I thought of him, and he slapped me, and then Patrick got up and hit him. It was wonderful! I mean, Patrick was such a gentle person, and Bruce was twice his size. Then Bruce started hitting him and winning the fight, until he threw some kind of fit and fell down, foaming at the mouth."

"But Patrick *said* something, didn't he?" Ashcroft, who had been standing aside, now came and sat by her, fixing her with a gaze every bit as intense as Zurer's had been. "Didn't he say something — a word — just before Bruce fell down?"

"Yes, I guess he did. But it wasn't really a word. It didn't mean anything. It was just —"

she shrugged — "a noise, that's all, a cry of anger."

"What did it sound like?" he persisted.

"I don't know!" It made her nervous, the way both of them scrambled to hang on words she didn't have. Zurer sat down on her other side. She bounced up and walked away from the settee to the french windows that opened on a quiet garden. She heard them muttering together behind her.

Zurer followed her. She was surprised to find herself comforted and even a bit thrilled when he put a fatherly arm around her shoulder. "Did Patrick ever mention a special book he had? A book that he may have found in the mill just before the tragedy unfolded?"

"No. Mostly he talked about a dream he'd been having, a dream about a beautiful woman with red hair. It bothered him because Frank — his father, he was a painter, you know — Frank started painting the same woman as the one in his dreams, independently."

"Mirdath," Zurer said.

"Do you really think so? Some people brought that up at the time, the story of the miller's bloodthirsty daughter, but I always thought that was . . . well. . . ."

"*The Miller's Bloodthirsty Daughter,*" Zurer said rather loudly, and Amy realized he was talking for the benefit of the tape recorder she had all but forgotten.

"Will that be the title of your book?"

He shrugged. "Of a chapter, perhaps. You'd be surprised, the unlikely places from which my ideas come to me. Sometimes I feel as if I'm only an instrument, a sensitive microphone that collects the whispered dreams of the people and broadcasts them back in a form made coherent by art."

Ashcroft had a coughing fit that began, Amy suspected, as a snigger. Like her, he probably thought that Zurer was more than a bit of a humbug; but that didn't diminish the force of his personality or the reality of his accomplishments.

"Are you one of Howard's followers?"

"Of course, my dear. My association with Howard changed my life, it was the source of my inspiration. Before I met him, I was the most pathetic sort of hack, grinding out do-it-yourself articles for homeowners' magazines — 'Perk Up Those Whitewashed Tires Lining Your Driveway!' — and the only fiction I ever sold were women's confession stories. Then I came to interview the Adept for a sleazy tabloid, and I stumbled upon a new direction for my life and my career."

Ashcroft cut in: "And Patrick mentioned nothing about a book, you saw no unusual book, either then or during the time you were in the cellar?"

"No." She shivered. "I don't remember about the cellar. But there was no book, none that I saw, anyway. It was dark."

Zurer, his arm still around her shoulders, propelled her back to the settee. "Howard could help you remember what happened in the cellar, you know."

"I'm not sure I want to."

"The reason it frightens you —"

He was interrupted by a commotion in the hallway. A red-faced man, gasping for air, burst into the room and cried out: "Doctor! Someone has found the book! He has it, he has it now, he came to me to interpret an astrological passage. It was nowhere in Spencer's house when I searched for it, I swear!"

"Did you actually see the book?" Zurer demanded.

"No, he'd copied the page, but —"

"We have company, Bob!" Ashcroft shouted.

Speak of the Devil, Amy thought, but she decided it might be considered in bad taste to say that here. She recognized the visitor as Mr. Bamberger, her high school English teacher. He looked just as she remembered him, sweaty and sullen and dim, except that he now wore black pajamas with a gold medallion around his neck, and sandals. He looked like nothing so much as an undercover narcotics agent whose information was woefully outdated.

He glanced her way, obviously not recognizing her, and acknowledged her presence with a surly grunt. As he stared at Ashcroft he shuffled his feet and fluttered his fingers impatiently, jerking his head meaningfully toward the door.

"You remember Amy Miniter, don't you, Bob?" She knew that Bamberger's news was important to Ashcroft. She could only assume that the book he was talking about was the same one the two men had just been so eager to find. But Ashcroft, perhaps to torment Bamberger, played the suave host whose only thought was the comfort of his guests. "If not from school, then surely from the Hallowe'en party at the Laughlins' mill? She was just telling us all about that, Bob. She remembers your part in that night vividly."

"Those little bastards! I haven't been the same since. Not you, Amy. How are you?"

"You look very 'with it,' Mr. Bamberger."

He tugged at his pajama sleeve as if wondering how it had got on his arm. "I don't teach anymore, that's a mug's game. I can dress to please myself nowadays. You've certainly grown. What —"

Ashcroft decided that was enough conviviality and steered Bamberger toward the door, apologizing to Amy. As they were leaving, Zurer called, "How's the work going, Bob?"

"Fine. I'm up to chapter —" With a glance at Amy, he cut off whatever he'd intended to say and concluded: "Just fine."

"Bob has been doing some research for me," Zurer explained, "mostly on the historical background of the mill, on Glendower and his daughter."

"You've started on it then," Amy said, nettled that the story she now thought of as hers — even if she didn't remember it — should have been started without her consent and cooperation.

"It could never be complete without your contribution, dear," he said, reading her mood. "But the book is already being written, yes."

She liked the way he had phrased that. It suggested that his humility might be no idle boast. She couldn't help contrasting it with the arrogance of Martin Paige, who had crammed all those 'I's' into one little letter.

She asked the great man about his life and works, and she found herself whirled away in a torrent of glittering anecdotes and persuasive opinions. She was told that all the famous writers she'd always wanted to meet were pompous frauds, drunken layabouts, envious plagiarists, and ungrateful pests, only one notch above the vilest scum, their editors, publishers, and agents. One man, however, Hogarth Zurer, had managed to wade through the dismal swamps of fame and fortune without compromising his honor or his lofty ideals. The next thing she knew, it was after four o'clock. She began to wonder whether Ashcroft would return to drive her home.

"Do you suppose they went somewhere together to get that book? I really ought to be getting home."

"I wouldn't be surprised. You see, the Laughlins may have found a book in the mill that rightfully belonged to our group. The information contained in it, misused by uninformed laymen, may have been responsible for the tragedy, and that's why we're particularly anxious to get it back and keep it safe from meddlesome fingers. Howard convinced himself that George Spencer stole it and refused to look any further when George disappeared. It was I who suggested that you might retain some memory of the book, and apparently my arrival on the scene with a fresh viewpoint and new ideas has borne fruit."

"I really can't hang around here all afternoon." Amy had nothing to do at home, and when she thought about her recent hallucinations and nightmares, the idea of going there was distasteful. But even that would be preferable to remaining here after dark.

"We were hoping you'd stay this evening. It's a night of some significance in our calendar, and rather an elaborate and exciting ceremony is planned. Oh, I know, you think this is just the maundering of an old intellectual fuddy-duddy, you'd rather be off rocking and rolling with your lively young friends, but I guarantee you, it will prove quite different from anything you've ever experienced."

"I couldn't!" she cried, distressed, but she was surprised to note that her distress wasn't extreme, nor was her refusal emphatic. She couldn't deny that she itched with curiosity to find out what these people actually *did.* Even if the ceremony proved to be in keeping with the bland atmosphere of their headquarters by day — and could the wickedness of any organization that numbered Bob Bamberger in its ranks be taken entirely seriously? — it was bound to be more interesting than her evening alone at home. She had planned to make a salad, eat it with a glass of Perrier while watching the news on television, shower, put on her night-gown, and read herself to sleep by ten o'clock. She had *The Pittsfield Ghouls* at home, but she hadn't found the nerve to start it. Maybe it would serve as a distraction from her own nightmares.

Because Hogarth Zurer had imputed a lively social life to her, she felt the urge to do something lively and unusual for once: to stay here for a Satanist ceremony. She also felt an urge to convince him that she didn't think of him at all as an old fuddy-duddy. He wasn't the least bit like her father or Peter Jennings, her two disparate ideals of what men should be like, but he did inspire admiration and even warmth. But she said, "I really couldn't."

"Oh, come now!" He seized her hand. "The reason you've been afraid to remember is that you've been alone. But you have friends here, good friends, Howard and myself, to protect you from your fears. Howard could unlock the secrets in your mind tonight, and help you master them." He had very nearly persuaded her when he added, "How do you expect to help me with my book if you can't remember anything, Emily?"

"I'm sorry, I have other plans —" as she jerked her hand away, she couldn't resist adding: "Mr. Zucker. And if Howard can't drive me, I'd better start walking."

"Of course I can drive you," Ashcroft said as he bustled into the room. "I'm terribly sorry about this, Amy, I didn't mean to maroon you here with Zurer. Something came up. Shall we go?"

Zurer seemed so desolated, and Ashcroft so unexpcctedly eager to get rid of her, that Amy very nearly sat down again and announced her decision to stay. But she distrusted her feelings for Zurer and she distrusted him. Even if he did like her, he wanted her to relive those mercifully forgotten horrors for the benefit of his bank account, and that was surely his only reason for asking her to stay.

"But the book — ?" he called after Ashcroft.

Perhaps deliberately misunderstanding, he all but snarled, "Don't worry about your book, Hogarth. I personally handcuffed Bob to his typewriter again."

Ashcroft drove in silence until she asked him, "Did you find the book you wanted?"

"I think someone was playing a joke on Bob, as often happens. Well, you know him. The first one to do it, of course, was God. At any rate, we couldn't locate the man he thought he saw. It's not important."

"Mr. Zurer said the book might have caused what happened at the mill. How is that possible?"

"Mr. Zurer doesn't always know what he's talking about, either."

"He said that *you* could help me remember. About the mill."

"It's not impossible. All of us together, directing our energies toward one purpose — some people even remember former lives. Say, I didn't drag you away, did I?" He slowed the car. "If you want to stay —"

"No, really, I don't." After a time she found the courage to ask, "What would it be, like a Black Mass?"

He laughed. "The Catholics flatter themselves, imagining that we have nothing better to do than mock their pathetic mumbo-jumbo. Just as with the psychiatrists, we've been around longer."

They had reached the entrance to Brooksprite Gardens. She was wondering how she could ask him if the ceremony involved sex, as Patrick had suggested long ago, and she had all but decided that she couldn't, when he said, "I have an idea. No matter what I could possibly tell you about the Natural Religion, you've been exposed to nothing but vicious, pornographic propaganda about us all your life — no, no, please don't interrupt, it's true of everyone in the Western world — and you just can't help suspecting, if only with a small part of your mind, that this invitation is nothing but a transparent ruse by a couple of dirty old men to trap you in an isolated house and pull your panties down."

Amy giggled wildly, making any subsequent denial impossible.

"So what I suggest, to set your mind completely at ease on that score, is that we bring the party to your place."

"My place?"

"Sure. You'd feel more secure, wouldn't you? You could invite a chaperone or a bodyguard — invite several, if you like — Miss Sloane from downstairs, for instance. We'll bring our own refreshments, you mustn't put yourself out, and we'll be careful not to annoy the neighbors. I won't even bring the goat, and I promise not to butcher any chickens on your carpet. This would be a splendid idea, now that I think about it. This place has a very special significance for us."

"*This* place?" She looked around in bewilderment at the cookie-cutter array of cedar-shingled barracks as he parked.

"It wasn't always like this," he said, smiling. "May we come?"

"Well . . . I guess so. All right, yes, I think I'd like that. What time?"

"Midnight, of course. When else?" He laughed. "We'll arrive a little early, say eleven-thirty."

Wondering if she could stay awake that late (but she had, after all, slept late this morning and even taken a nap), and wondering if she was doing the right thing, she got out of the car.

She was standing in the entryway and waving goodbye when Todd Farmer burst from his apartment and attacked her with a butcher knife.

Chapter Eleven

*T*odd stood above Toni's dismembered body for a long time. He had no desire whatever to look, but the powers that controlled his every movement did, and they made his eyes dart from one wound to another with eager curiosity. He nudged her severed head with his bare toe until it faced upright. Her face was unmarked, but it was hideously slack. Her eyes showed only dull white through narrow slits. If he'd had control of his own stomach, he would have thrown up.

The voices had closed a curtain in his mind. He was aware of them muttering to each other, but he couldn't overhear them. Abruptly the female voice shocked him by speaking clearly.

Dig a hole in the northeast corner of the storage room and bury it.

Reinforcing the command, the pain returned for an instant, and then he was free. He dropped hard to his knees, sobbing and spitting out the wad of ham and bread that had lain immobile in his mouth all during the butchery. The contents of his stomach followed. He'd have to clean up this filthy mess himself, he'd never get Toni. . . .

He laughed wildly at his mental lapse until his right arm, numb until now, returned to life and protested the agony it had suffered in wielding the demonic knife. With his left hand he had to pry loose the cramped fingers of his right, one by one, from the slimy red haft of the gouged and broken knife. Now both hands were bathed in blood. He had no idea where Toni's ended and his began.

He carried his soggy cut-offs to the kitchen and shoved them into a fresh plastic garbage bag from under the sink before they could drip elsewhere, and scrubbed his hands above the dirty dishes. Without looking, he put the bag near the place where he would need it next. On the television screen, the blond shrieked exultantly: she had, as Toni predicted, won the car.

He picked up the telephone and called the Adept, but he was told that he had gone out; where, no one knew. He hung up without leaving a message. Dr. Ashcroft was the only one who could conceivably release him from his demons. Since the Doctor was unavailable, he had to do their bidding and do it fast, before people started coming home to Brooksprite Gardens.

He showered thoroughly, bandaged his hand, and put on a sweatshirt and jeans. He drove to the nearest hardware store, where he bought a pick and shovel and a twenty-five pound bag of cement. He concentrated hard on each necessary step. He didn't permit himself to think of Toni or the forces that had stormed into his life. He believed he was acting coolly, admirably so. He resisted the desperate urge to scream and break things while he waited to be served, he endured the salesman's idiotic pleasantries and even contributed a few of his own, he didn't exceed the speed limit or run a single red light on his way home.

He carried his purchases through the laundry room, where both washing machines had stopped, and into the storage room beyond. The room was divided into cubicles with two-by-fours and chicken wire The compartment in the northeast corner, he was amused to note, was reserved for Gertner. Although the door was secured with an expensive padlock, he was able to unscrew the hasp that held it with a dime from his pocket. He entered the wire cage and pulled a heavy trunk away from the designated corner. He left his purchases there.

He stepped from the dry atmosphere of the storage room into the soapy heat of the laundry room. He transferred the loads from the washers to the driers and refilled the washers with the last of the dirty laundry His hand lingered on Toni's pink sheath, her favorite dress, for only a moment. He started all the machines. Anyone who came in with his laundry to find them all running would be unlikely to hang around. He didn't bolt the door. Whoever found it locked would knock persistently, demand to know why Todd had locked it, and probably snoop around.

It went without saying that anyone who blundered into the storage room would go into the hole with Toni. (Winking, he sidled up to Gertner, the peeping-Tom, and nudged him. "You want to sleep with Toni?")

He believed he had enough time for the job. It was only three o'clock. The history teacher who lived directly above the laundry room — Todd had grumbled about his goddamned motorcycle often enough to know — never came home until four. He was less sure of the people in the next entry, upstairs and down, but he thought they returned in the late afternoon. Their parking slots were now vacant.

Nevertheless he went to work promptly and vigorously with the pick, eager to get it over with. For once he felt grateful to the crooked contractors who had built Brooksprite Gardens so shoddily, laying this thin slab of concrete, so heavily laced with sand, for its foundation. Toni would have no use for a full-sized grave, and in less than half an hour he had cleared away sufficient concrete and gravel and was digging into the ground beneath.

It was less like earth than it was compacted rubbish. Broken glass and flattened metal were locked in a hard, rocky matrix. He had to break it up with the pick before he could dig it out. It proved far tougher than the contractor's slab had been, and he had to widen the hole in the concrete to give himself more elbow room. He tore off his soggy sweatshirt and threw it aside. His injured hand began to bleed through the bandage, and his left hand had developed a painful blister that soon broke and grew even more painful, but the remembered pain that his demons could inflict was a stronger incentive to keep going, and now the fear of discovery began to tingle his spine. He flung himself into the job with redoubled energy.

Two feet down, he broke through the compacted layer into a stratum whose consistency unnerved him. Black and rubbery, its appearance suggested tar, but the shovel sliced into it easily. The shiny, gelatinous wedges quivered when he slid them from the shovel, but they didn't break up.

Standing on the resilient surface of this congealed muck began to make him uneasy. Although it seemed capable of bearing his weight, the thought of breaking through — and how far would he sink? — scared him. He straddled the pit to dig it out, even though the work went slower and the strain on his back and thighs grew unendurable. He assumed that the layer comprised organic residue from the dump that had once occupied the site. Fortunately it didn't smell as bad as it looked, only mildly sulphurous with an undertone of rancidity.

He froze at the sound of a noisy engine outside. It couldn't be four o'clock yet! But that teacher — damn and blast him, and he might just go into the pit on general principles, him and his motorcycle and his unreliable habits! — was, he saw by his watch, fifteen minutes early. He paused in his work until his neighbor had stomped up the stairs and slammed his door behind him.

The hole was too deep now to be scooped out from above. Forcing himself to concentrate solely on getting the job done, Todd lowered himself to the quivering surface and began to smooth out the sides. Four feet down, he decided he had gone quite deep enough. He straightened up and wiped the sweat from his eyes. He was about to haul himself out when he saw something lying just a little further down in the muck.

He had no idea what it could be. The jelly-like stuff was dimly translucent, just enough to let him discern a more opaque object with apparently regular outlines. He supposed it was only trash, but since he had dug this deep, and the object lay no more than six inches deeper, he took up his shovel again to satisfy his curiosity.

It was, he soon saw, a blackened, human skeleton. He guessed that someone in the past, most probably before the apartments had been built, had used this spot for precisely the same purpose he intended. Of course, it might have been done more recently. Maybe it was Gertner's late wife, and the black stuff represented his ill-conceived attempt to dissolve the body in some ineffective chemicals.

As he scraped the muck away, he saw that there was something wrong with the skeleton. Only when he had bared the ribcage did he see that the body had been buried in a supine position, while the skull lay face down. He flung down the shovel and scrambled out of the hole, trembling. He knew the grave of a witch when he was standing in one, and the only notable witch ever buried near Mt. Tabor had been the unspeakable Mirdath Glendower. It was obvious why the voice — and he now suspected whose voice it was — had directed him to this particular spot.

Now he began to believe that he had acted foolishly, although that word scarcely served to reproach a man who had sought an unholy grail all his life and who, upon having it handed to him, had tried to throw it away. Long ago, before he had heard of Ashcroft and the Natural Religion, before he had heard of paranormal powers or suspected the existence of his own wild talents, when he was a small boy being pushed around by bullies and battered by drunken parents, he had been profoundly impressed by some stirring words: *for Thine is the Kingdom, and the Power, and the Glory. . . .* That, little Todd had thought, is exactly what I want out of life, just that and nothing less, the Kingdom, the Power, and the Glory. When those words were recited in Sunday school every week, Todd liked to imagine that the other children were addressing them directly to him, and that would soothe the sting of his latest black eye or bloody nose.

Ashcroft was the only man he had ever met with a power, but it was a power of the lowest sort. He could make others do his bidding, he could send them dreams or visions, he could hurt them at a distance, he could even heal them if he happened to be in a generous mood, but he couldn't whistle up storms or walk on water, he couldn't stand beyond the curve of space and time and bend it to his will, he wouldn't live forever, and he might never return from the dead. But Mirdath had commanded, by all accounts, a Power of an entirely different order.

Todd was now a mere suppliant in the faith. After fifteen years or so of intensive study, self-discipline and sacrifice, he might become, like Ashcroft, an Adept, but that was as far as he would probably go, and he doubted that the Doctor, a frivolous sort of person at heart, would go much further.

No Master of the Runes had walked the earth since the death, in 1847, of Mordred Glendower; but tradition maintained that his daughter, Mirdath, had been gifted with even greater talent at her birth than her father managed to achieve during his nearly three hundred years of life, and that she would have equalled his status if her life had not been cut short. To become a Master of the Runes — Todd's ambition had never soared so high — one ran a risk beside which the madness or suicide that the Doctor could inflict would seem inconsequential: the total and eternal disperson of one's consciousness into the Host of Ekron, a tormented state of being that is disingenuously glossed over in *II Kings* with a reference to Beelzebub, the Lord of the Flies.

He stared down at the black bones in the slimy hole. She'd had what he wanted. Maybe she could help him attain it. She wasn't all-powerful now. She had needed his help to dig her out. Maybe she needed his further help. He wondered if he ought to take out the bones, or at least turn the skull around the right way, but he was afraid to do anything more without instructions. "For Thine," he whispered fervently to the skeleton, "is the Kingdom, and the Power, and the Glory," and he squeezed his eyes shut and willed her to speak to him once more.

"Hello, there!" called a man's voice, and the storage room door slammed shut behind him. "Anybody home?"

Todd seized his shovel, then flung it aside and took up the pick-ax, holding it behind his back as he stalked into the corridor between the wire cages. He thought it would be the man upstairs, and he was poised to leap forward and strike him down. But it was somebody else, and that made him hesitate long enough for the intruder to turn and push his way blindly out the door.

"Jesus Christ!" the man choked. "What's that godawful smell?"

He hadn't seen a thing, and now he had left the room. Todd had at last recognized him as the spiffed-up Martin Paige. The enjoyment of bashing his skull in would have partly compensated him for the pain of losing Toni, but he knew that one corpse at a time was enough to worry about, and he threw the pick reluctantly back into Gertner's compartment. Martin retreated outside, looking distressed, when Todd followed him into the laundry room.

"Don't get too close," he said, waving his hand in front of his face as Todd followed him outside. "What the hell have you been doing? I don't mean to offend you, but you stink."

"Pipe busted. And if you need anything done in this shit-hole, you have to do it yourself."

Todd had noticed only a slight, unpleasant odor in the storage room, and now he smelled nothing. He raised his hand, smeared with the black muck from the pit, to his nose and sniffed it, but still he smelled nothing. Even so, Martin continued to edge away.

Todd said, "What do *you* want? You're not supposed to be in there. Or hanging around out here, either."

"Amy. Miss Miniter —"

"She's not here, so fuck off. Now!"

Martin retreated when Todd advanced, but it seemed as if he wasn't really intimidated, just pretending to be offended by an imaginary smell. Todd's anger boiled over.

"Go do your sniffing someplace else, you little faggot sissy! If you want to smell something, I'll cut your nose off and stick it in your asshole, how would you like that? Get the fuck outta here before I kick your fucking teeth in!"

Martin didn't seem to comprehend how angry Todd was, nor guess the sort of things he could do when he was angry, and that made Todd angrier. He wanted to grab Martin by his chickeny neck and grind his stupid cartoon-face into the blacktop of the parking lot. That he couldn't do so, mustn't do so, unless he wanted to draw attention to his guilty secret, drove his anger to the brink of frenzy.

"Hey! Watch out!" Martin cried in complete surprise as Todd gripped him by the lapels and flung him against the side of a car. "You can't do that!"

Upstairs, a window was flung up, and a woman shouted, "Hey! That's my car!"

She was a better judge of character than Martin. When Todd turned his face toward her, she retreated and shut up.

Todd feinted with his fist at Martin's head. Martin slipped away and galloped across the lot to his own car. "You can't do that!" he shouted from his safer distance.

"Go away, asshole. And don't come back."

"I've got a right to wait here," Martin said as he climbed into his car.

Todd picked up one of Toni's flowerpots and hurled it. The pot missed the driver's window he'd been aiming for and exploded on the trunk.

"Hey!" Martin shouted.

Todd's anger evaporated as he looked across at the pile of earth, the broken pot, the plant that would die. It was ludicrous, considering what he'd done — what he'd been made to do — to Toni herself, but he felt as if he'd just killed another part of her by destroying her pathetic geranium, and tears began to run down his cheeks.

He remembered the danger of his situation. What if that moron called the police?

He forced himself to shout, "I'm sorry."

"Don't mention it," Martin called sarcastically, and Todd felt his rage begin to flicker again, but he forced it down when Martin started his car at last and drove away, scattering dirt and shards of terra cotta from his trunk. Todd turned and stalked into his apartment.

Martin must have been smelling the apartment, he realized as he opened the door and the odor hit him like a fist, the reek of a human being torn inside out with all its blood and feces and urine, and rapidly going sour in warm weather. Without a glance at the fatal corner, he went into the kitchen and got a gallon of chlorine bleach and a roll of paper towels. He got the mop bucket and jammed it down among the dirty dishes, smashing them (*That will teach her to* — but no, she was beyond being taught) and filled it with hot water.

The television set bleated routine idiocies. He just couldn't take that nonsense now. Before doing anything else, he went to turn it off, wiping his hands first on his jeans. Only now did he know why he'd left the television on all this time. It was like her flowerpot. One of the last things Toni had done had been to turn on the damned TV. Turning it off would be cancelling her last action on earth, a meaningless action that assumed importance only because she was dead. To turn if off would be to admit that she was really, irrevocably dead.

He paused in mid-stride. A strikingly beautiful woman with a persuasive voice, an oddly familiar voice, was selling something. Her red hair glowed. Her eyes, dark and deep-set beneath a high forehead, held him.

"Do you find that you just can't get out of bed in the morning? Do your eyes, ears, mouth, and nose have that 'stopped-up' feeling? Do your loved ones ignore you completely, or burst into tears when they set eyes on you? Do your best friends, and people you don't even know, come in and walk off with your clothing, your TV, your stereo, and all your most cherished possessions? Do you have a mouldy, deliquescent look? Do you smell real bad? Are you starting to come apart altogether?"

What the hell *was* this?

"Chances are that you, like so much of the world's population, are afflicted with mortality. But don't despair! Thanks to the modern miracle of Mirdath's Life-in-Death, transitory relief is now available in mild cases of vital cessation. So when Old Man Death —" here she grinned brightly and held up a dripping red butcher knife that she proceeded to pound on her desk — "comes a-knock-knock-knocking at *your* door —"

Todd choked out a scream and jammed his fist at the *off* button. Breathing heavily, he stared at the blank, black screen and realized that he had just thrown aside his second chance for an immortal crown as if it were a rattlesnake.

He turned on the set to a perfectly ordinary commercial. It gave way to a familiar game-show, another of Toni's favorites. He turned it off. Mirdath didn't need the TV to contact him. She was just playing games, frisking with her powers after a century and a half in the ground. Todd felt the excitement of one present at a birth; or at a miraculous recovery. That she should even bother to tease him like this made him feel uniquely privileged.

But he was neglecting the order she had given him. She had told him to put Toni in the hole he had dug. He wished he had brought the shovel from the storage room to get all of her into the bag. He turned to survey what had to be done.

Toni was gone.

The blood was there, a lot of it, with shreds of flesh and clothing. The bag that held his bloody shorts was there, but now the pockets of those shorts had been turned inside-out, and the packet of tissue that had held Amy's pubic hairs was missing. The knife lay where he had dropped it, but now it was clean and unbroken, as if its latent spirit were signaling him to use it again.

He didn't know what to think. "Dig a hole in the northeast corner of the storage room and bury it," Mirdath had told him, so he didn't believe that she had moved the body. Of course she had appeared on television to taunt him about raising the dead, but that could very well have been a test, an experiment to see if he would still follow a clear order. He had to find Toni and put her where she belonged.

He went quickly to the bedroom and peered around a corner of the drapes. That idiot, Martin, had returned. He had apparently gone to buy an icecream cone, and he ate it while brushing the last of the dirt from the lid of his trunk.

It struck Todd only now that, despite his admirable coolness, his careful attention to detail, his iron self-control, he'd only had to turn the knob and open the door when he'd entered the apartment. He hadn't even locked it. In fact his keys weren't in his pocket. They must be in his car, on the ring with his car-keys, where he often forgetfully left them. Martin could have walked into his aparment and found the body. That nonsense about smelling something — of course, he'd been talking about the apartment! Martin had been needling him with his secret knowledge. He had probably transferred Toni's body to the trunk of his car.

He left the bedroom. For the first time he noticed a trail of blood leading through the kitchen into the bathroom. There wasn't much blood — there wouldn't have been much left — but it lay in a band, marking where the torso had been dragged.

It took him a moment to prepare himself, but he looked into the bathroom. Toni wasn't there, but the room was a bloody mess. When he turned on the light, he saw a small red handprint on the mirrored door of the medicine chest. He hadn't noticed that Martin's hands were so small. His own hands were three times as large as this print. It was as small as . . . as small as Toni's.

The bandages and adhesive tape that he had recently used on his own hand were missing from the cabinet. The bathroom towels were gone: all except one, wet and bloody, tossed in a rumpled wad in a corner. That was uncomfortably like Toni's style with soiled towels.

He had to clean this place. He had to find the body. He had no idea what he should do first. He made despairing gestures at the mess, wrung his hands, lurched first one way and then another, mumbled nonsense to himself, until it struck him forcibly that he was acting like a lunatic; and if he kept it up much longer, he wouldn't be acting. He brought himself sternly under control.

At the moment, it would be foolish to go hunting for the corpse. He couldn't charge across to Martin and demand to know what he'd done with it. He decided to concentrate on the cleaning. He performed the distasteful task of putting what fragments remained into the plastic bag and began swabbing the floor with the mop, using hot water and bleach. He was sure the landlord would have a lot to say about the condition of this floor when he tried to reclaim his security-deposit.

The phone rang. His first thought was to let it ring. It would be one of Toni's dumb friends. He would have to make up a story to account for her absence, a detail that hadn't even occurred to him until now. But it might be the Doctor. He hadn't left his name when he'd called the Institute, but his voice may have been recognized. Maybe the Doctor already knew what was going on here. If he didn't, Todd wouldn't tell him. He would keep his contact with Mirdath as his own secret, his own power.

He lunged for the phone on the seventh ring. "Hello?"

There was silence, but someone was on the line. He repeated, "Hello?"

"Todd . . . help me. . . ."

"What? Who is this?"

". . . you got to help me, Todd, you know about these kinds of things, I don't, I don't know what's happening to me."

"Who is this?" he screamed, but he knew who it was.

"I saw it all, that time at the Doctor's Christmas party, how you were going to kill me, but I didn't believe it, I thought it was just a bad trip. God knows I didn't believe *this* part. . . ."

The phone went dead. He shouted at it, rattled its cradle, but no one was there. The television set came suddenly to life. "Still another satisfied customer!" cried the red-haired beauty on the screen.

"If you'd like to make a call, please hang up and dial again," a recorded voice on the telephone told him. He hung up the phone. When he looked back at the TV, it was blank and silent.

Maybe Toni would call back. He would go to her, help her, take her to the hospital — where they would do what? Sew her head back on? He began to giggle. He wished Toni were here to put things into some kind of reasonable perspective with one of her sharp insights, one of her wise-cracks, so often annoying because they were so true. He realized that his laughter had changed to tears, and that he couldn't stop them. He felt an almost overwhelming urge to go and curl up in a ball in the corner of a dark closet until it should all blow over, as he had done so many times as a child.

He assumed a full lotus position on the floor and made his mind as blank as the television screen he faced. He waited for Mirdath's next apparition, either as a voice in his mind or an image on the screen, but all was still.

He heard a car door slam, and voices outside. He got up slowly and walked to the door. He hadn't noticed when he'd picked it up, but he was holding the miraculously restored knife.

He put his eye to the peep-hole. Amy Miniter stood on the sidewalk, waving: signaling to Martin Paige. In that instant he understood all. They were in collusion. Martin had stolen the body, Amy had provided the feminine handprint and made the phone call. She had made her voice weak, distant and slurred to cover the flaws in her mimicry. They had also done something to his television set. Their purpose was clear: to confuse him and make him disobey Mirdath's command, to bar his rightful way to the Kingdom, the Power, and the Glory.

He burst screaming from the door with the butcher knife raised above his head.

Chapter Twelve

*M*artin was already trotting across the blacktop toward Amy — who had just seen him, and his heart sank when he saw the undisguised dismay on her face — when Todd rushed at her with the knife.

This scene had been replayed a million times in his daydreams, perhaps a thousand times in the tales of adventure he had loved as a boy, and at least a hundred times in the detective stories and fantasies he couldn't sell. In all those instances, the heroes always knew just what to do and did it. Slade Bascomb, the hero of *Behold Now Behemoth*, when he wasn't boozing, philosophizing, or screwing (often doing all three at once), was a brawler without peer. And Pintar of Gemia, who saved Rhiannon MacLear's bacon more than once in *Swords of Winbourne*, had mastered a spell that enabled him to slow down the apparent passage of time when the going got rough, so that he always had leisure to plan the next murderous sweep of the two-hand sword, Wistinglass, that few other men could even lift.

But in actual practice, Martin knew nothing at all about fighting. He'd had only one real fight in his adult life. He and another drunk had stepped outside a bar to settle a dispute about whether the Battle of Waterloo should properly be considered a one- or three-day event. Each had brought a book that didn't really resolve the quibble to win a twenty-dollar bet. Martin's antagonist rushed him, and Martin unexpectedly extended his arm with a fist at the end to ward him off. It couldn't even be considered a punch, but it broke the other man's nose and ended the fight.

So he had often wondered what he would do in a situation like this. Being brutally honest with himself, he believed he would freeze and watch in impotent horror as the knife fell. Instead he raced forward with total disregard for Todd's size and strength, for the fact that he had already tossed him around like a rag doll today, for his maniacal fury, or for the evil-looking knife in his hand. He half fell the last few steps as his new plastic shoes slid out from under him, so that all his weight was concentrated behind the punch that he delivered to Todd's belly. Todd went down decisively, with Martin windmilling further, unnecessary blows on top of him.

Todd was obviously helpless, rocking and clutching his stomach while he gasped and grew whiter by the second, so Martin got up.

"He tried to kill you," Martin told Amy, who seemed bewildered.

"I didn't see —"

"Remarkable!" cried a man with a graying black beard who appeared at Martin's elbow. "I never saw such courage or quick thinking in all my life."

"What happened?" Amy asked.

"This man has just saved your life. He saw Todd coming at you with the knife — so did I, but I barely had time to stop my car, much less shout a warning — and ran in to disarm him with as nice a piece of work as I've ever seen."

Martin was alarmed to realize that this wasn't entirely true, for Todd still held the knife. At any moment he might get up and try to use it again. It took much more courage than it had to hit him in the first place, but he felt the need to live up to such praise, so he forced himself to kneel down and twist the weapon out of Todd's hand. Todd didn't resist. He managed to croak, "Kill!"

The man patted his back encouragingly, and Martin suspected that he had used the word "disarm" to cue his action without making him look like an idiot. He recognized him now as the man who had driven Amy home: her rich, middle-aged boyfriend, the true owner of that Porsche, he had thought, hating him, but now he felt nothing but warmth and gratitude toward him and wished he would continue to tell her how brave he was.

"Is he all right?" Amy asked, staring with deep concern at Todd.

"I'll kill the little cocksucker!" Todd gasped, struggling now to rise.

"Now, Todd," the bearded man said softly. He made an odd gesture with his hand — probably just a nervous tic, Martin thought — and Todd began to writhe as if in the grip of a relapse.

"I'm Howard Ashcroft, by the way."

"Oh." Martin was mildly shocked, and he had to do a bit of clumsy juggling to get the knife into his left hand and accept a handshake. "Martin Paige."

"Not *the* Martin Paige! The playwright?"

This threw Martin for a total loss. If someone had said, *the* Martin Paige, the pornographer, the bad-check writer, the sleazy magazine reporter, he would have responded, but *playwright?*

"Didn't you write a play a few years back called *The Wild Hunt?*"

"Oh. Yes, of course. It was a one-shot thing, a kind of favor for a girlfriend, who was an actress. I write mostly detective stories —"

"It was *brilliant!*" Ashcroft interrupted.

"It was? Nobody else thought so."

"That just goes to show how far ahead of your time you are. I've never seen anything that so beautifully captures the spirit of ancient so-called paganism and translates it into the present. That girl who played Hecate. . . ?"

"Oh, yeah, that was Margo Slye. My girlfriend." He glanced at Amy. "At the time."

"You are indeed a man of many gifts."

"I'd love to stand around and talk about me," Martin said, and indeed he would have, "but shouldn't we call the police? This man is a dangerous lunatic." He turned to Amy. "Do you have any idea why he would do this?"

"I didn't see him do *anything!* I wish. . . ." She didn't disclose her wish, but Martin suspected that she wished they would all drop dead and leave her alone.

"Truly remarkable!" Ashcroft said, gripping Martin's thin arm as if in wonder at its strength. He shoved him toward Amy. "You owe this brilliant young writer your life, young lady. He never gave a moment's thought to his own safety."

While she stared at Martin in perpelexity and exasperation, Ashcroft said, "Never mind the police. I know this fellow. He's just an excitable boy. He's been under a terrible strain. I've been helping him, and I'm sure I can take care of him. It won't happen again, you can be sure of that." He gave Todd a nudge that, from Todd's perspective, might have seemed like a kick, with the toe of his Wallabee. "Get up, Todd, you're coming with me."

"Yeah. Okay." He got painfully to his feet and stumbled toward his car. "Keys. Got to lock the front door."

Amy shrank reflexively toward Martin when Todd rose, and he slipped his arm around a waist as tense as bundle of wire. He guided her toward the stairs. She slipped out of his arm and ran up. He knew he should have remained and perhaps made an issue of notifying the police, but he was convinced that she planned to dash into her apartment and lock the door behind her, so he followed her hastily.

"Good show!" Ashcroft called after him. Whether he was referring to his recent actions or that dumb play, Martin couldn't tell, but he waved a deprecatory acknowledgment.

"Cut you in little pieces, asshole, and eat the little pieces with *dip,*" Todd managed to blurt out in strangled gasps, but he clutched his stomach and screamed when the Doctor shot him a reproving look, again making that odd twitch of his hand.

Martin caught up with her at the top of the stairs, but she ignored him for a moment as she stood with her key in the door and stared intently at Todd and the Doctor. Todd was following docilely, after an earnest, muttered conversation, but he glowered over his shoulder at Martin. He shivered. If he had really noticed how big and brutal Todd looked, he would have run home and hid under his bed, and he felt like doing that now.

"Did you really save my life?" Amy asked.

Although it wasn't his usual style, he felt that he had to say, "Of course I did. It all happened so fast, I guess you just didn't notice."

"Well, then, I guess you can come in." Frowning in thought for a moment, she added, "If you want to."

"I'd like to sit down for a moment. And wash my hands. And maybe have a glass of water. If you don't mind?"

She frowned again, as if these requests were outrageous, but she opened the door and let him follow her in. He stepped into a purple twilight, a cluttered but fastidious nest of frills and bric-a-brac and feminine scents. It all looked positively Victorian, but that impression was demolished when his eye was drawn to the dominant object in the room, a massive and ominous statue of a lion-headed figure on the bookcase. Amy's eye shot to it first, he saw, and then to the coffee-table. Whatever she saw, or didn't see, on that table seemed to relieve her.

"That was Ashcroft, huh? I saw him on television years ago, and he looked bigger and more sinister. The Devil-worshipper?"

"I've always thought he was a very nice man."

"You've known him long?"

"I met him once before. He was explaining to me that it isn't really Devil-worship. He makes it sound more like est, or Positive Thinking."

"I had always hoped it would be more fun. But maybe that comes with the territory."

"I don't know what you're talking about. I don't suppose you'd like some tea, would you?"

"Sure." He poked around the room. It made her nervous when he inspected the statue, so he stopped. "What I mean is, the Devil's agents had to sound quasi-clerical, and they used props like black cats and broomsticks, in a time and place when such things had some kind of superstitious validity. In the modern world, Satanists would have to come on like the Chamber of Commerce with a streak of California looniness."

He was pleased to hear her laugh from the kitchen. "I was thinking something like that myself when I saw his place. *The Famous Witches' School.*"

"And of course they'd play to your ego. 'Develop your hidden powers and you, too, can be as proud as Lucifer!' You'd get to thinking they were just like every other self-help program, unless you happened to notice, somewhere beyond the spotlights, the maniacs creeping around with knives. If my Catholic upbringing taught me anything, it was that the Devil is perpetually updating his inventory. He wouldn't be caught within ten miles of a broomstick or a black cat nowadays."

"Do you believe in the Devil?" She returned with a tray containing a tea service and cookies. He felt like one who, on a rare and privileged visit to the schoolmarm's house, had to be on his very best behavior; and the schoolmarm made his heart flutter. She said, "Do sit down."

"No, I don't believe in him, but I kind of regret it. It would be gratifying and cozy to imagine that some enormous, eternal, superhuman force took a personal interest in my damnation; or in my salvation, either. But, if you'll pardon me, nobody gives a damn. We're just arbitrary and transient patterns of electrical charges, whirling in one infinitesimal point on an infinite zero."

She shivered. "Even the Devil isn't as depressing as that."

"Exactly my point."

"What you said about maniacs with knives — weren't you implying before that Ashcroft's Devil is real, and that Todd is one of his agents?" The amused light in her eyes — were they green or blue? In this light, they looked almost violet — made him go hollow inside. He had to concentrate hard on taking his cup without rattling it on the saucer or spilling it.

"I'm just saying that Ashcroft is undoubtedly a much better theologian than I am, and that the Devil he serves up would be acceptable to the most discriminating Jesuit demonologist. He couldn't just sell repackaged Scientology, or the fish would all swim over to the original. He has to have some real craziness in the back room. Witchy stuff. You feel almost comfortable checking in at his super-slick Holiday Inn, but you have a sneaking suspicion that the guy behind the desk is Norman Bates. So you think twice about stiffing him for the bill." He asked with abrupt intensity: "Is he trying to convert you?"

It was her teacup that rattled. "No. At least, he says he isn't."

"But?"

"But I agreed to let him bring some people over here tonight. For a ceremony. He says that this place —" she rolled her eyes skeptically — "has some kind of special significance."

"Mirdath Hodgson, or Glendower — you've heard of her?"

"The miller's bloodthirsty daughter."

"Yes. She's supposedly buried somewhere underneath Brooksprite Gardens."

"Ugh. Anyway, he didn't twist my arm or anything. It was almost as if I had to twist his, even though I don't understand now why I wanted to do it."

"That follows from what I was saying. Salesmanship."

"Would you come?"

He answered instantly, "Yes, of course, I'd love to," before she could examine her own obvious surprise at having invited him and retract the invitation.

"If you have anything to wear, that is," she added, baffling him. He decided that she must have thought his new jacket was too flashy for a Black Mass.

"He said I should invite someone — a chaperone." She uttered a nervous cry that could have been interpreted as a laugh. "You seem, well, you seem at least to have thought about these things, witchcraft and whatnot." She stared at him speculatively for a long moment, and he was seized by a frightening suspicion that he might, under the full and direct impact of that stare, undo all that he had achieved through heroism and witty conversation by fainting. She looked away, and he breathed again. "You seem so sensible, so skeptical about these things, that I can hardly believe . . . well, never mind."

"You mean, how could I have sounded like such a damned fool when we first met?"

"Well, yes," she muttered, trying to hide in her teacup.

"The way I felt, the way I still feel —" When she winced, he hastened to add: "Don't worry, I won't start again. I don't think I will, anyway. But I was telling you how I felt, and you can't really be skeptical or sensible about emotions. When I saw you —"

"Please. Maybe you'd better go now."

He would have liked to stay and find out more, find out everything about her. From where he sat he could see Tolkien and T.H. White on the shelves beneath the menacing statue, and they might help create a bond of common interest. Perhaps it was hoping too much, but she might be the sort of person who would enjoy *Swords of Winbourne,* which owed a considerable debt to both those authors. But he sensed that he had already started to lose hard-won ground, and that he could only lose more if he stayed. He forced himself to his feet and dragged them to the door.

"All right. Tonight — what time is it, Ashcroft's gala?"

"Midnight. But he said he'd come a little early."

"Aside from tonight, do I have to save your life every time I want to see you?"

"We'll see."

"I will, if necessary," he said, but he spoke those words to the door that had been promptly closed behind him.

The door cracked open. "Thank you for that," she said hastily before closing it again.

He felt like bursting into song as he rattled down the steps. The meeting hadn't settled anything or even started anything, but it was an unqualified triumph when compared with their first encounter. He suspected that the heroic rescue, turning-point in so many fictional love-affairs, had little to do with her softened attitude. She'd hardly noticed it at the time, and seemed to have all but forgotten it. He wondered how much was due to his new clothes, his haircut, and his expensive cologne. He resolved to maintain his new look, no matter how difficult he knew it was to keep such trivialities in his mind.

The notable butcher knife lay where he had left it near the foot of the stairs. He picked it up. Even though the haft looked worn, the blade seemed brand new. Maybe he should ring the bell and return it to Toni. While Todd had been beating his chest and hurling flowerpots, Martin had caught a glimpse of her slipping behind her ape from the apartment to the laundry room. She had been wrapped in a robe, using a towel as a hood, presumably coming from the shower to fetch some clean clothes. Her manner had been furtive, and she had darted into the laundry room with remarkable speed, not pausing or even turning her head to observe the action in the parking lot.

Now that he thought about it, this all seemed odd. She wasn't the sort of girl who would bundle herself up like a modest mummy on a warm afternoon and hang her head to avoid notice. Nor, he would have been willing to bet, was she the sort of girl who could hurry past any altercation without putting in her two cents' worth. They had been making a horrific racket in their apartment during his previous visit. Maybe Todd had been beating her, and she was ashamed of showing her bruises.

He wished he had been able to hit Todd a lot harder.

She wasn't home now, he decided, because Todd had locked the door from the outside before leaving with Ashcroft. She must have collected her laundry and left during the time he had gone to buy an icecream cone at the Dairy Queen. He hoped she'd had the sense to leave for good.

He couldn't leave the knife with Amy. Either it would upset her, or it would look as if he were reminding her once too often of his selfless courage. He tossed it end-over-end into the air and caught it by the handle, only then realizing with a shiver what a dumb thing his high spirits had made him do, and how lucky he'd been to catch the right end. But . . . had his high spirits made him do it, or had the knife made him do it? He might write about magic swords, but he didn't believe in them, and much less would he believe in a magic butcher knife, but he couldn't deny that holding the knife gave him an odd feeling.

Exasperated by his vaporings, he threw it into the back seat of his car and drove off, wishing that his radio worked. Today, he knew, the stupidest love song would have sounded fit for angels. Unfortunately the only song that came into his mind was "Louie, Louie," but he sang that with exuberance as he pounded time on the steering wheel.

*H*e called Rod Usher from the pay phone in his rooming house and got the name and address of Usher's agent. As an afterthought, he got the same data on Hogarth Zurer's agent. The latter was big-time, but, Martin insisted to himself, so was his idea, and so would his book be. Italian film moguls and Arab sheiks, clawing their way over the bodies of their disappointed colleagues, would slobber on his feet as they begged him to take ever-higher percentages of the gross. That darling Amy herself had suggested a title to him seemed like an irresistible good-luck charm for the book, his fair one's handkerchief to fly from his freelance: *The Miller's Bloodthirsty Daughter.* Gwyneth Paltrow could play Amy. By spells to be found in the *Necronomicon,* Vanessa Redgrave would regain her youthful radiance to play Mirdath, Stanley Kubrick would be resurrected to direct. ("Don't give me this classical shit, Stanley, I want 'Louie, Louie' for the score.") If she agreed to sleep with him, Toni Sloane would get a bit part as a lap-dancer in a New England tavern, *circa* 1847. He ran upstairs to his typewriter (still there, thank God!) and flung himself into the task of composing letters.

Although he could write the better part of a long novel in two weeks, he found that business letters were harder. He drafted the first one six times, and each time he found words, sentences, whole paragraphs that weren't just right. He didn't have a letter that satisfied him to the point where he was willing to put it aside and reconsider it in the morning until ten o'clock.

Only then did it occur to him that he'd eaten nothing but an icecream cone all day. He wondered if he would find any place open, or if he could eat in time to catch the scheduled materialization of George Spencer at eleven.

His eye was drawn to the spurious phone book that squatted, fat and baleful, beneath the corner of his bed. He believed that George wouldn't simply turn up at the door of Ashcroft's Institute in the morning and announce that he had just blown in last night from the Fourth Dimension. No, as a dedicated psycho, he would make an effort to appear in the right place at the right time, perhaps by climbing up to his roof and entering through the door he'd put there. Perhaps a delegation of crackpots would be waiting to receive him. If Martin got there early, he might be able to conceal himself and overhear something of value. He decided to skip supper.

He had just snapped off his light and was about to leave when someone — he was sure it would be someone bitching about his typewriter — tapped on his door.

He didn't turn on the light. He would open the door by slow degrees to reveal a dark room and say, as Peter Lorre would, *You must excuse me, I always do my best work . . . in the dark.* That would start him off on the right foot with bothersome neighbors.

"You must excuse me, I always do my best work . . . in the dark."

It was perfect, he'd outdone himself; but he'd provoked no reaction at all. His guest neither spoke nor entered. He peeked around the edge of the door to see a woman — he believed it was a woman — muffled from head to foot in a black cloak. The bare, 25-watt bulb at the end of the corridor didn't reveal her face.

At last she said, "So do I."

He peered harder into the shadow of her hood. "I know you, don't I? Toni?"

"Aren't you going to ask me in?"

"Like a vampire?" he chuckled.

"Precisely."

"Well, then, come in." He turned and walked to the light on the desk. "Excuse me while I cover up the crucifix."

"*Don't* turn on the light. Please. It bothers me."

"What's wrong?"

"I'm not myself this evening."

"You sound like you have a cold."

"A very sore throat."

"Won't you sit down?"

"Standing is easier."

He leaned back on his desk, folding his arms. He couldn't imagine why she was here or how she'd found him. Now that she had entered and closed the door behind her, she stood as still as before and said nothing to satisfy his curiosity. A streetlight shining through the curtains showed her pale face. She looked quite different from this morning, her face totally immobile, glacially composed. Then he realized that her eyes were in constant, rapid motion, as if she could see perfectly well in the dark, even as if she could absorb visual impressions at a superhuman speed. He wouldn't have thought it possible, but Toni was beginning to give him the creeps.

"Okay, you win. I'm sorry about Peter Lorre. I thought you were a neighbor, coming to make a nuisance of himself."

"Who is Peter Lorre?"

He snorted. "Way before your time, of course. He was a movie actor who specialized in creepy roles. That's who I was imitating."

"Before my time." She had an incredibly sexy laugh. Her voice had a lubricious quality, too, and it was subtly different from the voice he remembered. Her sexiness was unlike her earlier, playful flirting. She seemed more serious, more mature. She hadn't denied his identification, but maybe she was Toni's sister, or even her mother. He couldn't say exactly why, but he was reluctant to step forward and try for a better look at her face.

"This Peter, he was frightening? Do you enjoy being frightened?"

"It depends. Women usually scare me quite enough without working at it. I wish you'd stop."

"Come here."

He pushed himself away from the desk and hesitantly went to stand close to her. He clearly remembered that Toni's eyes were blue. Even in the dim glow diffused through the curtains, it was plain now that this woman's were very dark. Accepting what seemed to be her dare, he bent forward and kissed her. Her lips were cool and unmoving, and when they remained so, he wondered if that was really what she had wanted him to do, despite all her apparent signals.

"Did that frighten you?"

"No, I guess not." He laughed nervously. "In a different way, maybe."

He noticed that the muffler she wore tightly around her neck in the shadow of her hood was made of terrycloth. He believed it was a towel. It was a warm night, and she seemed drastically overdressed, unless she was wearing only a bathrobe underneath her cloak. It was an odd getup for a seduction, if that was what this visit implied, but he couldn't deny that the idea *was* seductive. It must be the bathrobe he had last seen her wearing when she had dashed out of her house to the laundry room, probably distressed by her ape's barbarities. The cloak must have been improvised from a bedspread or a drapery, the first thing that came to hand, and she had fled Brooksprite Gardens without putting in the blue contact lenses she had been wearing when they first met. He breathed a little easier as he contrived these reasonable explanations. He touched the towel at her neck, meaning it undo it, but she fended off his hand.

"It helps my throat," she said.

"Maybe it's none of my business, but was Todd beating you?" He couldn't resist boasting: "If it makes you feel any better, I coldcocked him tonight. It was a lucky punch, but. . . ."

She laughed immoderately. "Todd will never beat me, no matter what he might think."

He supposed that she was making a pun. He was growing a little tired of her weird ways and cryptic remarks, so he said: "I don't mean to sound inhospitable or anything, I think it's really great that you came to see me, but the fact is, I was just going out and . . . well, what is it you want, if you didn't come here to talk or to neck?"

"*Neck.*" She laughed. "I don't understand. To neck someone, to cut off her head?"

"Now you're just being a wise-ass," he said, turning away. He stepped away from her and leaned on the desk again, even though the flimsy composition-board creaked at this fresh assault. He said, "Do you *know* what you want?"

She turned stiffly, moving her head with her body, and raised her arm to point directly to the disguised *Necronomicon.* That she could have seen through the false wrapping was impossible. He doubted that she could even see the book at all in this light, for he couldn't; but he knew where it was, and that was exactly where she was pointing.

"That is what I have come for."

"Is it yours?"

"It is not yours." She lowered her arm the same way she had raised it, as if her elbow didn't work. She continued to stand stiffly, her eyes apparently on the book.

"That's true."

"I would have it." Her cold, imperious voice wasn't at all sexy now.

"I have Spencer's diary, too, you know. You seem to know a lot."

"You may keep his diary. With my blessing."

"Thanks," he said sarcastically. "The problem is that the book you want might be the key to the code in his diary."

"The key to the code in his diary," she said promptly, "is the compact edition of *Webster's New World Dictionary*, printed in 1967."

"Are you kidding?"

"It is the truth."

It was convincing. Living under a mountain of bizarre books, George had chosen a commonplace one, one that held all the words he would need, for his book-code. The same devious turn of mind had led him to hide the *Necronomicon* in plain sight.

How she knew about the code was another question, but he presumed she was in league with the burglar who had contemptuously left the diary after inscribing it with his secret symbols.

"Are you — your people — planning on throwing a 'welcome home' party for George tonight? Is he coming back?"

"He will try. He is of no importance to me. I told you, *I would have the book!*"

He realized that she hadn't really been trying to scare him before. Now she was, and it worked. He shivered.

He managed to say, "So you did."

It didn't surprise him that R. Bamberger had apparently seen through him and tracked him down to this rooming-house. It did surprise him that the bouncy and apparently bubble-headed Toni Sloane had this odd side to her, so cold and creepy (but that could have been the effect of drugs), or that she should be a serious member of the group that wanted the book. When he considered that her boyfriend was a member, it made a little more sense.

None of that mattered. What did matter was that she and Bamberger and Todd and Ashcroft were local people. Not only that, they were agents of what the police chief himself had described as 'a respectable local industry,' while Martin was nothing but an out-of-town burglar with the loot in his possession. He hadn't wanted the damned book in the first place, he assured himself.

He said, "Okay, take it."

"You must do it," she said. "I suffer from a certain stiffness."

He sighed resignedly and yanked the book from under the bed. "Tell me —"

"I have told you enough." She snatched the book out of his hands. "If you would know more, we will meet again tonight at the Sabbat."

"You do know a lot about my business, don't you? Toni — wait!"

"I have no time!"

She opened the door and started through it. He reached out to stay her. She pulled. So did he. She broke free. He heard her footsteps retreating down the hall, down the stairs, and out the front door, but he didn't want to chase her, nor did he believe he could have done so.

Women had sometimes quitted his New York apartment leaving hand-bags, eyeglasses, bracelets, wristwatches, combs. He had always gathered them up and put them safely aside, secure in the Freudian knowledge that even though they might have fled in anger or boredom, they wanted to come back.

But he didn't want Toni Sloane to come back for what she had left in his hand, nor could he think where he might safely put it aside. If the *Necronomicon* had been only a rabbit hole, this was more persuasive evidence of Wonderland, this was the Cheshire Cat's grin hanging in the air after its owner had departed.

What he held and stared at in wild surmise — one end of it bound in the slovenly clump of adhesive tape that had held it on, its look and texture gray and bloodless and cold — was Toni Sloane's left forearm and hand.

Chapter Thirteen

*A*my hurried down the stairs in a foul mood to look for her laundry. She felt as if she had been manipulated into a series of progressively more invidious positions today. The latest, and worst, was being obliged to act grateful to that awful Martin Paige for something she wasn't even sure he had done. If it hadn't been for her dream, and the horrible sense of reliving it, which must have been only the latest of the dirty tricks her mind was playing on her, she wouldn't have believed for a minute that Todd Farmer had tried to kill her. And just because she'd had a recent nightmare was no reason to accept the word of Ashcroft, a snake-oil salesman, or Paige, a grubby hack.

That Todd and Ashcroft knew each other so well aroused her darkest suspicions. Could Todd have hypnotized her at some time and planted the suggestions for her crazy dreams? Dr. Ashcroft's pitch about people coming to him for help with dreams and hallucinations now seemed altogether too much of a coincidence, and she was glad she'd been too timid to rise to the bait at the time. Todd could have induced the dreams to make her more receptive to the Doctor's ideas.

But how could he have done that? Apart from fleeing encounters by the mailbox, she had never been alone with him. Had he made his hypnotic suggestions after breaking into her apartment to drug her food, or injecting some narcotic gas through a hole in the floor? She shuddered. The paranoid flavor of her theory scared her even more than the theory itself. She would simply have to stop putting off the call to her psychiatrist.

That all three of them, Todd, Martin, and Ashcroft had come together so conveniently for that (rehearsed?) scene suggested a real conspiracy, though. She couldn't quite grasp Martin's place in it, but Ashcroft's effusive praise for his action, whatever it had been, made him less credible. The Doctor had even praised a play he'd written. That she had never heard of it proved nothing, even though she did often skim the theater news, but she suspected now that Ashcroft and Martin were at least acquainted, and that Ashcroft's surprise at meeting the supposed playwright had been entirely bogus.

Much as she tried not to, she couldn't help remembering that Patrick Laughlin had believed someone was playing mind-games with him and his family just before the horror at the mill transpired. He had believed he was dreaming of a red-haired beauty and his father was painting the same person because someone had planted her image in their minds through hypnosis. Ashcroft had been present, too, the night Patrick had mentioned it, and he had supplied the information that Mirdath had been a redhead. He had brought it up casually, as if faintly amused at the idea that anyone might consider it important: just the way Martin had today brought up the fact that Mirdath was buried under Brooksprite Gardens.

She hesitated at the door of the laundry room. She saw that Gertner's car was gone (off to the dirty bookstore to get the latest by Martin Paige, no doubt), so she had time to put off opening the door and dashing into the awful place while she built up her courage. At last she pushed the door open at arm's length and slowly leaned after it. The machines were silent. The room seemed empty. She slipped inside and bolted the door behind her.

I can't wait to try on my new clothes.

What an odd thought! She didn't have any new clothes, at least none that she hadn't worn before. But as she'd entered the room, she'd been warmed by the thought that she had marvelous new clothing that she would soon be able to wear. It was a strong and lingering impression, too. Even though she knew perfectly well that no such clothing existed, she had to stop and visualize every garment she owned to back up her knowledge.

Martin Paige was the one who needed new clothes, she reflected. This afternoon he'd been wearing pants that didn't cover his white socks and a jacket, of a particularly offensive shade of blue, that looked as if it had been cut by a tailor with only a textbook knowledge of human anatomy; and the clothes looked as if he'd worn them while crawling around in a cellar. He'd gotten a haircut, too, apparently having stumbled upon Stan Laurel's old barber. Worst of all — it had taken an effort not to mention it — he smelled bad. The odor had seemed to come from the greasy black stains on his jacket.

She found most of her laundry in the dryers and the remainder in one of the washing machines. She transferred the wet wash into one of the dryers and began to fold the dry clothes at a table along the wall. She planned to wait here until everything was ready and save herself another trip to this damned place. She reassured herself with a glance that she had indeed bolted the door.

Someone had left a black velvet garment on the table. She picked it up and inspected it. It was a very expensive-looking hooded cloak with a lining of crimson silk, far too elegant or theatrical to wear while knocking around Mt. Tabor, and not at all the sort of thing one would ever put in a washing machine. She couldn't picture any of her neighbors wearing it, although it was true that she didn't know them all, even by sight. Encouraged by the locked door, she tried it on and found that it fell almost to the tops of her shoes in elegant lines. Its luxuriant folds swung gracefully when she executed a pirouette. Although she knew it was most unlikely, she felt that it gave her a look of mysterious and ever so faintly wicked enchantment.

"It is Mirdath's!" she hissed in a witchy voice made almost too effective by the harsh echoes of metal surfaces. She quickly folded the cloak and put it back where she'd found it.

My own new clothes. . . .

Damn! That feeling — it couldn't be called a thought, it wasn't expressed in words or in an image of the clothes in question — had persisted, defying her thorough mental inventory of her wardrobe. She perked up at the thought that it was a sign directing her to go out and buy some new clothes. She could do that tomorrow.

Having folded her own things, she went to the door of the storage room — and what on earth was she doing that for? She stopped cold with her hand on the doorknob. She had nothing to do in the storage room. She took her hand away and discovered that some slob had smeared the knob with red paint. Or something.

As she wiped her hand thoroughly with tissues from her purse, she noticed other red stains on the floor. Her hand went instantly to her nose. It hadn't been broken. None of that had happened; nor did the mess in her apartment exist. She reassured herself further by glancing down at her arm. There was no scab.

She found it hard to breathe as some of the terror she'd felt in this room this afternoon began to creep back. She was glad people would be visiting her tonight, any people. The thought of being alone in her apartment scared her.

She stared at the door of the storage room. She knew it was a perfectly ordinary room, she'd seen it dozens of times, its chicken-wire and bare bulbs, its dusty smell, there was nothing sinister about it. She remembered that Todd had been playing with a knife. He must have cut himself, and that accounted for the stains. Now that she thought about it, she remembered seeing a dirty bandage on his hand when he'd left with the Doctor, one that hadn't been there when she'd seen him in the laundry room.

She felt enormously relieved by the simple explanation; but when she began to fold Todd and Toni's dry clothes — she might as well, while she was waiting for her own to dry — she was very much aware of the storage room door behind her back. Without even looking, she could see the dull shine of its dark green paint, the scuffmarks at the foot, the dark discoloration from many hands near the handle. She could see it beginning to open. . . .

No, she couldn't! She whirled right around and stared at it, daring it to open, and it didn't. Of course it didn't. The room behind it was quite empty.

Folding Todd's shorts, while rigorously directing her mind away from the embarrassing thought that he had handled her most intimate articles of clothing, made her think of her imaginary husband. As they sat across from one another in the breakfast nook brimming with splashes of buttery sunlight, he looked concerned this morning.

> *There are no such things as witches, Amy. We are nothing but aggregations of atoms whirling at random in an infinite void.*

God *damn* it! Even though he still looked like Peter Jennings, he was unquestionably Martin Paige. He even had the silly haircut. Very, very tentatively, she changed the portrait to make it look more like Martin. She brought back the stubble on his cheeks. She had thought it looked scruffy this morning, but she decided she liked him better that way than clean-shaven. He was certainly intelligent. If you measured intelligence by one's ability to see oneself clearly (and she was inclined to do that), he was smarter than Hogarth Zurer, unlikely as that seemed. Martin apparently couldn't see himself in ordinary mirrors (she put a bit of egg on his necktie to make her portrait more realistic), but he seemed to have a truer image of himself than Zurer did. Just as Martin's stock rose when he wasn't around to leave inky fingerprints on her teacups, so the great man's dwindled when he couldn't overwhelm her with his personality: if he hadn't written *Behold Now Behemoth,* she would have thought him an ass.

"You remind me of Alice in Wonderland." Had Martin really said that? He couldn't have known that it was her all-time favorite book, that it had dictated the way she'd tried to speak between the ages of six and ten, which hadn't enhanced her popularity with her peers, and was still responsible for the way she wore her hair. It was the nicest and most perceptive thing anyone had said to her, not just in a long time, she was forced to admit, but ever.

It was pure idiocy, thinking of Martin as her husband, and she made herself stop. But if she was ever to have a husband other than the vague admirer who sat opposite her in the ideal breakfast nook of her daydreams, it would have to be someone from the real world. More specifically, it would have to be someone from the real world who took the slightest interest in her as a woman. Unless she counted Todd Farmer, and she certainly didn't, that narrowed the field down drastically to Martin Paige and Mr. Gertner. And Hogarth Zurer. But she suspected that Zurer's interest in her went no deeper than his need to have her help him with his book.

She didn't suppose that Martin had been trying to flatter her – or fluster her, that was more accurate – in an effort to win her help with his article for a "major crime magazine." Nobody would go to such lengths for a goal so trivial. The worst she could really say about his claim to have been smitten by a grand passion was that it indicated an unstable mind. She doubted that he had been merely repeating to her what he said to every woman he met: he just couldn't be made to fit her notion of a Don Juan.

It struck her for the first time that Ashcroft might bring Zurer with him tonight. She hadn't had the heart to tell Martin that a *real* author was working on an idea similiar to his. But the truth would certainly come out if they spent five minutes talking with each other. Zurer might decide he could write the book without her help if he supposed, even incorrectly, that she was telling her story to some wretched hack. At best Martin's feelings would be hurt, for she would have to tell him that Zurer's claim on her biography took the precedence of genius.

Of course, if both of them were involved in a plot with Ashcroft and Todd, they would both know what was going on; but there her conspiracy theory ran onto the rocks and sank. To imagine that four desirable men (well, three, and one who might be desirable if he paid the slightest attention to his appearance) had nothing better to do with their time than to hatch some dark plot aginst her involving hypnotism and drugs and prearranged scenes from melodrama – not only was it implausible, it was a scenario obviously inspired by sexual frustration and loneliness. To put it bluntly: no such luck.

When the dryer clicked off, the room fell suddenly and completely silent. She caught herself holding her breath and listening: more specifically, listening for some sound from the storage room. Exasperated with herself, she made a point of whistling loudly a spritely Mozart air as she jerked the last of her laundry out of the dryer and folded it.

She made a last confident, unhurried survey of the laundry room and saw to her horror that the green door stood ajar. She snatched up her clothes and ran, impeded for what seemed an intolerably long time by the bolt she had foolishly thrown. She didn't look over her shoulder as she fled up the stairs.

Her living room was just as it should be. Bozo (she winced as she remembered how Martin had studied the statue, no doubt drawing all sorts of improper conclusions from its brazen nudity) was unbroken.

When she put away her clothes in the bedroom, her hand strayed to the pearl-gray dress, but she had enough will-power not to pull it out and make sure that it wasn't ripped. Her new clothes. . . .

She sat in the wing chair by her bedroom window and closed her eyes, deliberately composing herself. *New clothes.* She made an effort to disengage her mind from every other concern and let it drift as it wished over that idea. She wanted to evoke an image of those clothes, she wanted to see just what it was that she imagined she owned. Blankness. Then . . . dancing. She was dancing with no clothes at all, not formally or in accordance with any recognized school, but flinging herself about joyfully, stretching her body, leaping, running, generally carrying on as she never would.

She opened her eyes and cursed as some inconsiderate neighbor slammed the laundry room door. Peeking around the corner of the drape, she saw that the owner of that cloak had retrieved it from the laundry and was hurrying down the walkway with an oddly halting stride.

The cloak with its hood made it impossible to say who it could be as she passed through the fans of light from the entryways. She turned into the last entry, where she mounted the three low steps with difficulty and vanished.

The only person Amy knew in that entry, and not very well at all, was Brenda Willy, who had been a teacher at the regional high school since she was a student there. Other kids used to say that Ms. Willy was weird, and they made odd faces or giggled when her name came up, but nobody had told Amy why they did that, nor had she asked, since she herself often evoked giggles and odd faces from those immature morons. Her clumsy gait and her difficulty with the steps suggested old age, but she was in her mid-thirties. Maybe she was drunk, and maybe that accounted for everything, even why she had left her expensive cloak in the laundry room in the first place.

She closed her eyes again and shoved her weird neighbor out of her mind, turning it deliberately once more to the nagging impression of *new clothes*. But that impression, as she had determined before, wasn't really defined by those words. It was new . . . something. It was something that she could put on like clothing, something that was fresh and new and excitingly free to move, to dance, to walk after such a long time . . . in the ground. When she let her mind drift, it dwelled lovingly on the surfaces and contours of her own pale skin, on the fine blue tracery of veins visible, as through milky glass, on the throb of the blood at her throat.

She looked down at her hand, palm upward, only it wasn't her hand. The three concentric arcs of ruptured blisters on the palm suggested that it was Toni Sloane's hand. It held a few short strands of fine, colorless hair that looked suspiciously like her own pubic hair. Her other hand made passes over the strands, weaving indecipherable figures in the air.

She sprang out of her chair, having apparently drifted from her meditation into a light sleep, and more distressed now than ever by her neurotic fantasies and her gift for cooking up unpalatable dreams.

She took her long-deferred shower, making it as hot as she could stand it. After that she wiped the steamy mirror on the inside of the door and made a more than casual survey of her pink body. She wondered why she had been obsessed with the simple, unremarkable fact that she possessed it, and why this fact had given her such joy. Although there was, she admitted wryly, no danger of mistaking her for one of the models in Martin's awful magazines — *high-class men's magazines* was an oxymoron, if ever she'd heard one — this was a perfectly healthy, serviceable, rather slim and long-legged female body. Daringly letting her mind edge toward a boundary she never let it cross, she believed a man would find it attractive.

"Well, don't you think it's about time you found out, Miss Priss?" she snapped at her naked reflection.

Having alarmed herself thoroughly, she bundled herself into her robe and hurried out to the comparative chill of the living room before that train of thought could go any further.

Only now remembering a thought that had come to her after meeting Zurer, she ran her hand along the top shelf of the case beneath Bozo until she came to a book hiding behind *Mistress Masham's Repose,* a paperback copy of *Behold Now Behemoth.* She knew that it didn't deserve such an honored position. Perhaps it belonged here with her favorite books, but on a less exalted shelf. She had merely stuck it here because the space had been available. She would leave it where it was this evening, and perhaps Zurer would be flattered if his eye happened to fall on it. She felt that asking for an autograph would be gauche, although she would have liked to have one.

As she had meant to do earlier, she opened the book with the thought of refreshing her memory. Her eye fell on the beginning of Chapter Six:

Bascomb took his steaming coffee to the wheelhouse, where Starke knew better than to say a word to him, and stared back into the unblinking eye of the sea. He wasn't himself in the morning. Who could say with any reasonable conviction that he was? Maybe he had been replaced in his bunk last night by some other person, or by some other sort of creature entirely, which had assumed the appearance, the memories, and the attitudes of Slade Bascomb. There was no way he could prove that this hadn't happened. The continuity of consciousness was the only proof that could sustain the pronominal erection that dominated his thoughts, and that continuity had been, as it was every night by sleep, cut off. The great gray shroud of the sea, shifting restlessly from pole to pole, wouldn't swear to his identity, couldn't even swear to its own, for it was no longer the same ocean he'd faced yesterday. He and the sea itself were nothing but shadows in the same, evanescent magic-lantern show called matter, renewed and replaced and intermingled with each other constantly by the wind of chaos that whistled through them both as they hurried, a meaningless swarm of electrical charges, to the ultimate Nowhere. The sea had suffered a change, and it was Bascomb: of its coral were his bones made.

Ugh! What a nasty idea! She snapped the book shut. The Shakespearean wordplay ended it on what sounded like an upbeat, but the despair remained unresolved, and it held the same gloomy view of existence that Martin had been advancing this afternoon. She didn't for a moment believe that Martin consciously went around spouting the wisdom of Zurer. It seemed likelier that they had both bought the childish Hallowe'en masks with which they tried to scare away the evil spirits of their psyches at the same cut-rate philosophy shop.

She couldn't deny the power of his prose, though. Even though Martin might share his outlook on life, she was sure he couldn't express it so eloquently. But that was obvious. Zurer wrote books like this, and Martin wrote for "major crime magazines." She returned the paperback to the shelf, placing it where it might be more easily noticed.

She saw that she'd missed Peter Jennings by almost three hours, and she'd done nothing about her dinner. She went to the bedroom and dressed: boldly choosing the pearl-gray dress as a way of scaring off her own evil spirits. As she had known it would, it annoyed her now to realize that all of her clothes weren't clean, and that she had discarded her underwear in the hamper before she showered. She was chilled to remember that she had anticipated that annoyance in a dream, not in real life. More proof — she certainly didn't need it! — that it had been a realistic dream. For the umpteenth time that day, she checked her arm and found no scab.

She passed the time by skimming *Behemoth,* struck anew by the vividness or insight of so many passages. A lot of it was commercial hogwash, of course, but she skipped the fist-fighting and bed-hopping parts. Zurer must have been playing the buffoon to tease her, or perhaps he habitually adopted that role to shield his sensitive nature. Whatever the reason, no self-absorbed windbag could have written a book like this.

When next she looked at the clock, it said eleven. She decided not to eat but to wait until Ashcroft came and nibble on whatever refreshments he might bring. On the chance that he would forget or bring something she didn't like, she went out to Leiber's Delicatessen for cold cuts and bread and a choice of dips.

When she returned, two police cars and an ambulance were parked in front of the first entry to her building, their lights flashing vigorously.

She had to drive carefully to get around them and to avoid her rubber-necking neighbors. She knew she was a poor driver, and it scared her to thread her way through the moving maze of people. ("Why don't all you nosy people stay home and read *True Detective Secrets?*" she thought with annoyance.) For the first time since she'd owned the car, she tapped the horn, earning herself some nasty looks and indelicate words.

After she had parked, it occurred to her that the activity was centered on Brenda Willy's entry. Maybe her odd behavior had signified illness. She should have run after her to offer help.

She was intensely curious, but even though she knew she was a busybody, she didn't want to get her mother's reputation for being one, so she walked hesitantly toward the activity, planning to drift at the edge of things and see whatever she could see. Her mother would have bulled right in and buttonholed a hapless cop.

"Think our place will be on *America's Most Wanted?*"

Damn damn *damn!* She had neglected her customary check for Mr. Gertner, and he had just sidled up to her shoulder, wrapped in his usual haze of gin-fumes and cigarette-smoke. He took her elbow companionably, and she was too polite to shrug off his hand.

Much as she hated to prolong the encounter, she asked, "What happened?"

"That schoolteacher, what's-her-name, somebody cut her throat from ear to ear."

"*Ew!*"

"Yeah, that's just what I said. Maybe she did it herself, of course. Some folks find odd ways to check out. You don't suppose your hippie boyfriend did it, do you?"

"My *what?*"

"You know, the guy with the beard. He brought you home this afternoon, and then there was all that fuss with the goon downstairs." He sniggered. "I figured it was a lovers' quarrel."

She found it hard to keep from laughing. Dr. Ashcroft looked more like a college professor or maybe a lawyer, but his beard had triggered the "hippie" reflex in this antiquated dumbbell.

She restrained herself from defending Ashcroft and said, "What makes you think he did it?"

"He was in and out of there all the time. Him and the goon both. Maybe that slut, the goon's girlfriend, got jealous and did it. It sounds like a job for that hotshot reporter for *True Murder Facts,* Martin Paige."

Good Lord, she thought, he really *is* a Martin Paige fan! Maybe she had been too hasty in dismissing her admirer as a pathetic nobody.

She said, "Was she wearing a cloak? A black cloak?"

"Who?"

"The teacher, Ms. Willy. Have you ever seen her wearing a black cloak?"

"She was probably wearing nothing. That's what she usually wears, the damn hussy, and she never pulls down her shades. One night I saw her out here, it was raining, and she was dancing around the parking lot in her birthday suit."

Amy knew her sarcasm would be wasted, but she said: "If I were you, I would have complained to the building management."

"Well, you know me. Live and let live. If that's how she wants to celebrate the Rite of Spring, that's her business."

Her mind boggled at Gertner's apparent reference to Stravinsky. He might not be a total idiot. But he had drawn her closer by her elbow, and now she found no difficulty in shaking his hand off.

"I have to go. I have some guests coming for a party."

"I'm not doing anything tonight."

She pretended she hadn't heard him as she dashed back to her entry.

She had just set out an appetizing spread on the coffee table with a bottle of rosé she'd been saving for a special occasion when the doorbell rang.

"I hope we're not too early. About this afternoon, I feel like a real jerk —"

"Don't mention it, Todd. I don't know what happened, really, and I don't want to." He looked so contrite and sheepish, so like the way he always looked in her Aunt Amy fantasies, that she didn't feel in the least menaced. She undid the chain-lock.

Her heart stopped for a moment as she saw that he was accompanied by woman in a black cloak. But then she recognized her, and she breathed a little easier. She would have some explaining to do about that cloak. But despite Gertner's hallucinations, she could have had nothing to do with the death of Ms. Willy.

"What are you waiting for, Toni, an engraved invitation? Come in."

Chapter Fourteen

*M*artin's lack of faith in the supernatural somehow managed to survive the shock of the severed arm. It had been a trick, a stage magician's trick: whether his visitor had been Toni or not, the arm she had been born with was still up her sleeve. However unsatisfactory or incomplete this explanation might be, it was the only one he would allow himself to accept.

But his hand remembered, even as his mind tried not to, exactly how it had felt to pull her dead arm free from its clumsy fastening. And on the relic that he forced himself to examine after she fled was a serious burn in the form of three concentric arcs: exactly the sort of burn one would get from an electric stove.

The arm could tell him nothing; George Spencer might tell him all. He wrapped the arm in the spare jersey he had bought today and hid it (insofar as anything could be hidden from those darting eyes that would haunt him forever) under the bed.

It was already 10:45 when he reached Spencer's house, but he forced himself to reconnoiter it thoroughly. The house was dark and looked empty. No cars were parked nearby, nor did he see any suspicious pedestrians. He parked in front to save time. Taking the flashlight from his glovebox, he walked to the rear of the house and the crawlspace he had used before. On the way he tried to see if the door in the roof was open, but the darkness and the angle of view frustrated his efforts. He didn't want to attract attention by playing the flashlight on the roof.

He was prepared this time for the long drop to the basement floor, and he entered silently. Using the flash sparingly, he made his way up into the kitchen. The icebox hummed, but he could hear no other sound in the house.

He mounted to the third floor, slowing his pace and stopping more often to listen as he went higher. At the door to the attic he paused for a minute until his breathing had quieted to the point where he could hear other sounds. He heard none.

He was probably on a wild goose chase. It was now eleven o'clock. Even if there were no reception committee milling around over his head, it seemed reasonable to suppose that George, if he were in the attic, would make some sound, or that a light would show around the door. R. Bamberger could have made a sloppy calculation; his own watch could be a few minutes off; and maybe George and his friends were already on their way to the Black Mass at Amy's place. That thought gave him the push he needed (he realized only now that he was wasting time because he was afraid of what might wait for him in the attic), and he opened the door and climbed stealthily into the darkness, which seemed oddly less dark than the third floor.

Halfway up he saw that the door in the roof was open. When he first saw it, and for only an instant, it seemed that the sky was bright with a shifting confusion of unfamiliar lights. Like a continuation of the ladder, a crystal shaft rose to the zenith of a weirdly different sky, but now the illusion was over. It passed so quickly that he could ascribe it to a combination of retinal impressions from his flashlight and vertigo from his exertions. He rubbed his eyes. Now the open door showed a conventional patch of dully glowing sky and a few dim stars. The fact remained, however, that the door was open, and he had securely closed it this afternoon.

He took two more cautious steps and froze. He heard an ambient undercurrent of sound that could have been whispers. It was only the buzzing of flies. He sensed more of them, many more of them, than there had been this afternoon, and he believed it was odd that they should be so active in the dark, but these seemed to be facts of no great significance. The flies brushed his face disquietingly as he continued to the top of the stairs and, after a moment of hesitation, probed the attic with his light.

"Who – ?"

The flashlight clattered to the floor and went out. The voice had come from a figure lying at the foot of the ladder. In the moment he had glimpsed him and been shocked out of his wits, Martin had gathered the impression that he was an old man, naked and emaciated. Beyond that . . . something was wrong with him. Perhaps it was merely his twisted posture that had disturbed him. He had looked as if he had fallen down the ladder and broken, at least, a leg. But beyond that lurked an anomaly that hadn't registered completely on his conscious mind, perhaps one that he resisted. He retrieved the flashlight.

"No light, if you please. It will only hasten my dissolution."

Martin obeyed. He found it hard to think of the dim figure by the ladder as a demented mass murderer, a cannibal who flaunted the relic of his enormity on his bookshelf. He was just an injured old man, more afraid than Martin was. He inched his way forward through the murmurous, tickling darkness.

"George Spencer? Don't worry, I'm not here to hurt you. Are you okay?"

It might have been laughter that answered his question. It might also have been dry leaves rustling across the attic floor, or a sudden agitation of the flies. If it was laughter, it conveyed no mirth.

"Mr. Spencer?"

"For the moment, I am he. Why have you come, to gloat? Is it you, Ashcroft?"

"My name's Martin Paige. I'm a writer. I have nothing to do with Ashcroft. Don't worry, I'll get help for you."

It was a laugh, and it was surely the most unpleasant one he had ever heard. "Don't trouble yourself. What is happening to me is slow, but it is sure. Do you want something of me?"

Martin stood over George, who was no more than a pale blur in the darkness, a blur whose outlines he couldn't quite delimit. His shape seemed to be in continuous flux. Martin realized in horror that the man's extremities were blotted by a black, shifting, buzzing mass. He bent and tried to wave the flies away.

"Don't!" The command was so sharp that he straightened reflexively. "You will only speed the process. You find me in the unique, and I must say, painful condition of giving birth to myself. If you want something, ask. I am in a generous mood. It is, after all, my birthday."

Distressing though it was to accept this nonsense and do nothing to relive his condition, Martin forced himself to humor him. He took him at his word and came to the point: "I want to write something about the murders at the mill. Did you kill the Laughlins and Mrs. Miniter?"

"Mirdath killed them."

"Do you mean. . . ?" He couldn't decide how to word the question, nor could he see what worth the answer would have, but he wanted to ask: *Did you kill them, acting under Mirdath's imagined influence?*

"By that I mean that Mirdath Glendower, imperfectly raised from the dead by Mordred Glendower, her father, killed those people. She also killed Rupert, my son, and the young woman with whom he was incorrectly believed to have eloped. Rupert was an utter fool, but he was a good man. He would never have involved himself with a high-school girl."

He wanted to get George's story first-hand, however senseless it might be (and it was obvious that the man was every bit as crazy as he'd supposed); but even though going for help would end his chance for an exclusive interview, the revulsion he felt for George's affliction was more than he could bear. He wanted to run down the stairs and out the door and scream for the medics. That, at least, would get him away from these damned flies, which seemed determined to crawl into his nose and ears.

"Try to rest easy, Mr. Spencer, I'll go and phone —"

"No one can help me, you idiot!" When he raised his voice it evoked a buzzing echo, as if the flies mocked him. "Stay and watch, and see what will become of you if you would be a Master of the Runes."

"All I want to do is write a book. Really. But you need —"

"I want for nothing but company, and even yours will do. I'm not dying." Again that laugh, and again its rustling echo. "There is no danger at all of that, I fear. I should be indebted to you if you would stay."

Martin decided to grit his teeth and stay a little longer. That George could lie here like this, twisted and aswarm with insects, and still find the energy to talk like a book, indicated that he might not be so badly off as Martin imagined. He could wait a few minutes before running out to make an anonymous call for help.

"If that's what you want, all right." He figured he might as well spend the time by getting some information, even though it might be worthless. "How could Mordred raise her from the dead? Wasn't he dead, too? Who raised him?"

"The essence of his being — the cellular memory of Mordred, if you will — lived on in his descendants. It was concentrated in Patrick Laughlin to the point were it possessed him completely."

"And he. . . ." Even in this black attic teeming with unnaturally active life and littered with wizardly paraphernalia, even after he had held Toni's severed arm in his hands, Martin couldn't take this conversation seriously, but he struggled to seem solemn. "And he raised Mirdath?"

"It was an indiscriminate resurrection. Her remains had become contaminated with the remains of every manner of creeping, crawling thing. Her only wish then was to return to oblivion, and she killed whoever got in her way. No one canceled Mordred's work, however. In a way — in more than one way, for a creature like Mirdath has extensions beyond your world of five senses — she still lives. She plots now to return in a more suitable form, by seizing the body of a living person."

The taste of Toni's cold, still lips returned so vividly that it didn't seem absurd to ask: "Or a dead one?"

Martin resisted the urge to stop his ears against that laugh. George cackled, "I infer that you have met her! That would be simple for her, but unsatisfying. She craves a new life, craves it to the point where she has pledged herself to the ultimate horror, the force that would smooth out all differences and resolve all contradictions in our chaotic universe."

"Would that be so bad?"

"After the fact, you wouldn't think so. You wouldn't be able to discern the difference between good and bad in a world without youth or age, male or female, light or dark, life or death. Contrast is our natural element. Whatever joy we take from life, whatever meaning we find in it, comes from our knowledge of its alternative. Wise from the memory of pain, we seize and enjoy pleasure; and we endure pain in the hope, however false it might be, that pleasure will return. Such opposites would be resolved in a world sucked dry by the great leveler, the same-maker, the vampire of life's essence, Zurvan, That Which Is (Not)."

Martin couldn't believe or even envision what Spencer was talking about, but it nevertheless chilled him. Before he could phrase a question, George continued: "You may find it amusing, perhaps even instructive, to learn something of the path that has led me to my wretched state. Don't worry, young man, I won't burden you with the story of my life. Except to note that I was uncommonly rich in those things the world values. Even though I had wealth, honor, and love, I saw the conditions of my existence as a prison. I longed for the extraordinary, the transcendent, for the powers and pleasures — and, in my foolishness, even the horrors — that other men have only imagined.

"I never tasted those things. I read, I studied, I experimented with drugs and mystical disciplines. But I remained a temporal being, a mortal man, and one morning the adolescent enthusiast that I had never quite outgrown looked in the mirror to see an old and dying man. The only things of this world that I really cared for, my wife and my son, had been taken from me.

"But, as if in compensation, I had acquired a certain book, a book in whose existence I had never fully believed, a book that might grant me the transcendent sensations for which I had always longed. It may have been a Satanic temptation. *The Book of Job* would have made a better story, don't you think, if Job had been tempted with the power to strike back at his sanctimonious tormentor?"

"This book . . . the *Necronomicon?*"

He was silent for so long that Martin suspected he had lost consciousness. He was about to speak when George said, "Have you come to taunt me? Who are you?"

"I'm not here to taunt you. I found your diary, that's all, where you wrote that you found it."

A touch of that buzzing echo lurked in the sigh that George heaved. "That you should be here at all, at just this time — but I have to trust you. The *Necronomicon* will be found eventually, whether I tell you where it is or not. *It must be destroyed!* Mirdath can do nothing without it. More important, she cannot forward the destiny of Zurvan without that book."

While George went on to tell him about the location of the bogus phone book, Martin struggled with his conscience. George believed passionately in all this nonsense. For Martin to tell him that he had given the book to . . . to whomever he had given it to, would compound the pain of the sick old man's delusions. But what if those delusions were true? If the book was so dangerous, and if he had in fact given it to Mirdath, George was the only man who might know how to repair the disaster.

"I've already found the book, Mr. Spencer." He had found it by pure chance, but he saw no harm in embellishing his achievement: "I applied

Poe's theory that the best place to hide something is in plain sight." He concluded sheepishly, "And now someone else has it."

"It is minimally gratifying to receive proof that my ability to judge human nature remains unimpaired," he said with surprising calm. "I took you for a meddlesome dunce, and so you are."

"And I think you're a nut, but it won't help anything to call each other names. If I've done any damage, how can I undo it?"

Seeming to speak more to himself than to Martin, he said, "Mirdath needs assistance. Ashcroft would provide it, he's the sort of man who would bid on the contract for his own execution. The time must be right. No time would be better than this very night, at about midnight. The place would be her grave, the Mt. Tabor Landfill."

"It's not there anymore. They built apartments on the site."

"How obliging of them! The final thing she needs, a living body, an innocent bystander, would be readily available."

"Anyone at all?"

"She can seize on anyone for a short time and bend him to her will. For a permanent bond, a perfect fit, she would need a susceptible young woman. She would need some part of that person — hair, fingernail parings, whatever — to effect the spell."

"What do you mean, *susceptible?*"

"Someone accustomed to a submissive role. An introverted, neurotic sort of person. Preferably a virgin."

"They must be rarer than copies of the *Necronomicon.*"

"You won't like Zurvan's world, young man. Cynicism, depending as it does on an implied contrast between the real and the ideal, would have no point."

Martin didn't hear him. He had realized who the victim would be. She wasn't in danger from Mirdath, of course, but from crackpots who shared Spencer's delusions: Ashcroft, for instance.

"For Christ's sake, what can I do about it?"

"Kill yourself before the changes begin. It may take ten years or twenty to accomplish them, but once they are well under way, you will no longer have that option."

It took all his will power not to grab the sick old man and shake him silly. "What can I do to stop them?" he shouted.

"Become a Master of the Runes. Like me." It was an intermittent, insectile buzzing now, not a human laugh at all. "But if you wish to oppose them. . . ."

"God damn it, that's what I'm telling you! I do!"

"If you wish to take on the infinite powers of Outer Darkness from a position of weakness and ignorance, with only one chance in a billion of success, then listen to me."

"I'm listening."

"Ten Words comprise the Litany of Hastur. Even Mordred Glendower, the last Archimage, knew only One. Mirdath may know as many as Three. And in 1869 a fool named Davis published a book called *Wonders of the Unknown Underworld* that contained the First Three. You will find them on page 354 of that book, which is on the top shelf on the north wall of this room."

"Your books are lying all over the floor. Thousands of them."

"Perhaps you can do without them. Here is the much more terrible Fourth Word."

George extended his right hand, or what would have been his right hand, for it was only a black blur that shifted constantly, confusingly, as if covered with the flies whose buzz was now nearly deafening, and a thin line of blue light appeared on the floor to form the letters of a Word.

"Quiet!" he said urgently as Martin began to mouth the grotesque syllables. "You will be able to speak it only once, and you must speak it directly to Mirdath."

"And what will happen?"

"That remains to be seen. Constantly refining her powers in the grave these past four years, she may have grown beyond the reach of incantation."

The glowing word had faded. As Martin repeated it in his mind, his stomach soured. The nausea intensified with each repetition. This, he told himself, was due to the power of suggestion, and it would have an even worse effect on someone who thoroughly believed in it. When he stopped thinking of the Word, the sickness passed.

"Find Davis's book, if you can, and the other Three Words. If she speaks them — and it may not even occur to her to speak them to a person like you — knowing them may save you. But as I said, your chance of success is virtually nil. You may already have unwittingly sprung some trap in this house that they laid against my return. Have you passed through any doors in this house that were inscribed with odd symbols?"

"Uh . . . no," Martin said, not wanting to add to his distress.

Pintar of Gemia, hero of *Swords of Winbourne,* never asked for better odds than *nil,* Martin reflected wryly; but he clung, or tried to cling, to the conviction that his skepticism was a secret weapon that evened the odds. More potent than any meaningless Word George might produce with some phosphorescent magic-store gimmick would be his own steadfast refusal to be fooled by any more sleight-of-hand. The danger to Amy was real, but it was a danger generated by contemporary lunatics and tricksters, not by long-dead witches and maleficent Beings.

As he used his flashlight to rummage through the welter of ill-assorted books across the room, George's voice droned on. He must have bought the gadget that altered his voice and made it sound like something filtered through a kazoo in that same magic-store. "She may already have isolated her victim with the same sort of trap, probably a loop in time," George said. "No matter what you do, if you once step into such a trap, you will remain an hour, a year, or a thousand years removed from Mirdath until her purpose is achieved."

Time was the only word of importance in that speech, Martin was sure. His watch said eleven-thirty. The sabbat would soon begin. "How can I avoid it?" he asked, desperately trying to read the titles of all the books at once as he waded through them, kicking or hurling them aside.

"By possessing all of my knowledge. Having met you, she may reasonably believe that you pose no threat to her, so perhaps she's been careless."

"Screw the book." Martin had absorbed his quota of insults. "When I run into the room, wild-eyed and shouting this gobbledygook, that's when Allen Funt will come out, right, and tell me I'm on *Candid Camera?*" Getting no answer, he started for the stairs and said, "I'll send help for you, George. Mr. Spencer?"

Shocked by what he thought he had seen in the reflected glow of the dimming flashlight, he turned it directly on the old man. Not a bit of him showed. He was covered from head to foot with a squirming mass that glittered blue and black and green in the beam of his light. Fighting back his revulsion, he ran to George's side and tried to bat the insects away. He hated to touch the undulant mass, but he forced himself to plunge his hand in and brush the flies from the old man's face. The swarm exploded, momentarily blinding him. He spat and snorted and retched with loathing as he felt strays crawling in his mouth and nostrils. When he groped for George's face, his fingers touched only bare floorboards.

He picked up the flashlight he'd dropped in his brief struggle. George was nowhere to be seen. An irregular patch of the floor was clear of dust, indicating that someone had recently lain there, but that was all that remained.

He checked the ladder to the roof and probed the dark corners of the attic with his fan of light, even though he was certain that no one, surely no one in George's apparent condition, would have had time to conceal himself or escape during the moment he'd been fending off the flies.

"Yeah, very good, George, worthy of Houdini," he called. "But he got paid for his tricks, and what did it cost you to rig this one? Come out and take your bow, I promise to clap."

If the trick had been planned to scare him, it had failed. He felt only actute exasperation. They were wasting his time by playing dumb jokes on him. Diversion was the key to illusion. Just as he had been distracted by the flies to permit George, far spryer then he'd seemed, to make his escape, so this whole insane scene must have been arranged to distract him from whatever was going on at Brooksprite Gardens.

He was already leaving — by the front door this time, but with all due caution — when it occurred to him to wonder why anyone should go to such trouble to mystify him. He could think of no convincing reason. He began to wonder if he had spoken to George at all, or if he had merely been talking to himself in an empty attic. Had he really spoken to Toni? What had he really concealed under his bed in the rooming house?

Such doubts might be worth examining later, but he had no time to spare for them now.

Chapter Fifteen

*T*he lot beside Amy's building was blocked by a police car, its dome-light washing a red stain on the shingled walls. Martin saw the reflection of more flashing red or blue lights from the rear of the building. He was momentarily relieved to see that the trouble involved an apartment separated from Amy's by four entries. Then it struck him that this might be still another diversion, one staged to draw his attention from another trick. He abandoned his car in one of the coyly meandering lanes and dashed across the manicured lawn to the other end of the parking lot.

"You, there! Stop!"

It wasn't, as he had anticipated, a policeman. A white patch bobbed angrily toward him through the murk, resolving itself at last into a bandage on Mr. Gertner's head.

"What's going on here?" Martin asked.

"Some silly cunt did the Dutch by diving off her balcony, what else is new? What I want to know is, what's going on in your girlfriend's apartment? They've been making that godawful racket —"

"*Evoë! Evoë! Saboi!*" It was a chant. Half-hysterical voices, accompanied by the boom of a drum and and a thin, off-key pipe or flute, came from behind the tightly-drawn curtains of Amy's apartment. "*Evoë! Evoë! Saboi!*"

"Get out of my way!"

"Don't you lay your hands on me, you rotten punk! The cops are right here, and they know how to deal with your kind of city-slicker con-men. They know how to deal with that goddamn nigger-music up there, too!" Gertner shrieked, clawing at Martin, blocking his way. "And don't think for a minute I'm not going to stop payment on that *oof!*"

"*Evoë! Evoë! Saboi!*"

"Help! Police! Assault! He hit me! Murder! Extortion!"

Martin scrambled up the stairs and flung himself against the door, slamming it with his open palms to be heard above the thunder of voices and instruments. It seemed impossible that the small apartment could have held even a tenth of the people implied by the din. He heard heavy bodies bumping the walls, making them vibrate, suggesting restless animals in a barn. He heard a clatter that might have been hooves.

He thought at last to try the knob. The door was unlocked. He burst into a silent and empty apartment. The only sounds he heard now were Gertner's thin cries and the squawk of emergency radios at the other end of the lot. He closed the door behind him.

"Amy?"

All the lights burned. The apartment was disorderly, but only by comparison with its previous tidiness. He saw nothing to suggest the pandemonium he had heard outside. The stereo was off. He stepped forward and touched the amplifier. It was quite cool. But even if it had been going, he was sure, it could never have produced the volume and quantity of sound he'd heard. A clock on the shelf beside the amplifier said one. He looked at his watch in panic; but his watch said exactly twelve, and the second-hand was moving.

The ominous statue lay in fragments on the floor with those of a broken cup and saucer. The cocoa spilled from the cup seemed to have dried a long time ago. The mirror behind the statue had been broken. A chest on the far side of the room had been forced. Clothing, papers, and books, and a Raggedy Ann doll, faded with age, lay tumbled nearby. A photo album and a stack of pictures lay on the coffee table. The place was messy, but he saw nothing to suggest a wild party, or even a few decorous visitors.

He walked cautiously through the kitchen to the bedroom. From what he had seen of Amy and her apartment, he knew that she was the sort of person who would clean up spilled cocoa and broken dishes immediately: unless someone prevented her from cleaning up. The evidence suggested that an intruder had surprised her and either taken her away or. . . . He tried not to think of the alternative, but the trick Toni had played on him had required *someone's* arm.

"Amy!"

The bed was unmade. The bedside clock said five past one. He consulted the phone book on the bedside table, then dialed for the time. A recorded voice said, "When you hear the tone, the time will be one-oh-three a.m. and thirty seconds. . . ." Had he been so stupid as to neglect to wind his watch when time meant everything? But his watch was still going; it said twelve-oh-five. He must have inadvertantly put his watch an hour back when he was winding it this morning. Donovan hadn't mentioned that he was an hour late for his appointment, probably out of courtesy; and George could have arrived from "ye Outside" an hour before he found him. He rejected the silly notion that he had fallen into any such thing as a "time loop" while he hurriedly searched the closets without result.

Of course, he had walked through a couple of doors inscribed with symbols in blood today, and he had omitted to tell George. . . . But George *knew* that, of course, which was why he'd mentioned it, and all this confusion about the time was just another feat of parlor-magic.

He returned to the living room and opened the drapes on the doors to the balcony. Red lights flashed outside. He slid back the glass door and the screen door and stepped out. Leaning over the rail, he saw an ambulance parked on the grass at the rear of the building, several entries down. A gurney with a wrapped body was being loaded into the ambulance.

In the woods directly opposite Amy's balcony was a second scene of activity: figures, mostly policemen, cast giant shadows from portable floodlights set up around an object covered by a sheet. He saw a bulky shape that could have been Donovan's.

"Donovan! Hey, Chief!" He cupped his hands beside his mouth, filled his lungs, and roared: "Chief Donovan! Police!"

Nobody, not the man he took for Donovan, the other policemen, nor the EMS volunteers who had just finished loading the ambulance at the other site, took the least notice of him. A police radio was blatting, he could hear subdued conversation, but none of those sounds could have drowned out his yells.

He had arrived at Brooksprite Gardens at midnight. The cops had been here at midnight. But inside the apartment now, and on the balcony where he stood, it was ostensibly after one in the morning. He still refused to believe in time loops, to believe that he was shouting at people who only existed in the past. Obviously he had fallen into another net of prankish obfuscation, this one woven with the collusion of the police. Ashcroft's Institute was a major local industry, as he had been told, one that might be hurt by his snooping, and the whole town had got together to discredit him and make him believe he had gone crazy.

"Donovan!" he screamed in anger. "Are you deaf, you stupid flatfoot?"

He ran through the living room. He tore open the front door and ran outside. He should have been standing on a concrete landing at the head of the stairs, facing the parking lot. But he found himself inside the living room, facing the curtained glass doors. The front door stood closed behind him.

Forcing himself to be calm and deliberate about it, he turned around and opened the front door again. He stepped toward what appeared to be the top of the stairs leading down to the parking lot; and he entered the living room. He still held the door open behind him. He looked back over his shoulder at the stairs, the parking lot, the building where Gertner lived, a dully glowing sky and a few dim stars. He pulled the door quietly shut behind him.

"Fuck you and your dumb games," he said calmly, "whoever you are. I will not panic."

Except that the drapes and the sliding glass doors behind them were closed, this was just like the room he had originally left. Yet it was subtly different. Colors were duller, edges less crisp. It was as if the second copy had lost some of the clarity and definition of the original. His eye was drawn to the bookcase. The titles of the books were, on close examination, just smudges that appeared, from a distance, to be English letters. Inside the books, the pages were all blank.

Then he spotted one whose title he could read: *Behold Now Behemoth*, by Hogarth Zurer.

He pulled out the paperback and opened it to Chapter One, where he read: "In the mind of Zurvan are many chambers. In the mind of Zurvan are many chambers. In —" He flipped through the book and found the same phrase repeated over and over again.

He thought at first, and not at all unsurprisingly, that he could hear his heart pounding, but now he recognized the sound as the thud of a drum. It got louder. The thin, off-key pipe wailed. The voices surged, a whisper of tightly leashed ferocity: *"Evoë! Evoë! Saboi!"*

An unshakable faith in the essential banality of existence made him glance at the stereo. It was, as he had known it would be, off. What he saw wasn't at all funny, but it made him laugh: the face of the amplifier was just a sketchy suggestion, the knobs and dials only meaningless blobs. It was as if he were standing inside his own mind, or someone else's, closely examining a memory of a room and discovering that he couldn't fill in all the precise details.

The noise now filled the empty room. He heard screams and snatches of spoken words: *Hanging Tree . . . bloodthirsty daughter . . . Lovecraft . . . and then I says to him . . . Detective Secrets . . . Yog-Sothoth will get you, if you don't watch out. . . .* He heard the bleating of a goat, the rattle of hooves, woven into the thudding beat and hysterical chanting.

He couldn't doubt that all this noise came from beyond the glass doors to the balcony. He stepped across and jerked the drapes open. On the balcony, it seemed, a crowd of naked people, some wearing snatches of bizarre costumes, outlandish maks, the heads of goats, deer, asses, apes, milled in uncertain time to the music, their backs to him.

"Iä! Crom Cruach! EVOË! EVOË! SABOI!"

His first impression had been wrong. This crowd wasn't on the balcony. Beyond their fantastically horned and antlered heads, partly hidden by clouds of blue smoke, he saw the ceiling and the walls of a room, a duplicate of the one in which he stood. The bodies shifted, giving him a glimpse that drove him to a frenzy. In the center of the pack Amy lay on the floor, struggling wildly but ineffectively, her blood-smeared face turned to him, her pale eyes *seeing* him and lighting for a moment with hope, her mouth stretched wide in a scream that he couldn't hear over the noise. He had never seen R. Bamberger's fat, hairy ass, but he suspected that the one that jerked spasmodically as he thrust between her squirming thighs was none other than his. He determined this even before he saw that the rapist was wearing sandals with white socks.

Martin wrenched the glass door open on darkness and silence. It was as if he had been fooled by a reflection in the glass. But there was no one in the room behind him to cast a reflection, and nothing was now visible in the glass. A gust of malodorous vapor, similar to the stench from the page he'd found in the mill, wafted around him and was gone.

He stepped onto the balcony. The ambulance and the police were gone from both locations. Before he had been able to see lighted windows in this building, the lights of other buildings and parking areas, but now he could see nothing beyond the rail: nothing, that is, but a dark forest in place of Brooksprite Gardens. He could see no trace of the apartment complex except the balcony where he stood and the lighted room behind him. Only that fragment of his world seemed to hang suspended in a forest, a much deeper and older forest than the scruffy wood that had faced the balcony.

Below the balcony ran a dirt lane, little more than a pair of wheel-ruts between deeply mossy banks. It extended ahead of him past a gnarled and ancient oak tree, twined with mistletoe, and into the shadowy green gloom of the wood. A mist hung stilly in the farther groves. He could see surprisingly well. The road glowed, hoarding in the light of the pale sky. Glossy leaves, red berries, white flowers stood out with vibrant clarity. It looked like the hour before dawn, but his watch said twelve-forty-five.

Toward him up the lane wound the tinny noise of a parade: pipes and drums and tambourines, louder and more erratic than before; wild voices laughing, shrieking, braying their nonsense-words with no regard for the formerly tight rhythm. The mob was almost upon him. Shadows and pale shapes cavorted through the wood beside the lane.

He might have shouted curses, threats, questions — but to what purpose? He had grown resigned to whatever might happen when the parade should at last arrive and engulf him. And it would flow around him: how and when, he couldn't say, but Amy's apartment and its balcony had faded into oblivion. He stood with the dirt of the lane beneath his feet.

The happy music swelled, and it was ineed happy music: primitive, exuberant, amateurish, the sound of fairyland as it might be depicted in a children's backyard theatrical. It was even infectious. His rage and his terror, much as he wanted to cling to them as his last links to the real world, were dissolving in the spell of the music.

The capering pageant burst upon him: satyrs, fauns — were they only costumes? It wasn't light enough to be sure — naked nymphs with garlands in their tangled hair, men and women with horns or hoofs or tails or the heads of beasts, all of them just as jolly and playful as could be: no witches here, they seemed eager to assert, nobody but us joyous pagans. The ragged line of march shifted and twisted upon itself, contracted and expanded, as individuals chased one another, as small groups of the horde splintered into mock fights with wineskins or flowers, as men and women fell aside, apparently with the most readily available person or group of persons, to make love on the inviting moss. It was as if Walt Disney had made a dirty movie, and as if it were coming off the screen to get him.

In the advancing pageant he saw clearly depicted the resolution of the central struggle of his life, the tension that generated his work, the essence of his own (as he secretly thought of it) blighted genius. *Swords of Winbourne* was a frantic attempt to recapture the innocence of his child-hood, just as the works of Tanya Hyde and Dick Standing were equally frantic attempts to master the messy secret that had ended that innocence. But now peace, happiness, love, and the end of all struggle and confusion were within his grasp. An exultation compounded by a painful longing, a desire to belong, to go to all the wild parties he'd never been invited to, swelled in him until he thought he would burst. With no conscious thought or purpose, only as a release for this expanding emotion, he began to tear off his clothing.

Still, in a cold corner of his mind, a voice told him not to join the orgy. This vision of the earthly paradise that now swirled around him (hands tugged at him; voices whispered, *"Martin! Martin!"*; wanting lips caressed his face) was too blatantly his own, too like his adolescent dreams come true. It wasn't so familiar and comfortable because its roots lay in some atavistically recalled festival of his Druid ancestors, but because these clever devils had served him up a temptation cut from the meat of his own imagination. The temptation was not merely to join the party; but, by joining it wholeheartedly, and with the full knowledge that it was his personal vision, to blot out the real world and live solely in his fantasies.

The sky flushed as if one drop of omnipotent blood had tinged its dark crystal. He saw a nymph skipping into the forest, where each leaf had become a tongue of green flame, with the red vinyl *My Diary*. She ripped and balled the pages and strewed them like flowers as she pranced away.

That didn't seem to matter, for Amy Miniter, lodestar of the surging horde, its goddess or perhaps its sacrifice to the new god, Martin Paige, sat astride a pony that ambled shyly up the lane. Her hair, no longer colorless, burned with red glints gathered from the sky. He wanted her, and she him. He saw it in her eyes . . . in her dark eyes. She flaunted her nudity in a way that Amy never could have done. She grinned in a wicked way that Amy never could have grinned.

He knew her.

He managed to screw up the courage and will-power necessary to shout the Fourth of the Ten Words that are the Litany of Hastur, and his skull exploded.

"... *J*ust in time. You're darned lucky."

"... don't know ... thank you ... seemed like such a harmless little man."

"It's all my fault. Your neighbors would still be alive if I'd recognized him this morning. Bastard had the balls — I beg your pardon — had the nerve to walk into my office, just as bold as brass, and chat about the magazine where I saw his picture."

Martin's eye opened against the red and yellow weave of Amy's oriental carpet. Every thread was just as it should be: this was no slipshod copy of an image inside the mind of Zurvan. He lay on his side. His head throbbed intolerably, and he couldn't move his hands. He found that his wrists were shackled.

"Awake, are you?" A heavy foot kicked him in the small of the back. "On your feet, pervert."

"Don't — don't hurt him." Amy's voice ... but not quite.

"These scumbag so-called psychos make me sick. He knows what he does, and he does it because he likes it, but they'll just stick him back into his rubber room, and some day he'll take it into his head to waltz out again, just mark my words. I'd be serving justice if I dragged him outside and shot him down like a mad dog." Donovan's voice.

Martin rolled over and started to rise. The chief grabbed his collar and jerked him upright as handily as if he were a rag doll.

"Very funny," Donovan snarled, waving something under Martin's nose.

He couldn't focus his eyes. He squeezed them shut and shook his head. When he opened them, he was looking at the clock beside the amplifier, which said one a.m. The statue stood unbroken in the bookcase. Beside it lay a plastic bag he hadn't seen before. He stepped toward it for a better look.

Donovan shoved him back. "Sorry, sport, we have to keep your little toy."

In the translucent bag he had seen a knife: gouged, broken, and stained, not at all like the shiny new blade he'd put in the back of his car and forgotten, the one Todd had dropped, but the handle was similar.

"What's going on?"

Martin asked the question of Amy. But then he noticed her reddish hair, her dark eyes, her expression of sly malice. He turned away from her. He tried to think of the Word he had spoken so he could give it another try, but it was gone from his mind as completely as if it had never existed.

At last he was able to focus on the object Donovan had been waving under his nose. It was a copy of a magazine he knew very well, *Detective Secrets,* an old and well-thumbed copy.

Donovan held it open to a story headlined, "The Girl Who Couldn't

Say Maybe," by Merry Treece. She hadn't written for that magazine, he knew, for five years.

The headline was splashed across a photo of Martin's own New York apartment, its disorder and squalor emphasized by the stark, head-on flash of a police photograph. The picture contained two things he had never seen in his apartment. The first — he guessed it was Mirdath's playful signature on her work — was the Manhattan telephone directory supporting a broken leg of his desk. The second, sprawled across the bed, was the bruised, torn, and unquestionably dead body of his exasperating former friend, Margo Slye.

"Yeah, I remembered seeing your name in *Detective Secrets,* all right," Donovan said. "You miserable son of a bitch. Sorry, miss."

"That didn't happen," Martin said earnestly, looking the chief straight in the eye but finding neither sympathy nor even comprehension. "It didn't happen! I thought about killing her, maybe I could have done it, but the point is, I didn't. I knew her five years ago. She's still alive and well, as far as I know. And I left that very apartment — without any corpses in it — this morning."

"You walked out of some zoo in New York this morning, you mean, stole a car, and came up here to play mystery-writer. Then you met Antoinette Sloane and decided it would be more fun to play Jack the Ripper again. If Miss Miniter hadn't been cool and smart enough to turn up her radio full-blast and get you to sing and dance along with it, so we got complaints from the neighbors, she would have had her picture in the next issue of this rag."

Martin said nothing. Over Donovan's shoulder, he looked at Amy. She winked at him.

The chief said, "After I made the connection between you and this story, I went looking for you. I found Miss Sloane's arm under your bed. Wrapped in your shirt. What the hell was in your mind, I wonder — no, don't tell me, I'm sick enough. The rest of her was in the woods behind this building. Maybe you'd like to tell me when you cut Brenda Willy's throat, though, I'd like to hear that."

"Who?"

"The schoolteacher who lived down the way. We found her out back."

"Somebody told me she jumped off her balcony."

"She wasn't about to do any jumping. Doc Keller — but he's senile, so we'll have to get a second opinion — said she got her throat slit at least a year ago. How did you rig that one?"

"It was Zurvan!" Martin screamed, struggling past him to get at Amy; but the chief easily knocked him sprawling, and he enjoyed doing it.

"Who?"

"I think he means *Zurer,*" Amy — but Amy was no more, he knew that now, and each graceful gesture that the ineffable Mirdath made with the once charmingly awkward body was like another nail in her coffin – said. "Hogarth Zurer? He's a popular novelist." Each elegantly modulated word she spoke in that once-loved voice was like another shovel of earth on that coffin. "When he burst in here this evening, he was raving about Zurer, how he'd stolen his work. He claimed that I reminded him – or rather, that I *was* the model for the cover."

Martin rose cautiously to his knees, resolving to make no more foolish moves. Donovan didn't stop him. The chief frowned at the paperback that Mirdath had fetched from the bookcase.

"That's the nuttiest thing he said yet. You're a lot prettier."

Mirdath blushed and modestly averted her eyes.

There had been no woman on the cover of *Behold Now Behemoth,* and this book seemed much thicker. Martin said, "May I see that?"

He had spoken to Donovan, but Mirdath took the book from the chief's hand and, with sadness and compassion in her dark eyes, showed it to him.

Eventually, he supposed, he could have come to terms with a past rearranged to include the murder of Margo Slye. There had been times when he had wanted to kill her, when he had gone so far as to consider the various ways of doing it. Such schemes had always foundered on the question of what to do with the body. Apparently he hadn't answered that question in his new past, either. The punishment would be out of all proportion to his guilt, but the guilt was there.

But there was no way he could ever accept this, no way he could ever learn to live with it.

The book that the sad-eyed witch extended was a door to the destruction of his soul. He lunged at her, planning to tear out her throat with the only weapons left to him, his teeth. It seemed as if a wall rose out of nowhere to stop him. As he lay on his back, choking on a mouthful of blood and hard, jagged objects, he realized that Donovan had stripped him of even those weapons.

Dim through a lens of tears, Mirdath still held out the book for him to see. Amy, that Amy who no longer existed, was pictured on the cover, clinging in her sorcerous, pearl-gray gown to the mighty arm of a man with a two-hand sword, who looked not unlike an apotheosis of Martin Paige.

The title of the book was *Swords of Winbourne,* and its author was Hogarth Zurer.

About the Author

Brian McNaughton was born in Red Bank, New Jersey, and attended Harvard. He worked for ten years as a reporter for the *Newark Evening News* and has since held all sorts of other jobs while publishing some 200 stories in a variety of magazines and books. He recently ended a ten-year stint as night manager at a decrepit seaside hotel, where he once had the honor of helping his hero, Warren Zevon, break into a stubborn soda machine. *The Throne of Bones* won the World Fantasy and the International Horror Guild awards in 1998 for best collection.

www.ingramcontent.com/pod-product-compliance
Lightning Source LLC
Chambersburg PA
CBHW050752250626
47155CB00005B/2031